CARRION SHADOWS

JONAH BUCK

SEVERED PRESS
HOBART TASMANIA

CARRION SHADOWS

WWW.SEVEREDPRESS.COM

ISBN: 978-1-925597-82-0

For Jones and Marilyn

And from this chasm, with ceaseless turmoil seething,
As if this earth in fast thick pants were breathing,
A mighty fountain momently was forced:
Amid whose swift half-intermitted burst
Huge fragments vaulted like rebounding hail,
Or chaffy grain beneath the thresher's flail:
And mid these dancing rocks at once and ever
It flung up momently the sacred river.
Five miles meandering with a mazy motion
Through wood and dale the sacred river ran,
Then reached the caverns measureless to man,
And sank in tumult to a lifeless ocean;
And 'mid this tumult Kubla heard from far
Ancestral voices prophesying war!

-       *Samuel Taylor Coleridge, Kubla Khan*

ONE

NOTES ON THE NARROWLY AVOIDED EXPEDITION TO SATAN'S BUTT CRACK AND THE GREAT SPIDER MIGRATION OF '25

December 9, 1925

"I came to ask you about my application," Denise DeMarco said.

Gunder Kirkeberg, Ranger Station Thirteen's chief of operations, glanced up from the papers he was reading. "Mmm," he said, looking right back down at the field reports.

"To the new anti-poaching unit the park is putting together," Denise continued.

The Dracobly Hessler Game Preserve took up a significant portion of South Africa's northeastern frontier. The park's grounds stretched for thousands of square miles, covering everything from the craggy grasslands that gave way to African savanna further north to mountainous peaks and ridges and verdant river valleys. The park contained everything from lions to elephants to water buffalo to crocodiles to white rhinos to leopards to hyenas. Denise wanted to work here because it was one of the greatest centers of biological importance anywhere in the world, protecting dozens of rare species.

The great diversity of wildlife had also attracted the inevitable, though. Poachers took hundreds of animals per year. They moved in fast, rugged vehicles, killing dozens of animals at a time. Then they cut off whatever parts were most valuable from the downed and dying creatures, brought the spoils back to their well-hidden camps, and smuggled the parts out of the country at enormous profit.

Denise sat on the other side of Kirkeberg's long, heavily polished desk. A stuffed giraffe head hung from the wall directly behind Kirkeberg. Denise always wondered about the giraffe. The creatures were primarily known for their long necks, but Kirkeberg just had the head mounted on his wall.

Maybe the office would have been too cramped trying to mount any more of the animal's length up on the wall. Maybe Kirkeberg simply didn't care how the animal was displayed so long as it was there for the world to see, evidence of his hunting prowess. Either way, it seemed odd to Denise to kill a giant animal simply to harvest the top two percent of its height for a wall decoration. What had happened to the rest of the giraffe? Left to rot? Carved up into steaks?

The giraffe's eyes always seemed to watch her whenever she was in Kirkeberg's office. Denise shifted in her chair. The chair squeaked in protest. Up on the wall, the giraffe's eyes looked like they tracked after Denise. Kirkeberg circled something on the report in front of him.

Several other trophies lined the walls, but none of them watched Denise quite like the giraffe. Most of the offices in Ranger Station Thirteen bore similar decorations, the walls littered with prizes and relics from feats of outdoorsmanship.

Denise's tiny corner of the building was the only space that was free of hunting trophies. The only thing she kept on the wall was a picture of Teddy Roosevelt standing in front of a downed rhino, grinning as he held a long rifle. Another man stood next to the former American president, an equally large smile planted on his face. That was her father, Cedric DeMarco, founder of DeMarco & Company Hunting Tours. Denise was in the picture, too. A gawky teenage girl standing near the rhino's corpse. She was the "& Company" part of DeMarco & Company Hunting Tours.

Her father had been the best hunter in Cape Town until he disappeared on an expedition into the Namib Desert some years ago. Then that title passed to Denise until she gave it up.

She made a noise in her throat, a polite way of informing that Kirkeberg that he had about ten seconds until she ripped that report out of his hands and smacked him upside the head with it.

He looked up again. "Yes, your application. *That*." He said the word as if referencing something that a cat had barfed up into his slippers. "I threw it away."

"You what?"

"I threw it away," he said, gesturing toward his trashcan. "I knew what it was before I even opened the envelope, so I simply deposited it where it belonged. The poaching squad is made up of the best of the best. The men on the shortlist for the position are mostly either ex-military or police, or they're some of the best hunters we could recruit. It will be the park's most elite group of rangers. I knew you weren't qualified, so I threw your application away. It's not a particularly mysterious concept, Ms. DeMarco."

"Wait, wait, wait. Hold on there a red hot second. I'm qualified. I used to be the best hunter in Cape Town. I can out track most of the guys on your short list, and I can out shoot the rest."

"Used to be the best hunter in Cape Town, Ms. DeMarco. Used to be. Your words, not mine. That was before you lost your nerve."

2

"I didn't lose my nerve," Denise said, her voice rising. "I left the hunting business for different reasons."

"You can frame it however you want. It's none of my business how you explain it. I've seen it before, though." Kirkeberg touched the set of long scars that ran down his cheeks, coming within a hair's breadth of his right eye. Claw marks. Denise doubted he was even aware of what his hand was doing.

"I don't hunt, anymore. That's true," Denise said, trying to lasso her temper and wrangle it to the ground. Her fingers dug into her palms. "But this isn't a hunting unit. It's an investigation and prevention unit."

"You're partly right." Kirkeberg took his hand away from the claw marks that marred his leathery skin. "Mostly you're wrong, though. This will be a hunting unit. You'll be hunting the most voracious and deadly creature God ever saw to curse the earth with. Mankind. I saw your file when I hired you. You've got some skill, sure. But I don't give a damn. Your file also said you were squeamish about hunting and didn't work well with others."

"I work great with others," she half-shouted. She looked around, suddenly realizing she was standing up and had a fist raised in Kirkeberg's direction. "Admittedly, I can be a little passionate sometimes," she said, sitting herself back down.

Kirkeberg raised an eyebrow.

Denise sucked in her lips. "Look, I don't want to turn this into something it's not. The park has a problem. A big problem. We're losing hundreds of animals per year. I haven't been here very long, but it's obvious we're not going to have a game preserve in a couple of decades if this keeps up at its current rate. I have skills that you need. Skills that the park needs. Skills a lot of your so-called elite guys don't have. Give me a chance. That's all I really want. A chance."

"I already am giving you a chance. You're here. I wouldn't have hired you if Balthazar van Rensburg hadn't given me his word about you. He and I go way back." Kirkeberg's hand fluttered up toward the scars on his face again. This time, he seemed to notice and his hand snatched up a pen instead. His fingers fiddled with the cap as he continued speaking. "Balthazar is a good man and a better hunter. Even so, I didn't like bringing you on board. Not with your record. Your father's hunting expedition company in Cape Town failed after you lost your nerve."

There was that phrase again. Denise gritted her teeth, knowing Kirkeberg was testing her.

Kirkeberg smiled briefly, maybe pleased she hadn't risen to the bait he'd placed in front of her. Or maybe just enjoying himself during the lashing. "And then you were involved with Yersinia Bioresearch, briefly."

"Emphasis on 'briefly.' That was a mistake."

"Indeed. I've been told that the court records are sealed on that incident, and you're not allowed to talk about it unless you want to be sued out of existence, so I won't dwell. But they're unpleasant characters, and their business does unpleasant things. I would normally not care to associate with anyone involved in one of their projects."

"I'd just like to add--"

Kirkeberg cut Denise off. "Your history paints the picture of a woman who is unreliable, difficult to work with, and prideful. Perhaps rightfully so on that last count. But the anti-poaching squad will need teamwork and discipline, through good times and bad. You haven't been here at the game preserve very long, Denise. Certainly not long enough for me to gain a fuller picture of you as a person. I think a lot of my first impressions might be right. Maybe you shouldn't be here at all."

"But what I really--"

"Even though that is what it is, I agree that you have potential. Maybe. Your talents alone won't get you very far here. Not very far at all. I hired you because someone I trust said you had a good head on your shoulders to match those talents. Plus, I owed him some favors."

"Not exactly a ringing endorsement of Cornelia and me."

"No, it's not. Just of you, though. I probably would have hired Cornelia, regardless. We needed someone with more field medicine experience."

Cornelia van Rensburg was Balthazar's daughter. She'd been hired at the same time as Denise. Even though she was the daughter of one of the best big game hunters in Pretoria, she hadn't met him until a few months ago. They'd been separated during the Second Boer War when she was a young girl. A paperwork mix-up said Balthazar died in the fighting, and Cornelia was adopted out.

"Gee, thanks," Denise said. Her initial anger ebbed out of her, leaving her feeling vaguely sick inside. It felt like someone had opened her up and scooped all the fire out of her, leaving only ashes and burnt residue. The problem was that Denise recognized Kirkeberg was at least a little right. Maybe he'd put the worst face on things, but he wasn't entirely wrong. She knew her own flaws.

"Know thyself," the ancient Greeks said, intending it as one of the keys to wisdom and happiness. Sometimes knowing oneself wasn't all it was cracked up to be.

"I have a task for you and Cornelia," Kirkeberg said, pulling a single sheet of paper off his desk.

"I hope it's not giving another tour to some scientist. You remember what happened to the last one."

Kirkeberg laid the sheet of paper back on the desk. "Hmm. I suppose so. I seem to recall you describing him as 'handsy.'"

"I seem to recall the doctor describing him as 'requiring a few weeks in a neck brace' after that. I suppose that counts as another black mark on my record."

"Well, you kind of proved some of my points with that one. I actually marked that incident down as a plus in your record, though. He deserved that. Maybe you'll make it someday, despite yourself."

"Regardless, I'm not sure whoever is touring the park today would be thrilled to know what happened to the last guy."

"This one comes highly recommended. Dr. Albert Neville Thornber. He's Dr. Rumson's replacement from the United States Geological Survey after you and Dr. Rumson...disagreed on matters of his personal conduct. I was going to reassign you and Cornelia because of her science background, but maybe you're right. Dr. Thornber might take a disliking to you after what happened to his colleague. I'll reassign Hartzell and Planck. You'll pick up their tasks for the day."

"Thanks. I appreciate it. What were they assigned to?"

"They were tracking the spider migrations."

"Oh. Oh good."

"I'd recommend you wear long sleeves and maybe a veiled hat. There's a lot of spiders out there."

"Perfect." Denise tried to hitch her mouth into something resembling a smile. She was fairly certain she missed a gear and got stuck somewhere around a rictus, though.

"Do you need anything else?" Kirkeberg picked up his pile of reports again, indicating that the conversation was effectively over.

"Nothing for now. I'll go tell Cornelia that we're riding spider duty. I'm sure she'll be so...thrilled."

"Good. Here, take this to Hartzell and Planck. They'll need to meet Dr. Thornber and help him with his equipment when he arrives." Kirkeberg handed a sheet of paper to Denise. She took it and walked out the door, Kirkeberg's giraffe still watching her as she went.

She glanced down at the paper as she walked. Whoever Dr. Thornber was, he was headed to Sulfur Springs, a poisonous cave near the dam. Apparently, the seismographs or whatever geological equipment he was using had picked up some unusual activity from below the park's surface, and he was investigating.

Denise wasn't a geologist, but Cornelia might have found it interesting stuff. She'd studied paleontology before she became a

5

military nurse and then a park ranger. Denise might owe her an apology for getting them on the team tracking the spider migration.

She found Hartzell in Ranger Station Thirteen's common area, sipping on a cup of coffee that smelled like emulsified asphalt.

"Here, you're off the spider study today. Kirkeberg reassigned you to babysit some geologist instead."

"Hey, alright. I won't be sorry to get away from that section of the park. I brushed my hair last night and had ten or fifteen baby spiders caught up in the teeth of my comb. Who got the spider job?"

"Me."

"Wow. What did you do?"

"I asked to switch duties with someone else. Possibly a mistake."

"No kidding."

"The scientist is going down into Sulfur Springs, though. You're not exactly landing a plum assignment."

"Hey, at least there won't be any spiders down there. Nothing can live down there."

Denise handed off the sheet of paper directing Hartzell and Planck where and when to pick up Dr. Thornber. His equipment had already been shipped ahead and was waiting in the vehicle depot. The man had everything from pickaxes to sample cases to a rowboat and dive suit. Denise didn't know what he planned to do with those last two in a poisonous cave, but the man obviously came prepared.

Then she moved off to find Cornelia. They had a long day of spider watching to attend to. Better to tell her sooner rather than spring it on her at the last second. She found Cornelia van Rensburg waiting by Denise's office.

The tall blonde woman smiled upon seeing her. Cornelia was about the same age as Denise, roughly thirty, but she wasn't as worn from a lifetime spent on the veldt and game trails. She was plenty tough, but not as weather-beaten. "Hey, how did it go? What's the word on your application?"

"The word is, Kirkeberg doesn't trust me with anything more dangerous than a couple of rubber bands and some lint. He threw my application away without looking at it."

"Oh. I'm sorry. Who pooped in his cornflakes this morning?"

"Yeah. Things didn't exactly go as I hoped. I'm not really sure what to do with myself. Part of me is pretty upset, but part of me thinks maybe he's a little right about some of the things he said."

"Oh, nope. No way. Nuh-uh. Trust me, Denise. I know you. You've gotten through situations by being smarter and tougher than a raft-load of the guys Kirkeberg probably has on his shortlist. My dad, my biological

6

dad that is, has told me stories about what you two did together when you were stuck with Yersinia Bioresearch. Hell, just all the creative paperwork and records juggling you did to reunite me and my father shows you know how to get a lot of complex, mind-numbing stuff done. You'd be great as a field investigator and tracker. The park needs people like that."

"I can be a little hot-headed sometimes."

"Good. We need someone to get out there and kick some asses. There's whole piles of asses that need kicking."

"And I don't always work well with others."

"Fields of asses. Great, vast expanses of asses, swaying peacefully in the breeze."

"And there's another thing."

"Do tell."

"Kirkeberg was going to assign us to help out the new scientist from the geological survey."

"He's given us a string of those. I'm not exactly thrilled to keep playing tour guide myself. You said he was 'going to,' though?"

"Yeah. Do you want the good news first, or would you like the bad news first?"

"Let's roll the dice. Give me the bad news."

"I asked if we could have a different assignment, given that any colleague of Dr. Rumson probably wasn't going to like me very much."

"Fair enough. What's the part that's so bad about that?"

"He gave us Hartzell and Planck's assignment instead."

"Hartzell and Planck? What were they doing lately? They needed one of the cars to go out to the lowlands and...oh goddammit."

"Yeah. We're going to be tracking the spider migration."

"Beautiful. Alright, so what's the good news?"

"The alternative was staying with the visiting geologist and going down into Sulfur Springs."

"Ah, I see. So our choices were between riding up and down the spider trails and spelunking up Satan's butt crack. Neither one is exactly appealing."

"No, not especially."

"I suppose I'd rather be out in the fresh air. The worst-case scenario out there is that maybe you swallow one of the little eight-legged darlings and choke. If something goes wrong with your equipment in Sulfur Springs, it would be like a mustard gas attack."

"Yeah, the air down there will jelly your lungs."

"Alright, let's get to the motor pool and grab a car. There's about a billion baby spiders out there, and they aren't going to track themselves."

"Oh boy. Just a second, let me get my hat and some eye protection." Denise opened the door to her tiny office and grabbed her slouch hat off her desk and secured it over her dark hair.

She looked out the window toward the mountains and the Verschoor Dam. Sulfur Springs lay near the dam, though she couldn't see the tiny cavern entrance from a couple miles away.

Then she looked at the picture on the wall, of her father and Teddy Roosevelt smiling over their success on the trail, of her smiling in the background along with them. Was this really what she wanted to do with her life?

She'd been educated on her father's knee out on the veldt. The grasslands and open sky were what she knew best, trekking across the landscape miles from the nearest hints of civilization. She spoke English, Afrikaans, and some of the Bantu languages, mostly Zulu and Xhosa, enough for her to travel freely across the African expanses.

It was what she knew how to do. She'd start chewing the paint off the walls if she was stuck in a city the rest of her life, working some job in a shirt factory or caring for a couple of runny-nosed children. Being tied to the same plot of land on a farm didn't hold much more appeal, either. She needed to trammel to the dark corners of the earth and see what was there.

Could she stay here at Dracobly Hessler Game Preserve? Maybe. Cornelia's words made her feel better about herself, but they didn't necessarily bode well for her fitting into an institutional culture. The game preserve was fantastic, and it did important work, but Denise wasn't sure she fit in here.

Would she be any happier here if she knew she couldn't succeed to her potential? Would she be any happier here knowing that she'd only been hired in the first place because Gunder Kirkeberg owed one of her friends a favor? Was that how she wanted to live out her life, as the fly in the soup of whoever was in charge here?

She looked at the picture again. Her father. So proud and happy. A younger version of herself, certain how the future would turn out and happy to follow along on the ride.

Maybe she should go back to hunting.

No. Denise knew she couldn't hunt for sport anymore. Simply thinking about it made her thoughts travel back to that day by the river. To the steady booming of elephant guns. To the scent of blood sinking into hot, parched soil. The memories made her insides roil.

This is what she had now, and she would try to make the very best of it. She donned a pair of goggles and grabbed a map of the park to mark up. Hopefully, things would start to look up soon.

TWO

SCUM OF THE EARTH

Dr. Albert Neville Thornber watched the two park rangers who'd been pressed into his service carry the equipment up to the cavern entrance. The roar of water cascading down the side of the Verschoor Dam was little more than a dull rumble in the distance. But for the smell, the path up to the rocky outcropping might have been pleasant.

The smell was like rotting eggs mixed with hellfire. Thornber didn't so much sniff it as it barged into his nose and started brawling with his mucous membranes. Even from a distance, his eyes watered every time the breeze sent a puff of the caustic effluvia his way.

That's what the gasmasks were for. Army surplus. Meant to protect troops against German chlorine gas attacks. Of course, in the summer heat, they were almost as unpleasant as the smell they were meant to combat.

He would have to put it on sooner or later, though. The air deeper inside Sulfur Springs was completely toxic, utterly unbreathable. The underground chamber had been trapped beneath the surface, isolated from the world above for millions and millions of years. The atmosphere within was fed by hydrothermal vents that belched out fumes and chemicals from deeper within the earth, a hot spot for low-level volcanism.

At least that was what the notes he had read said. He wasn't an expert in matters of geology. The biological sciences were his field of expertise, not that these men from the nature preserve needed to know that.

"So, you're some kind of geology expert, right?" Myron Hartzell asked.

"Yes, indeed I am," Thornber lied.

"What exactly are you studying in there? Why do you need a boat?" The ranger gestured up the path in the direction of the cavern's entrance.

"I believe you'll understand best once you actually see inside the cavern system itself. Lately, our equipment has been picking up some small disturbances in the area that we believe are linked to the geothermal hotspots down there."

"Does that mean there's a volcano that's going to erupt down there or something?" Hartzell looked over his shoulder at the entrance again as his partner carried the last of the gear up.

"No, no. Highly unlikely. Although a major disturbance might produce a localized lava flow," Thornber said, repeating something he'd read in the notes.

"Well, that doesn't sound good," Hartzell said.

"It's extremely unlikely. This chamber has survived millions of years without it happening. The odds of the earth opening up and swallowing us while we're down there are about the same as the odds we'll be hit by lightning that far underground."

"Alright. That's something at least."

"That looks like the last of the equipment. Are you ready to enter the caves with me?"

Myron looked over his shoulder again and then wiped his brow. "Yeah, I guess so."

"Good. You and your friend can carry the essential equipment as my bearers while I lead the way down there."

The ranger nodded and wiped more sweat off his brow. His expression said this wasn't what he'd been expecting, but Thornber didn't care. He couldn't carry everything down himself, and there was important work to be done down there. Hopefully, the grunt work of lugging everything around would tire the rangers enough that they wouldn't ask too many probing questions.

He moved further up the craggy slope, picking his way up the rough path. The smell grew stronger as he went. His innards started to clench up, squirming like a litter of newborn puppies as his body tried to decide whether or not it should vomit.

Slipping the mask on, he cinched the straps tight around his head. The rubber sucked tight against the sides of his face. He immediately began to sweat, turning the inside of the mask into a damp second skin.

However, the filtered air the mask provided was worth it. Thornber paused for a second as his stomach stopped lurching. The slightly stale air from the gasmask was a great improvement over the belches emanating from Sulfur Springs.

The human body was a remarkable machine, but it was easy to short circuit. Millions of years of evolution, of fighting for the basest of survival on African landscapes just like this, had taught the human body to throw up when it thought it was being poisoned. The reflex had probably saved countless primitives who had sampled poisonous berries or eaten spoiled meat in the hunter-gatherers' constant search for food.

However, it was almost more of a nuisance in the modern day. Dizziness was a common symptom of poisoning. Thus, when the inner ear became agitated from motion, the body often thought it was being poisoned and induced forced vomiting. That was why people became sick from the effects of traveling by sea or car or plane. The idiot forces of evolution had perfected a system that now made the body believe its only chance for survival on a rocking boat was to become violently ill.

The truly devious machinations of men could take advantage of that, too. During the Great War, many of the chemical arms lobbed between the trenches weren't dangerous in and of themselves. One side would begin their bombardment by hurling chemicals that were harmless but for their ability to cause vomiting. Anyone who caught even a whiff would fall down and puke their guts into the mud. That's when the mustard gas and chlorine would start to rain down. Troops who put their gasmasks on would simply have to whip them right off again as they threw up into the filters, and then they would choke to death on the real poisons.

The exact same thing could happen here. Throwing up in his mask deep in the tunnels would be a death sentence. The air down there was brutally poisonous. Amazing how a system designed to protect his ancestors against the dangers of spoiled food might accidentally kill him. Evolution was both remarkable and profoundly stupid.

Thornber was here to study one of the remarkable aspects, not that the rangers needed to know that part. Nobody at the Dracobly Hessler Game Preserve needed to know exactly what was going on down there. Everything would work better if they continued to believe he was merely a geologist interested in rock samples and seismic data.

Taking a few more deep breaths, he adjusted himself to the musty air that filtered through the mask. Then he took the last few steps up to the rim of the cave.

Warm air wafted out of the crevice. The entrance to Sulfur Springs was less of a cave and more of a hole. They'd have to march down the steep incline into the dark fissure before they could set out deeper into the cave system.

Thornber wore long sleeves and a hat to protect himself against any caustic chemicals that might drip from the ceiling or smear onto his clothes. He also wore gloves and thick boots. The rangers were similarly equipped as they carried the small rowboat above their heads and more gear in packs on their back.

He took the first step down into the crater and began the short descent. Hot air hit him as if he were sitting in the front row at a politician's speech. The warm, wet breeze bubbled up from below as he found his footing on the damp rocks.

Sulfur Springs wasn't a natural cave, as was evident from the blast marks all along the entrance. Engineers building Verschoor Dam blew the little pocket of rock apart by mistake. Before that, the interior of the cavern system had been almost completely cut off from the outside world for millions of years, accessible only from tiny cracks in the rock. Thornber and the rangers would be only the second team to ever traverse much further than the entrance.

Moving downward, the ground leveled off, but the air only became hotter and stickier. The atmosphere was more like a swamp in the summer rather than a typical cave. That was due to the hydrothermal vents deeper down in the system, spewing heat and gases from down in the earth into the cave.

As he came to a stop at the base of the hole, Thornber noticed how sterile the mouth of the cave was. No moss clung to the rocks. No bats had left piles of guano about. No plants or animals of any sort had made their homes here; the atmosphere was too poisonous for anything from the surface to tolerate here.

The cave entrance was like a brackish estuary on the edge of the deep, dark sea. Around an estuary, animals spread in abundance on the land near the water, and they swam and slithered and crawled in vast, uncountable numbers down in the depths, but few things were hardy enough to survive in the transition zone where those worlds converged. This was nature's no man's land, where not even the imbecilic genius of evolution could produce something that could survive trapped between two extremes.

Deeper, though, deeper there might be possibilities.

Thornber turned his flashlight on and shone it around the darkness. He spotted the tunnel he was looking for, leading deeper into the mountain and gradually downward.

"This way," he said, pointing the way ahead for the park rangers. One of them grunted in acknowledgement, and Thornber began walking down the tunnel, shining his light back and forth.

Once he stepped free of the rubble near the entrance, the path was mostly smooth. Long ago, sometime before mammals inherited the earth, water had washed away sandstone or some other soluble rock and left an easy path ahead. Outcroppings and rough patches had been ground smooth over a vast geological timescale until the route was a meandering tube crisscrossed with smaller capillaries and offshoots.

Sticking to the main path though, Thornber didn't take any detours. He continued down the primary section of the cave. The air grew warmer and more fetid around him. The atmosphere was starting to feel almost like a slow cooker, and they were the ingredients. Warm water dripped down onto their heads from above.

They wouldn't be able to stay below the surface for too long at a time. On this trip, Thornber just wanted to confirm what the studies he'd seen hinted at and take some initial measurements and samples. Then they'd head straight back up to the surface and check their gear. He wasn't even sure how much of this the gasmasks could take, being designed for brief chemical attacks rather than meandering strolls through the outskirts of Hell.

He saw the first signs of life a couple hundred yards into the cave system. "Wait, hold on," Thornber said, holding up a hand. The rangers behind him stumbled to a halt, half-blind from their masks. They eased the boat they were carrying onto the cavern floor, and Thornber could hear them panting.

Dropping down onto one knee, Thornber looked down at a little puddle of water lying in a pothole. The shallow, yellow-tinged water had some sort of simple lichen-like fuzz growing around its edges. Dark red in color, the mossy strands clung to the surrounding rock for dear life. Thornber was tempted to grab a sample case and scoop some of the unknown plant life up, but his time down here was limited.

This was promising, though. Very promising. Down here in the darkness, depths untouched by the sun since time immemorial, the plant couldn't be photosynthetic. There was no sunlight to draw energy from down here in the cave. That meant it was surviving off some other energy source.

Maybe thermosynthesis.

Maybe chemosynthesis.

Maybe something entirely unknown.

Thornber smiled behind his mask. That little patch of maroon fuzz was worth a dozen years of study to a botanist. Someone would win awards and grants out the whazoo for unlocking the secrets of that tiny, exotic lichen.

He was here after a bigger prize though, and he wouldn't be satisfied with anything less. More to the point, the powers behind this expedition wouldn't be satisfied with anything less. He was here to find the big enchilada, the motherlode the last expedition hadn't understood, and stick his flag there. If everything went according to plan, this place would be far more valuable than any mere gold mine, though.

"Let's keep going," Thornber said, shining his light further down the shaft. He heard one of the rangers mutter something under his breath as they hefted the rowboat again, but the words were too muffled by the man's gasmask to understand, not that Thornber particularly cared what he said.

Further down the tunnel, Thornber found more of the crimson lichen. It appeared in little isolated clumps and wads. Soon, though, it was much more common. It existed in mats on the floor, the walls, even the ceiling. Tendrils hung down and tried to tickle the backs of their necks. More warm water dripped down from overhead, pattering the rocky floor and their clothing.

Thornber realized they must have passed some sort of tipping point. The gases from the thermal vents somewhere ahead had finally reached a high enough concentration to support these plants. They were now in a completely different environment, one nothing like the surface.

If they took off their masks now, they'd probably choke on the cocktail of noxious fumes before they could make it back to the cavern entrance. This was some primeval land from an earth that never was. Pellucidar, ahoy!

Soon, the passage ahead was almost choked with the strange vegetation. Thornber couldn't tell if the walls of the tunnel had grown tighter or if the lichen had simply grown to the point where it clogged their path forward. Now, the journey downward was reminiscent of nothing so much as a trip down an oversized drain, clogged with bizarre effluence.

He was going underground. It never occurred to him that he might need a machete down here. Jungle equipment was just about the only thing he hadn't brought with him on this expedition.

Just as he was growing concerned that the path forward might become impossible to traverse, the path opened up into a large cistern. The lichen retreated away from them as the path opened up into a sizable chamber.

Yes, this was what Thornber was looking for. This is what the previous notes had indicated lay down here.

At the center of the cistern lay a lake. Thornber shone his light across the surface. The liquid in the lake wasn't water. It was some sort of tar or slime, perfectly black and opaque. The lichen stopped short of the lake's edge, creating a smooth, stone beach down to the edge of the tar pit.

The surface of the lake wasn't still. A point near the center constantly boiled and bubbled like a witch's cauldron full of some deadly brew. Other parts of the lake occasionally released a fat bubble of gas with a noise like a cow flop plopping onto the slaughter house's concrete floor. The hydrothermal vents must be somewhere below the surface of the lake, spewing their gases out into the tar. Eventually, the sulfur and other gases filtered their way up through the slurry of discharge and ooze and emerged here. This was the beating, geothermic heart of Sulfur Springs.

And it was all his.

"You can put that down near the shore," Thornber said. The rangers lugged the metal-framed rowboat a little further and laid it down near the edge of the tar pit. "I wouldn't touch anything if I were you, though," he added.

He was already thinking about the risk of contamination. Not to himself or the rangers. Anything they brought up to the surface would be evolved for this particular environment and would probably die as soon as they brought it to the sunlight. No, he didn't want anything from up above to poison this pristine environment before he could study it.

Odd to think that it was possible to contaminate a toxic biome, but this place was untouched by human hands, an *Urwelt*. Primal. Wild. Alien. They needed to minimize their impact in case the situation down here was more fragile than they realized. At least until he got what he needed from this place.

The rangers set his boat down with a grunt and opened up the equipment packs. Thornber stepped over and removed the items he needed for his initial work.

Today, he would only need the basics to test the lake. Sample cases. Measuring tools. A battery of field testing equipment.

After a few minutes of preparation, he was ready. Everyone piled into the boat and pushed it away from the stony shore, moving out onto the sludge lake.

Despite its appearance, the lake wasn't a tar pit. The ooze within wasn't oil. The substance clung to the boat's oars as the rangers rowed, as if the blackness below was trying to suck the oars off the boat. However, they moved far too smoothly to be on a true tar pit.

Thornber had been briefed on what the tar pit probably really was. Collecting some samples was his top priority. They rowed out toward the center of the lake, steering between the massive columns of rock that supported the chamber's ceiling.

They stayed well clear of where the bubbles from the thermal vents were most intense, however. The heat and commotion would be extreme there, and the last thing any of them wanted was to be flung overboard into the sludge.

Unscrewing a specimen jar, Thornber pulled a pipette out of one of his pockets. He leaned over just as a bubble reached the surface and burst right in front of him. A burp of fetid air hit him as he reached down and sucked some of the ooze into the pipette.

Squirting the black slime into his specimen jar, he took his flashlight to get a better look at the substance. It looked like it had a couple of components, the way salad dressing sat if no one shook it for a while. The base component, the part that made the slime more viscous, looked like it was probably just dirty water, stained vaguely yellow by the minerals and chemical ejaculations from below.

The remainder of the substance, the dark part, reminded Thornber of melted wax. Globules drifted off and rejoined the main amorphous mass. Ripples moved separately through the black substance but not through the water. After the sample had settled in the jar for a few seconds, both components mixed back together into the same slumgullion as before. Thornber shook the jar, and they separated again before merging back into a single dark blob.

As he watched, it almost seemed like the ooze was trying to climb the sides of the jar. The substance refused to sit still inside the container. Thornber couldn't tell if that was because his hand was trembling slightly or due to the gentle rocking of the boat or simply his own imagination, overworked by the strange environment.

He took several more samples. Before he stuffed each jar back in his pack, he double-checked that each lid was screwed on tight. No one knew very much about this stuff, but his superiors thought it could be worth a fortune if some of their theories turned out to be correct. If some of their theories turned out to be correct, it could also be hellaciously dangerous.

Thornber eyed his pipette. A thin layer of black ooze remained inside, clinging to the interior space. He didn't want to stick the tool back in his pocket, not where that black slime would be only a couple of layers of cloth away from his bare skin, and he didn't have any specimen jars large enough to fit the pipette.

He tossed it overboard. It landed on the slime with a plop and floated there for half a second before sliding underneath the ooze, never to be seen again. Wilhelm Planck, the ranger on the right side of the boat, gave Thornber a *do you mind* look through his mask. Thornber pretended not to see it. He'd changed his mind since earlier. A little contamination of the site would be fine. A little littering never hurt anybody. There was no way he wanted that obsidian goop on his person.

A gentle wave rocked the boat. Thornber and the two rangers looked up from where the pipette had disappeared. Shining his light around, Thornber searched for whatever had caused the disruption on the pool's surface. The powerful beam cut into the darkness, but not far enough to reveal the far end of the cavern. All he could see was the shore they'd set off from and the various support columns. There was no sign of whatever caused the boat to sway and bob.

Frowning, Thornber tried to bite his lip but failed under the restrictive mask. He wanted to tear the damn thing off. With it pressed warm and tight around his head, he felt like a team of leeches had covered his entire face in their unctuous embrace, pinching and slurping as they pressed in tight. Taking the mask off now would be suicide, though. After a few more preliminary studies, he was more than ready to pack it in and make for the surface.

Part of him wanted to break for the daylight right now, though. And not just because it felt like he was being slowly roasted down here in the heat. He didn't like this weird oleaginous lake. The strange black scum seemed like something that might explode out of a giant zit on the planet's face.

Nor did the wave that had just rocked them back and forth comfort him any. He tried to explain it to himself. Most likely, a gas bubble had formed and broken just below their boat, sending them wobbling slightly on the surface.

That answer sounded good, but he'd watched the wave continue onward into the darkness for some distance. A massive ripple. The disruption was much larger than any other he had seen from the various gas bubbles that rose to the surface and popped.

Thornber took a deep breath to keep his nerves from galloping away from him. He eyed the two park rangers. Even though he still had a few basic measurements he wanted to take, that didn't mean he couldn't find a way to speed them up a little. More hands lightened the load.

"Here, take this," Thornber said, handing a rope to Hartzell. A weight hung from one end of the rope, and regular markings noted the rope's length. "Toss that end over the side and tell me when it hits the bottom. I want to know how deep this lake is."

The ranger nodded and chucked the weighted end over the side of the rowboat. Thornber turned his attention to pulling his next item out of his pack, like a magician reaching down to pull a rabbit out of his hat.

"Twenty feet and falling," Hartzell said.

"Hmmph." Thornber was surprised. He knew the lake was supposed to be deep, but he didn't expect it to fall out from under them so fast. They weren't all that far from shore. He had thought the bottom was no more than ten feet beneath them.

"Forty feet and falling," Hartzell updated them.

Thornber pulled a rock hammer out of his bag and then looked down at it, unsure why he'd chosen that item. His brain was clouded by a vague sense of unease, and his hands were moving without much thought.

"Sixty feet and falling," Hartzell said, looking at Thornber as if to make sure he was using the readings correctly.

"That's deep. Are we going to need more rope?" Planck asked in a low voice.

"Eighty feet and falling," Hartzell said.

Thornber looked at the unspooling rope. The entire rope was only about two hundred feet long. What would he do if they couldn't find the bottom? What if those black depths were fathomless?

He didn't care for the idea that they were above some sort of trench. His brain conjured up the image of his pipette sinking down and down and down, finally hitting some distant depths. Perhaps something would take notice of the glass instrument landing next to the entrance of its black abode and swim up to investigate. Perhaps there was already something on its way.

Shaking such nonsense thoughts out of his head, Thornber realized that the bigger threat was from falling overboard. If the sludge was difficult to move in, like quicksand, anyone who fell off the boat would never be seen again. They'd sink straight to the bottom in short order.

The mental image of thrashing against that soupy blackness only to be inexorably dragged further and further downward turned his sweat suddenly cold. Thornber stuffed the rock hammer back in his bag. That was it. He'd let his nerves get the better of him. Even though his rational mind knew he was being silly, his underbrain was whispering all sorts of dire warnings.

Just like the ancient urge to throw up under certain circumstances, even when doing so was more dangerous than keeping one's gorge tamped firmly down, evolution hadn't gotten rid of that whispering reptile voice that was afraid of the dark, despite the harm it sometimes did. Thornber needed a quick jaunt to the surface to peel off his mask and feel the sunlight on his skin again. Thinking about that shadowy abyss below them anymore would only work his ancient and useless prey instincts into an unnecessary conniption fit.

"One hundred feet and falling," Hartzell said.

"Alright, alright. Reel it in. We're done here. Short break back to the surface to make sure our masks are in top shape and regroup," Thornber said, trying to sound authoritative. Both Hartzell and Planck looked relieved.

"Fine by me. Hey, wait. I think it just hit bottom. Just over one hundred feet down," Hartzell said. The rope had stopped moving in his hands.

Thornber looked at the stilled rope and felt a soothing touch stroke his fidgeting underbrain. Just knowing the lake below wasn't truly bottomless, something he'd obviously known intellectually but was almost starting to doubt, felt good and calming. He chided himself for getting ready to leave so quickly.

The rope jerked a couple of inches in Hartzell's hands. A rapid, quick movement. Like a snake darting back in a burrow as a hawk flew past.

"Wait, maybe it just--" Hartzell said.

Suddenly, the rope started to unspool at full speed. The fibers flew through the ranger's grip as if someone had attached the other end of the rope to a race car. He tried to grab the rope but hissed in pain as the rough cord chewed apart his gloves and took a layer of skin off his palms instead.

Frozen in surprise for a second, Thornber looked down and realized that Planck's foot was resting in a coil of the rapidly disappearing rope. A split second later, the rope tightened around the second ranger's foot like a kraken's tentacle. The rope kept going, yanking Wilhelm out of his seat before he even had time to realize what was happening.

Wilhelm screamed. The boat rocked violently to the side as he was pulled overboard, nearly capsizing the little vessel.

Thornber looked over the side as the boat rocked back to its center. The ranger's yelp of surprise cut off almost as soon as it began. He'd been sucked under the black muck before he could even try to grab onto anything.

"Oh shit," Hartzell said. The echoes of Planck's scream rebounded off the walls, seeming to come at them from every direction before dying away for good a second later.

"Grab the oars," Thornber ordered.

"But something took Wilhelm," Hartzell said, leaning over the edge of the boat to look down into the blackness below. The remaining ranger dipped his hands down into the sludge as if he expected his friend to be right there, covered by only a thin layer of slime, hoping to catch an outstretched hand and haul Planck back aboard. "We have to do something."

"No, don't," Thornber said, trying to haul Hartzell back from the edge of the little rowboat.

A second later, the park ranger reared back on his own, his hands covered in black ooze. The slime had found its way inside his shredded gloves and the raw spots on his hands. Hartzell screamed and clawed at his hands like an animal caught in a trap trying to chew its own leg off.

He pawed at one hand with a black-encrusted claw and then at the other hand.

Cursing, Thornber grabbed the oars himself and started to paddle the boat back around toward shore. He'd have to deal with Hartzell later, but right now, he needed to get back to dry land. Whatever had inadvertently dragged Planck away was still down there, somewhere under their tiny boat.

He succeeded in spinning the craft around and then made a mad dash for shore. The oars dipped in and out of the Stygian mire, the black goop fighting his every movement.

Each breath he took as he exerted himself with the oars now had a slightly different odor than the usual musty gasmask smell. The sweat pouring down his face from the heat and effort was now tinged with sour undertones of adrenaline and fear.

More bubbles rose up around the rowboat, bursting all around them. A particularly large one swelled up next to the boat, growing and expanding like a tumor before popping and threating to spray Thornber with a small amount of the black slime. Hot air bombarded them like the scene around a crashed zeppelin.

Hartzell was still screaming as a swell hit them. Thornber felt the boat lifting up on the crest of the wave. They were drawing closer to shore now, so tantalizingly close to some modicum of safety. If he could only make the boat move faster. He put all his strength into moving the oars, feeling the muscles in his chest straining as he fought to push the boat across the surface.

Something rose up directly next to the boat. At first, Thornber thought that it was some sort of geyser erupting next to them, a column of filth straight from the overworked septic system of hell's ninth circle. The tower of slime swept up and up and up.

Thornber had enough time to gather the brief impression of a long, crocodile-like snout, claws like brutalist farming equipment, and teeth the size of his thumbs.

Then the filthy mass came crashing down. Thornber watched in horror, feeling like a kayaker realizing that a whale was about to breach directly on top of him. The mass of slime and fangs slammed downward directly next to them.

Those terrible teeth caught Hartzell on the way down, tearing him off his seat and ripping him overboard. They took part of the boat with them, too.

Slime sprayed outward in a goopy splash. Thornber threw his arms up to protect himself, but the ooze splattered him anyway.

For a second, he was blind. He rubbed the glass view ports on his mask, and the world smeared back into focus. Checking himself, Thornber realized that he'd been splattered all over with slime from the lake, but it was all on his clothes rather than directly on his flesh. Thank God for small favors, but he still didn't have long. The ooze on his mask choked the air intake, making it difficult to breathe, and it wouldn't take long for the black gunk to reach his skin.

And that was completely ignoring the creature in the lake. Thornber grabbed the oars again and slapped at the lake's surface, rowing as hard as he could.

Slime started to slip in through the hole the creature tore in the boat. It pooled on the floor near where Hartzell had so recently sat. If Thornber didn't move fast, the rowboat would sink out from underneath him, leaving him to be sucked below the lake's bubbling surface.

Stroking hard, Thornber aimed for the nearest outcropping of shore. The rocky boundary of safety drew closer. A mere forty feet away.

Thornber's lungs struggled to suck down air. The slime clogging his mask made it difficult to breathe. Each inhale caused a sucking, gurgling noise and precious little breathable oxygen. Each exhale produced a rude raspberry noise, and then the desperate struggle repeated itself all over again, with seemingly less air each time.

The shore drew closer. Twenty feet away.

The bottom of the lake must be shallowing out. Surely something as large as the creature that took Hartzell couldn't come this close to shore. If the lake was composed merely of water, Thornber might have considered ditching the boat and wading the last few yards to safety in the shallows, moving faster and freer.

But the lake wasn't water. Jumping out into that would leave him exposed to the slime, and then he would be in even worse trouble than Hartzell when he got some of the gunk on his hands. Thornber's clothes clung wet and heavy on his skin, reminding him that he only had a short amount of time before the slime reached his own skin anyway.

The rowboat bumped against the edge of the lake. Thornber stood up and vaulted over the rapidly growing puddle of sludge that had leaked in through the torn hull. He scrambled forward and leapt over the hull onto the solid stone shore.

He took two steps in the direction of the tunnel they'd walked down earlier, back when there were three men in his party. That was his exit out of here. He staggered in that direction. Then he stopped and looked back, his vision still partially obscured by the slime stuck to his mask.

His pack still sat on the boat's seat, and his sample cases were still in the pack. Lurching backward, he leaned over and grabbed the pack.

He needed those samples. Every fiber of his being wanted to take off down the tunnel to the surface, but he was safe on the shore now.

He'd dash over, grab the pack, and dash right back. It would only take a couple of seconds. Then he'd be on his way out of here. Spinning around, he ran up to the disabled rowboat.

Thornber's mind raced as he grabbed the pack. He needed to get out of this chamber. He needed to run down the tunnel and rip his mask off as soon as he hit the entrance so he could actually breathe again. He needed to rip his clothes off and throw them away as soon as he could, before any of the slime worked its way down to direct contact with his skin.

What was he going to do about the dead park rangers? How was he going to explain that? Screw 'em. He had the samples. That was all he needed to bring back to his superiors. He'd hijack the ranger car, steal some new clothes, and use his contacts to slip out of South Africa quietly. The game preserve never needed to know what had happened here. If they thought he disappeared along with two of their park rangers, that was just fine by him. Probably for the best, actually.

Now, it was time to get the hell out of here. He looked up from the pack in his hands just in time to see a surge of black ooze speeding directly for the shore. The wave grew higher and higher as it drew nearer to the shore, turning into an ebony tsunami.

Thornber turned around to run just as the creature started to emerge from the cresting wave, but it was already too late. A second later, the wall of sludge smashed into him, and then everything was burning black agony.

THREE

THREE DAYS LATER

"So, it was a pretty quiet day. The usual artillery duels and some machinegun fire. Pretty much par for the course. A couple of casualties coming into the field hospital each hour, but nothing like the big offensives. Practically a pleasant day as far as the frontlines went," Cornelia van Rensburg said, picking at the sandwich she'd packed herself.

"Uh huh," Denise said between a bite of her own lunch. They were sitting in one of the game preserve's cars down by the edge of the river.

A lot of the park was dry grassland and bushveldt, often baked brown and dry by the African sun. Further north, the land would flatten out into the great savannas, but the land here was more varied, and many sections of the park were thick with trees. The car was parked not far from the river's edge, where the grass grew high and the trees hung their branches low. Denise and Cornelia sat in the dappled sunlight beneath the trees, their vehicle all but hidden amid the greenery.

They were a bit north of Ranger Station Thirteen and east of the Verschoor Dam. This stretch of the river was part of the dam's outflow, not that they could even see the dam from here behind all the vegetation. The only sign of any human presence at all was the lines of power cables that led from the dam out toward some of the ranger stations, the wires overhead humming in the summer warmth.

"But then I hear all this shouting near the front of the tents. It sounds like a couple of guys are getting ready to start a fist fight. I didn't pay much attention because I figure it's just some sort of argument between a couple of enlisted men. Maybe some orderlies had a disagreement or a couple of the patients had gotten sick of each other. Those sorts of things happened from time to time, so I didn't think about it too much. But then the shouting kept getting closer. Both guys are shouting their lungs out at each other.

"Then a stretcher bursts straight through the tent flaps right in front of me, and there's our staff surgeon arguing with the guy I was dating at the time, who was part of the munitions disposal team. A bomb expert, basically. A couple of medics are hauling a stretcher along, and Mike and the surgeon are both walking beside it, yelling and waving their arms around like the world is about to end and there's only room for one of them on the ark."

Denise brushed some crumbs off her safari jacket. Their current task had kept them away from the spider migration, so at least she was only dealing with crumbs today, not baby spiders.

At certain times of the year, millions of egg sacs broke open and released even more millions of baby spiders. The local area never had enough aphids or other tiny insects to support the sudden burst of tiny spiders, so the infant arachnids spun a little circle of silk and cast it to the wind.

The silk wasn't meant as a web. The silk actually caught the wind like a little kite, and the breeze sent hundreds of thousands of spiders ballooning away at once. The sight was like some sort of bizarre hot air balloon festival, with the spiders riding the breeze to new homes, spreading out across the landscape. A lot of the baby spiders weren't much bigger than a mote of dust, but some of them were closer in size to a raisin.

She couldn't say she was unhappy to be clear of their wind patterns. Her first day of the job of tracking the spider migration, she'd looked up and caught a baby spider squarely in her eye. Any time the heavens opened up and it started raining spiders, it wasn't going to appear on her list of top ten best days ever.

That being said, she'd rather still be tracking the spider swarms if it removed the necessity of their current assignment. Myron Hartzell and Wilhelm Planck had gone missing along with that geologist, Thornber.

The rangers and geologist hadn't returned to Ranger Station Thirteen at their appointed time. Initially, no one thought very much about it one way or the other. Almost everyone there had escorted someone through the park who insisted on taking over their lives for the day. Sometimes a car simply became stuck in a mud hole. There were dangerous animals in the park, certainly; but both Hartzell and Planck were experienced and knew how to steer clear of danger. Even in a worst-case scenario, they were armed with rifles in their car, so it wasn't at all likely that lions could drag them both away.

By nightfall, it was clear something was wrong, though. Kirkeberg sent out every available ranger in their section of the park to investigate Sulfur Springs and the path to and from the cave.

They found most of Thornber's equipment stacked near the entrance to Sulfur Springs, but there was no sign of the geologist or the rangers.

The cave entrance was smeared with some sort of dried black goo. Hours of exposure to sunlight had turned it into a strange, crusty coating, like an old scab. Kirkeberg ordered everyone to stay out of the cave until he could get in touch with some of Thornber's people and maybe learn if the black gunk was dangerous or not. He didn't want more people wandering inside if they might be facing some grave and unknown danger, just in case it was poisonous and Thornber's team had been overwhelmed by the toxins.

Perhaps the oddest thing about the scene at the entrance to Sulfur Springs was the single set of footprints. In places, the desiccated slime on the floor was scuffed and worn away in such a way that it was obvious that someone wearing boots had tromped out of the entrance. By the look of the footsteps, whoever walked out of that cave hadn't been very steady on their feet. In fact, they'd been moving in more of a determined shamble down the slope. That was all they could tell, though.

From the footprints alone, it was impossible to tell if the boots belonged to Hartzell or Planck or Thornber. Whoever had wandered down from Sulfur Springs hadn't returned to the ranger station, so that meant they were out here in the wilderness somewhere, possibly injured. Possibly dead.

Kirkeberg had every ranger he could borrow from the other stations and outposts beating through the brush, looking for whoever had wandered out of that cave. Three days later, no one had found a single thing. No body. No torn clothing. Nothing. If their possible injuries hadn't killed them already, every hour the stranded survivor spent out here exposed him to the elements. Denise didn't have much hope for finding a warm body at this point, but she and Cornelia would resume their search along the river as soon as they'd refueled on some food.

"But the weird part was, there was a man on the stretcher. A soldier. Obviously in bad shape. He had some sort of wound on the right side of his belly. My first guess was shrapnel or something. We saw a lot of shrapnel wounds near the front lines. However, the surgeon and Mike seem to be arguing about the guy. Technically, Mike should have stood down because the surgeon outranked him, but they were all but grabbing scalpels off the tables and dueling."

"What exactly was the problem?" Denise asked.

"A mortar had landed on the soldier. Right on top of him. It didn't explode, though. Instead, the damn thing got wedged most of the way inside him. The fact that his body softened the impact enough that the thing didn't explode probably saved the other guys who were in the trench with him, but it wasn't exactly a good situation. He had a live bomb inside his body."

"That sounds...unpleasant."

"No kidding. They'd sedated him, but he was still conscious somehow. The surgeon and Mike were arguing over whether they needed to operate on him first or defuse the bomb first. If they operated without defusing the bomb, there was the slight chance it would blow up one of their operating rooms. If they took the time to defuse the bomb, the man would probably die from the trauma and blood loss."

"I'm starting to see why you gave up on nursing to pursue something else."

"Yeah. I think that was the moment I decided I didn't want to be involved with the practice of medicine anymore. I mean, I'd seen plenty of bad business treating war wounds fresh off the battlefield, but this was different somehow. Standing right over an injured man arguing about whether they should treat him or not, and pretty seriously thinking they should probably not act in that man's personal best interest, made me realize I probably don't have what it takes to do that for the rest of my life."

"You thought they should defuse the bomb first? Even if it meant he might die before they could finish? I guess I can see why, though."

"I mean, the way I figured it, there were a few different outcomes possible there. The first was the one the surgeon wanted. They'd treat it basically like a regular shrapnel wound and just ignore the fact that they were dealing with live explosives. The mortar would be safely removed, and they'd patch the soldier up and send him home.

"The second outcome was what Mike was arguing for. Defuse the mortar, even if it meant the man it was buried in had to wait longer for the medical treatment that might save his life. He'd already lost a lot of blood, and he probably wouldn't have lasted through the defusing process, given the complications of having the mortar buried inside him."

"So who won the argument?"

"The surgeon. Which was inevitable really, given their respective ranks. He ordered some MPs to go drag Mike out of the hospital so he could save the man's life. A few minutes later, the third possible outcome happened. The mortar blew up while the surgeon was trying to remove it. The explosion killed the patient, smeared the doctor across half the operation room, and destroyed most of the equipment in there," Cornelia said.

Denise didn't say anything for a moment.

"Some days, I think that must have been the dumbest surgeon who ever passed his medical exams to take a risk like that. Other days, I think maybe that's the bravest thing I've ever seen, trying to save a man's life at such a risk to his own. Maybe there's some overlap in there. That was pretty much the final straw, though."

"Saw too much?"

"Not so much that, although it was tough having to hose the surgeon out of our operating room. I'd seen plenty of gruesome injuries from the war already. Saw some more before it ended and I went back to school for paleontology. No, I just knew I could never be that high-minded all the time. I was with Mike all the way on that call. Defuse the mortar even if it meant probably killing the patient. I just didn't want such an obvious example of my own failings hanging over my head every day if I stayed in nursing."

"I'm not sure that being practical counts as a failing."

"Not usually. Still, I didn't want to be the person in the room telling everyone else we should back off and let people bleed out, though. On the plus side though, Mike taught me how to defuse a lot of simple explosives after that. I can assemble the things too, so I'm the wrong lady to piss off. Mike learned that the hard way when I found out he was sleeping with some French doxie. I blew up his locker a couple of times after that."

Denise chuckled for a moment, but it didn't last long. Everyone's mood was dark after the three disappearances in Sulfur Springs. That was how she and Cornelia had gotten onto this topic in the first place.

"So, I know you've skirted around it before, but you've never told me exactly how you ended up working here at the game preserve," Cornelia said.

"Well, that's not a particularly fun story, either," Denise said, thinking back to the day she knew she had to give up big game hunting. The hunting expedition company in Cape Town had been all hers for a few years at that point, long enough to establish a reputation of her own by then.

"It hasn't exactly been a fun few days," Cornelia said.

"Alright, I was out on a hunt. I'd been hired by a group of--"

Suddenly, Denise heard a noise out in the distance. She'd spent most of her life wandering one stretch of the veldt or another, and she knew the sounds associated with it. This was something else though, a low rumble growing louder, almost like the growl of a hungry beast prowling the night.

"Wait," Denise said, listening. Cornelia tilted her head slightly, straining to pick up the sound above the rustle of the plants all around them. A few seconds later, the rumbling noise was much louder.

That was a truck engine. Big and powerful. But the ranger stations didn't maintain any trails through this part of the park. Was someone coming to recall them back to Station Thirteen? Had someone found the owner of those tracks from Sulfur Springs?

She checked the car's radio, but it was functioning. If someone had found anything, the ranger station would have contacted them directly rather than send someone out to bring them back.

A few minutes later, the large truck pushed its way forward through the grasses near the edge of the river. The military transport-style vehicle snorted its way forward like a large hog searching for truffles, shoving its way through the path of least resistance. Denise watched in fascination as the truck passed within one hundred feet of their parked car, apparently not noticing them amid the foliage.

The Dracobly Hessler Game Preserve didn't own any vehicles like that. Denise didn't move as the truck lumbered past, its suspension squeaking as it clambered over the uneven ground. The truck slipped out of sight through the greenery. Off in the distance, the sound of the truck's engine began to fade away into a low growl again.

"That wasn't one of ours," Cornelia said.

"I know." Denise let out the breath she hadn't realized she'd been holding and listened. The sound of the truck's engine had faded away to nothing. She stabbed the keys into the ignition, and their touring car grunted and coughed to life. "Let's go find out who that was," she said.

She eased the car forward. At the same time, Cornelia twisted around and reached into the back seat. Leaning back around, she had a .577 Nitro Express elephant gun in her hands.

The huge rifle was designed to bring down some of the massive African game that roamed the park. Each and every round it fired wasn't much smaller than a salt shaker, and the recoil could break a man's arm if the weapon wasn't held properly.

Such weapons weren't simply designed to kill large animals, they were meant to stop them in their tracks. Regular bullets would eventually kill an enraged bull elephant, but the Nitro Express was meant to make it fall over dead mid-charge. Denise had seen the power a full blast from an elephant gun could inflict, and it wasn't pretty. On a large target, they could blow out an exit wound you could throw a medium-sized dog through. On a man-sized target, the gun would blow off limbs, rip bodies in half, or turn the unfortunate victim more inside-out than not.

Obviously, Dracobly Hessler Game Preserve didn't use the guns for hunting. Their job involved protecting the natural beauty of the park and the populations of rare animals that lived there. However, that didn't mean all the animals appreciated it. Sometimes rangers found themselves suddenly face-to-snout with a herd of white rhinos or other territorial creatures who didn't take kindly to the sudden intrusion. Sometimes, there was the risk that one of the big cats in the park might develop a broader palette and become a man eater. Usually, the cars could speed away from the large animals before they became too agitated, but not always. Given the choices, the park preferred potentially losing a couple of animals over finding a carload of rangers and park guests rended limb from limb.

There were other uses for such a rifle, though. Denise picked up the car's radio and sent in their location and what they'd seen. She eased the car through the shielding screen of greenery and started to follow the truck's tracks.

Denise and Cornelia bounced in their seats as the car purred forward over the rough terrain. The park vehicles were designed to handle a certain amount of off-road activity, but this was rougher ground than they normally traversed. The big truck they were following was built to rumble around craters and shell-blasted mud, though. It wasn't as nimble, but it would be steadier on the path than the ranger vehicle.

The ranger car slid along the bank of the river like a lioness tracking an antelope across the plains, moving low and slow. Of course, Denise didn't think they were following something as simple and docile as an antelope. Whoever was in that truck, they weren't supposed to be here.

A layer of sweat formed on Denise's hands as the steering wheel rocked in her grip. She licked her lips once. There were a few different possibilities about who might be inside that truck. The first was that the mysterious driver was somehow involved with the disappearance of Thornber, Hartzell, and Planck. If they were, then they would almost certainly be unsavory customers.

The second possibility was that they were poachers. The criminal gangs that operated poaching operations might be even more dangerous. They were sure to be well-armed, under some sort of central direction, and not the least bit adverse to violence.

Denise licked her lips again. She'd wanted to prove that she could work on the anti-poaching squad. This might very well be her chance. She hoped it wasn't, though. It wasn't that she wasn't champing at the bit to prove Kirkeberg wrong. She most certainly was.

No, she hoped that whoever was driving that vehicle could tell her something more about what happened to her fellow park rangers and Dr. Thornber. The truck was an old cargo transport. Maybe Thornber and his guides were tied up in the back, bound, gagged, and rattled but basically okay. That was the best-case scenario.

She barely touched the accelerator except to rev out of the occasional rut. The path was rough, but the truck was easy enough to follow. Where it strayed close to the river, it left thick tire tracks in the mud. Where the truck was forced to veer away from the river, due to rocks or fallen logs, it carved a path through the tall grass and reeds. The broken branches and mashed reeds were easy enough to follow, even though she couldn't see the truck itself anymore.

Cornelia sat in silence in the passenger seat, her hands locked tight around the elephant gun. The same worried thoughts that had buzz sawed through Denise's mind flashed behind Cornelia's eyes. What if the team from Sulfur Springs was lying in the back of that truck, stone dead? What if the truck had ten poachers sitting in the back, armed with rifles and machine pistols? Maybe there was a perfectly mundane explanation for all of this, but it wasn't obvious on the surface, and the number of bad possibilities seemed to outweigh any innocent ones.

The car slid around another wall of foliage, and Denise suddenly heard the truck start up right in front of them. A muffled voice shouted something as the truck roared to life.

Denise slammed the car into park and opened the door, already moving low through the grass. The truck must have come to a stop somewhere just ahead, but she'd been too far behind to hear the engine shut off. Whoever was driving hadn't been aware of her until her own vehicle's engine noise alerted them that they'd been followed. Now, instead of getting the drop on her quarry, they had a few seconds of warning that she was coming. That meant they'd either try to run or they'd try to fight.

She leapt through a row of bushes, and then the truck was directly in front of her, black exhaust pumping out of its tailpipe. A smaller personal truck was parked nearby, hidden from surveillance under the boughs of a tree.

An Asian man ran toward the smaller truck, vaulting through the grass. Even from here, Denise could see that the back of the truck was loaded with several sets of large elephant tusks. The ivory gleamed dully in the muted sunlight. Despite the distance, Denise could see blood splatters covering the stumps where the tusks ended. The blood had dried and coagulated until it was a gruesome maroon.

Her more immediate concern was the elephant gun propped up next to the driver's door on the smaller truck. Denise couldn't tell if the man was running to hop in his truck or if he was going for the gun.

"Stop," she yelled, raising a revolver. The man didn't stop. He didn't even give any indication he'd heard her as he barreled straight for the ivory-laden truck.

She raised the revolver above her head and fired a warning shot. A severed leaf drifted down from overhead as the report from the revolver faded away. The man still didn't stop, moving straight for the truck. Straight for the gun.

The driver of the old transport truck threw himself out of the vehicle. Denise spun the revolver onto him. Her first impression was of carefully combed, dark blond hair. His hands shot up into the air in surrender, waving in please-don't-shoot gyrations.

Her attention snapped back to the running man. He was no more than ten feet from the truck's front door, no more than ten feet away from the long-barreled elephant gun.

Denise clenched her jaw and levelled her revolver at the man's back. A crash of gunfire filled the clearing, industrial thunder cascading down on them.

Cornelia rocked backward from the impact of the .577 Nitro Express, nearly falling down before she wobbled back to solid footing. Across the clearing, the small truck rocked up on its side as a hole appeared in its front hood. Flanged metal chaff and jagged spall blew out the far side of the engine block and spun off into the grass. Gasoline and radiator fluid bled out into the dirt in spurts and dribbles.

The running man skidded to a stop and turned around, giving Denise her first good look at him. He was dressed in a khaki vest and wore his hair cut short. He raised his hands slowly to about the height of his shoulders, but he didn't move any closer to Denise. He didn't move away from the elephant gun that had fallen to the ground, knocked loose when the truck jolted. Denise couldn't see the rifle anymore to tell exactly where it was in relation to the man. She didn't like that.

"Step closer," she shouted at the man. "Move away from the truck."

Denise didn't move any closer herself. That would start to put the cargo truck's blond driver behind her, and she didn't trust him any more than she did the runner. She wanted them both right where she could see them, where she could swivel her revolver from one to the other with just a flick of her wrist.

The man didn't step any closer. His hands remained raised only to the height of his shoulders.

"C'mon. Hands up high," she said, gesturing with the revolver for emphasis. From this distance, she would have rather had a .577 Nitro Express of her own in her hands. The long barrel was more accurate than the revolver's. Plus, there was a certain reassurance that came from holding a weapon that could blow a hole in a tank's armor.

The man raised his hands a little higher. Not as much as Denise would have liked, but if he wanted to lunge for the elephant gun or some hidden backup weapon, she'd have an extra split second to lodge a couple of formal complaints directly into his chest.

He still wasn't moving away from the disabled truck. She told him to move closer again, but he didn't budge. She tried in Afrikaans next. Then Zulu, which was a long shot.

The blond man said something in a language that was probably Mandarin. Denise didn't speak a lick of Mandarin.

Without taking her eyes away from the runner, she turned her head in the direction of the blond man. "What did you say to him?"

"I'm just repeating your order that he move closer. He doesn't speak English." The blond man spoke with an accent. Denise plugged it as Australian and tucked that information away.

She turned all of her attention to the Australian for a second. "Go stand over there next to him. Get him to step closer, too. I want you both where I can see you, and I want you away from the trucks." The Australian walked over toward his silent colleague.

Denise looked back at the other man and narrowed her eyes. She couldn't tell for sure, but it looked like the first man had inched half a step backwards toward the truck while she was talking to the Australian.

The man's eyes were staring at her. No, not at her. Through her. He was thinking about something. Maybe he was imagining just how much trouble he was in. Maybe he was picturing his next move in his head, visualizing scooping up the rifle and leveling it in one smooth, fluid movement.

Maybe option one. Maybe option two.

Maybe they should defuse the bomb. Maybe they should try to save the patient.

The Australian stopped a few feet away from the Asian man and said something in Mandarin again. The runner gave a one-word response. The Australian said something back, tilting his head in the direction of Denise and Cornelia, both of them armed and not in the mood.

Scowling, the runner took two shuffling steps away from the truck and stood a little closer to the blond Australian. He didn't look happy about it, though.

Somewhere off in the distance, Denise could hear engines racing. That would be the other rangers, converging on her position. They'd reach the river in a couple of minutes.

At least, she hoped it was more rangers. If the poachers had sent out a message to their people too, Denise and Cornelia might be well and truly screwed.

Still pointing her revolver in their direction, Denise eyed her two prisoners. She had to assume that was her back-up arriving. If she tried to shuffle the two men into the bushes, one or both of them would probably bolt and disappear into the thick underbrush and she'd never see them again.

"What are your names?" She glanced at the blond man, not expecting any response from his colleague.

"I'm Dr. Skipworth. Lyndon Skipworth. This is Lin."

"Doctor Skipworth, is it? Doctor? As in 'Doctor Livingston, I presume?' Count me as skeptical."

"Yes, I suppose the circumstances here do look just a tad peculiar. I am a doctor, though. I have a medical degree."

"Uh huh. And I suppose you and your friend here simply got lost on your way to a Johannesburg medical conference."

Lin's scowl intensified at the back and forth going on.

"Would you let us go if I said yes?"

"Not a chance."

"Then no, that isn't quite why we're out here."

Just then, two ranger cars nosed their way through the underbrush, churning grass and small shrubs beneath their wheels. Two large park rangers emerged from each vehicle with weapons of their own, surveying the tableau before them. Denise and Cornelia. Two strange men. A truck full of blood-speckled ivory and a larger cargo truck, contents unknown. And guns.

"You can inform me and my friends about what you're doing here back at the ranger station then, Dr. Skipworth." The other rangers approached and grabbed both men, securing their hands and dragging them back toward the cars.

Cornelia dropped her weapon to her side and rubbed where her shoulder had absorbed the impact from the elephant gun. She grimaced, but it turned into a grin as she looked over at Denise. Pausing from tending to her arm, she flashed a thumbs up.

Denise returned the gesture. Cornelia had done well. Very well. The knowledge gave Denise a certain amount of pride. She considered the woman to be a sort of understudy. Balthazar van Rensburg had hoped they'd work well together when he pulled the strings to get this job, and it looked like it was paying off.

She also felt a sly little satisfaction, though. This was the first time anyone had managed to track down any of the gang of poachers plaguing the game preserve. Maybe capturing this Dr. Lyndon Skipworth and Lin would lead to something on Thornber and the missing rangers. Maybe not. Either way, it would be a huge boon to the park if someone could crack the poachers apart and send them packing. And it looked like she was the one who got the ball rolling on that investigation.

Ambling back to the ranger car, she picked up the radio and called in to Ranger Station Thirteen. "Hey, Kirkeberg, guess what?"

FOUR

THORNBER RETURNS

"What do you make of them?" Kirkeberg asked.

"The one, Skipworth, gave up as soon as I walked into the clearing. He wasn't interested in putting up any sort of fight. I think he might be helpful."

"Hrmmph." Kirkeberg grunted. "Maybe. The Pretoria police are sending a unit to take them off our hands, including a translator fluent in Mandarin. It'll be a while before they get here, though. What about the other one, Lin?"

Kirkeberg and Denise stood in his office. Both cells in the tiny holding area down the hall were now in use. Each room had a ranger standing in front of it. Ranger Station Thirteen wasn't really meant to serve as a jail, or even a police station, but it could temporarily serve those roles until more conventional law enforcement arrived to pick up the mess.

Right now, the break room was in the process of being transformed into a makeshift interrogation unit. Most of the amenities were being removed, leaving behind a single table and a set of chairs. Catching a couple of poachers red-handed was a start, but they weren't working alone. The rest of their team would be somewhere in the game preserve or nearby. The two men in the holding cells almost certainly knew where.

Of course, once the rest of the poachers realized that two of their number had been captured, they might very well scatter and regroup elsewhere. Kirkeberg had made the decision that they wouldn't wait for the police units to gather more information. If they could break this now, they might be able to lead the full police team straight to the main poacher camp.

"I don't think we're going to get much of anything from Lin."

"We could have this Skipworth character translate for us. It's not ideal, but we don't have anyone who speaks Mandarin here."

"That's not what I meant," Denise said. "Skipworth pretty much rolled over and showed his belly as soon as we found him. Lin took off running. I'm pretty sure he would have taken us out if we gave him the chance. He didn't do much to cooperate, even with Skipworth translating for him."

"You really think he would have shot the two of you?"

"Hard to say for sure, but he seemed like he was at least tempted by the idea. Maybe he would have just fled in his truck, but something about the way he moved seemed like he was thinking awfully hard about whether he could reach his rifle or not."

Kirkeberg grimaced. "I guess that settles it. We need to get as much information from these two clowns as quick as we can. Maybe they know what happened out at Sulfur Springs. Maybe they can point us to where to find Hartzell and Planck, even if they're dead in a ditch somewhere."

The grimace spread to Denise's face. She didn't care to think about that possibility, though every hour the three men were missing, it seemed more and more likely.

"Alright, tell Cornelia to bring Skipworth in, assuming that's his real name. I think you're right. We're not going to get anything out of the other one, not when we have to translate everything through his accomplice. We'll work over Skipworth on his own."

A few minutes later, Lyndon Skipworth was sitting in front of them. Cornelia and another ranger stood in opposite corners of the room, and there was a third ranger outside the door.

Skipworth didn't exactly look like maximum security material. Skinny, freckled, and sunburned, he looked younger than his age. Denise could more easily picture him as a chartered accountant than as a hardened hunter.

"So, uh, what can I help you with, officers?"

"We're not police officers," Kirkeberg said. "Although they'll be along to ask you more questions later. We're rangers here at the Dracobly Hessler Game Preserve. Did you know you were on protected land when we found you with all those elephant tusks?"

"Well, yes. My, shall we say, 'associates' chose the area because they knew the hunting would be good here. Look, I don't want this to get worse than it already is. I'd like to help you, if you help me a little bit. Believe me, this is not what I want to be doing with my life. This is one of the last things I'd like to be doing."

"We'll see," Kirkeberg said. "We'll see. And who exactly are these associates of yours? Lin, for instance."

"They're members of the Sun Yee On Triads."

Denise blinked. Skipworth was proving more forthright than she could have hoped. But this wasn't good news. Triads were Chinese gangsters. Criminal syndicates with operations and connections around the world. They weren't so very different from the organized crime consortiums that caused trouble in cities like New York and Chicago.

They dealt in contraband and intimidation, and they weren't shy about violence. If Thornber, Hartzell, and Planck ran afoul of a group of Triad-affiliated poachers near Sulfur Springs, that didn't help the odds of finding them alive.

Kirkeberg seemed to be thinking along the same track. He pulled out a staff folder and removed pictures of Hartzell and Planck. "Have you ever seen either of these men?"

Skipworth looked at the two photos for a moment and then shook his head. "I can't say that I have. Are they involved with the poaching trade, too?"

"No, they're rangers here at the game preserve."

"What do they have to do with any of this, then?"

"They're missing."

"Oh."

"Anything you might know about them could save their lives. You said you'd be interested in helping us out. This is our top priority right now," Kirkeberg said. "If you have something on them and don't share it now, we'll find out about it, and you'll be the first in line when the axe drops."

"I've honestly never seen either of them before. I'm sorry they're missing, but I don't know anything about that one way or the other. I'm a doctor. Zhang would have called me if he decided to take a couple of park rangers hostage for some reason."

"Zhang?" Kirkeberg asked.

"Zhang Dong. He's in charge of this operation."

"Let's start from the beginning here," Denise said. "I gather from your accent that you're not from around here."

"Melbourne, Australia," Skipworth said.

Denise nodded as if this was something important. The good cop to Kirkeberg's bad cop. The old Jeff and Mutt routine. She'd be friendlier and more approachable, and Kirkeberg would goad and push him.

Normally, Denise wouldn't have much interest in the role. She'd go far for her friends, but everyone else could take a flying leap up their own butts. A lion might eat her face off because it was hungry. Another person might do it for fun. Sometimes, she thought that was what really distinguished mankind from the other orders of life. Poachers weren't very high up her list of all-time best buddies.

She found that she basically believed Skipworth, though. He seemed eager to spill his guts so long as he could find a way to save some stretch of his own hide. So long as there was some possibility he could scrape through this, Skipworth would keep talking. A lot of it would probably even be the truth, too.

"How long have you had your medical degree?"

"About two years now. I was doing a residency in Port Elizabeth. Obviously, things didn't quite work out."

"What happened? How does somebody go from a medical degree and residency to running with See Yee On Triads out in the wilderness?"

"It's a complicated story."

"We've got the time," Kirkeberg said.

"Yeah, I guess we do. Cripes. How do I get into these messes? Alright, so it goes something like this. I specifically came to Port Elizabeth because I thought I could do the most good in a place like that. South Africa has a lot of shanty towns and neglected areas, the segregated black areas. They don't see a lot of proper medical care out there."

Skipworth was referring to the reservations and the homelands the South African government had set aside for the black populations. Part of the idea was to segregate the indigenous elements from the white British and Dutch-descended populace. The relatively small stretches of land had few opportunities for education or advancement. Some of South African's politicians wanted to make the regions nominally independent, which would strip the residents of their citizenship and other rights while still leaving them wholly dependent on South Africa. Only about thirteen percent of South Africa's land was reserved for the black populace, which accounted for about eighty percent of the overall population.

Denise didn't care for the system, but it didn't show any signs of changing. Blacks couldn't purchase land outside of the reserves, and they required passes to even enter many of the areas reserved for whites. Laws prohibited black workers from practicing skilled trade, and other restrictions were designed to perpetuate a system of indentured servitude that looked more like slavery.

She squinted at Skipworth, trying to see where this was going. Someone who started out trying to administer medicine to the indigent didn't seem like an obvious recruit for a Triad gang.

"I know. I know," Skipworth said. "I've fallen a long way, and most of it's my own damn fault. You see, I have a problem. A gambling problem. Because the Bantu settlements are able to come up with some of their own legislation, they'll scrounge for any opportunity they can to find some independent revenue. Some of their laws are much less restrictive on gaming establishments and other forms of entertainment than the rest of South Africa."

"So you blew all your pay from the hospital at some casino," Kirkeberg said. "I thought doctors were supposed to be smarter than that."

"Oh no. You underestimate me," Skipworth said. "I didn't just squander my paycheck from the hospital. I managed to squander an entire lifetime's worth of money at those places. When I couldn't get any more credit, I turned to less reputable lenders and gambling dens that wouldn't even pass the reservation's lax laws. Shadier underground establishments run by even shadier people."

"And you ended up eyeball-deep in debt to some tough guys," Denise concluded.

"Right. I didn't know they had connections to a Triad organization at the time. I'm not sure it would have stopped me even if I did know. I was so convinced my big break was right around the corner, and the system I was working on would turn things around for me, that I just thought I'd pay everything off with no problem. I never thought there would be any consequences, because I'd have the money back in my hands with the next shuffle of the cards."

"To reiterate, I thought doctors were supposed to be smart," Kirkeberg said.

"Smart doesn't always intersect with good sense," Skipworth said, looking down at his hands folded on the table.

Denise could tell the matter had eaten him up for a long time. He'd obviously had time to think about it and ponder on his mistakes.

"Hindsight has a way of highlighting your worst choices, am I right?" Skipworth said. "I was taking money from one loan shark at exorbitant interest rates to pay off the last loan shark and his exorbitant interest rates. Never underestimate the power of compound interest. Eventually, it got to the point where I had to deal with the lenders of last resort, the sort of people you normally only meet when you need a telescope and some good eyes to figure out just how high rock bottom is above you. That's how I became good buddies with folks like my pal, Lin."

"That still doesn't exactly explain how you ended up in the poaching business."

"Normally, they would have just terrorized someone who owed as much money as me. Find a way to pay up or we break your kneecaps. That sort of thing. The normal cheap thug routine. Of course, being professionals, they had connections who were a bit more creative with their solutions in case I still couldn't pay up. It's my understanding that they scrapped all the skin off the bottom of one man's feet, tied him to the back of a truck, and forced some of their other debtors to take bets on just how long he could walk before the truck dragged him to death."

"Charming," Denise said.

"Yes, they're not exactly pleasant people. I suppose I'm lucky in that regard. They thought I might be more valuable in some capacity other than roadkill. The made me an offer. Work as one of their fixers, and they'd simply allow my interest to continue accumulating instead of slicing me open and feeding my organs to pigs one at a time. Very persuasive, those Triads."

"If your interest rate is still running, how much do you owe today?"

"Probably somewhere north of South Africa's gross domestic product. I lost track a while ago. The point was, I was never going to pay it all off, and that meant I'd be their plaything for the rest of my life. Being white and having a reputable career, I could make connections and access areas most of their contacts in the reservations couldn't. Smuggling drugs out of the hospital? Bringing suitcases of money to Boer hitmen in Pretoria? Driving cargo trucks full of contraband out to the ports? I could travel freely and without suspicion, unlike a lot of their lap dogs, so I was tasked with all sorts of fun jobs. Since the hospital fired me, I mostly work with Zhang Dong, though."

"Tell us about Zhang Dong."

"He's in charge of the Sun Yee On's poaching operations out here. It's by far their most profitable business in South Africa. Probably one of the most profitable operations in the entire organization, inside of China or out. Without the hospital to keep me in the country anymore, they're worried I might try to quietly disappear, but Zhang has enough people to always keep an eye on me out here."

"Just how many men does he have?"

"At any given time, there's probably fifty Triads working for him. A few are transporters and work the logistics of keeping his camps supplied and mobile. There's a few scouts, usually recruited locally rather than brought in from Shanghai, to track the most valuable animals and keep watch on the ranger patrols. Most of his people are hunters, though."

"What about their camps?" Kirkeberg asked. "How hard would it be to round them up?"

"If I tell you, will you help me out?"

"Depends on the value of the information," Kirkeberg said.

"That doesn't give me a lot of reason to trust you."

"Too bad. You can either tell us and maybe it'll be useful enough that you'll get out of this with our recommendation to go easy on the charges, or you can keep the information to yourself. You'd go to prison along with everyone else, and the Triads would assume you'd ratted them out anyway."

Cornelia fidgeted in the corner where she'd been standing. Denise glanced at Kirkeberg. "Do you mind if we step out briefly to discuss something?"

"I'm the one who has the final say on what we do this matter."

Denise gritted her teeth. Kirkeberg meant well in his own way, but he also had the bad habit of taking his own word as law. "I know. Given that I brought this matter to you, I'd appreciate it if you'd humor some input."

"Very well. Cornelia. Basil. See to it that the prisoner remains where he is while I discuss something." Cornelia and the other ranger both nodded.

Standing up from their seats, Denise and Kirkeberg pushed open the door and moved down the hall far enough that Skipworth couldn't hear what they were saying.

Taking a deep breath, Denise launched into her argument. "I think we should go ahead and promise Dr. Skipworth that we'll recommend lighter charges for him if he cooperates."

"Do you now?"

"Yes, he clearly wants to cut some sort of deal. The police units will be here in a few hours. If he spills his guts now, we can use the police to help us go after the poacher camps."

"I was thinking something similar about the police units. I requested that they send a large team with a few prisoner vans. With a little luck, we'll have broken the poaching ring by nightfall."

"So we're in agreement, then? Because in there I really didn't think you were going to offer any sort of deal to the doctor."

"We're in agreement about the police. But, no, I don't plan to offer any sort of deal to Skipworth."

"Why not? He could be the wedge we use to blast this thing apart, and it doesn't sound like he's a willing part of it anyway."

"Maybe he was forced to help out. Maybe he wasn't. I don't particularly care either way, but I'm not going to take his word for it. My job is to protect this stretch of land. He's been an active participant in destroying it. For all I care, the Triads are welcome to put a shank in him in prison. I won't say anything more than I would be willing to consider offering him a deal. Considering a deal. Not offering a deal. He'll sing like a canary either way because he'll do anything to save his own skin at this point. We've got him over a barrel, and I don't intend to relieve the pressure by giving him any direct assurances."

Denise clacked her jaw shut. Kirkeberg could get exactly what he wanted without having to give up a thing.

"Look, I want this Zhang Dong character's head on a pike just as much as you do, but I think Skipworth is right. If we don't give him a little bit of slack, he probably won't survive his first week of prison. I've heard stories about the Triad gangs, none of them pleasant. The fact that they have a substantial program set up here is surprising."

A ranger walked into the hallway. "Mr. Kirkeberg, we've lost contact with one of the patrols out near Sulfur Springs."

"What happened?"

"We don't know. It might be nothing, but Crane and De Hoog didn't radio in when they were supposed to. It's been over an hour now."

Kirkeberg squeezed his eyes shut for a second. When they opened back up, he looked very tired. "Send the closest two teams out to Crane and De Hoog's last known location. Tell them to keep their wits about them and come prepared for action. It might be more poachers. If they see anything, tell them to get back here on the double and report it in. We can't afford to have anyone lost out there."

"Very good." The ranger nodded and retreated back down the hall.

Kirkeberg's face was hard as he turned back to Denise. The scars down his cheek stood out as white streaks as his cheeks turned red. A vein pulses along his temple.

"This is what I'm talking about. There's something called a felony-murder rule. Two robbers walk into a bank, and to the surprise of the first robber, the second robber shoots the bank clerk. Both get charged with murder. Dr. Thornber, Hartzell, and Planck are still missing out there somewhere, and now I learn that two more of my rangers might be gone. If I find out that this Skipworth had anything to do with this, if one of his Triad friends so much as whispered their names to him, and it turns out that something happened to any of them, I want him strung up by his thumbs right there with the rest of them. If he gives us useful information right now, I don't plan on cutting him any sort of deal. If he later turns out to be some tiny cog in this big machine and the barristers want to cut him a deal of their own, fine. But right now, I just want to find my friends alive, and I want a map of where I can find those poaching camps. Everything else is secondary. Do you understand?"

Denise nodded.

She understood Kirkeberg's position. Getting Thornber and the other rangers back was just as important to her as it was to Kirkeberg. Hartzell and Planck were good men. She didn't know Dr. Thornber from Adam, but she obviously wouldn't wish whatever unpleasant fate Zhang Dong and his Sun Yee On Triads might come up with on him. She just thought there was a better way to go about the situation.

She wasn't about to win that argument, though.

"Let's get back in there before he can get comfortable with the situation and starts trying to make demands," Kirkeberg said. Denise followed him as he stomped back toward the makeshift interrogation room, still feeling glum about the situation.

It wasn't that she had some great reservoir of pity for Skipworth himself. He'd screwed up his own life plenty without their help, and he deserved a fitting punishment for helping to despoil the park. Had he gone for a gun like his friend Lin earlier today, Denise would have shot him dead without a second thought, sad story or no.

She didn't like dangling false hope out in front of him, though. Kirkeberg wasn't offering a square deal, and that violated her basic sense of fairness.

Unfair dealings were something she understood all too well. Before she signed on with the Dracobly Hessler Game Preserve, Yersinia Bioresearch had offered her a deal. The only problem was, they'd obfuscated a few salient points in their contract, and the next thing she knew, she'd been marooned on an island full of aberrant biology. She barely survived the ordeal, so she didn't like participating in Kirkeberg's elaborate dance of baited non-promises.

Kirkeberg opened the door and blew into the interrogation room like a typhoon. He took out a map of the park and slammed it down on the desk.

"Show us where to find the poacher camp."

"Do I have your word that you'll help me if I help you?"

"Listen," Kirkeberg said in a deceptively cool voice. "I've just been informed that two more of my rangers haven't reported in. Maybe it's nothing, but they were out looking for the first group of men to go missing. So help me God, if something has happened to a single one of them, I'll be using you and your friends as lion bait. Show me where to find the camp, and then maybe we can talk. I'm a results-oriented man. If you help me roll this up quick and clean, before something happens to anyone else, I *might* remember your contributions when this comes to a close. If you refuse me now, and it costs one of those men his life because we were delayed, I'll stake you out right next to Zhang Dong for the lions."

Denise knew that Kirkeberg didn't have much real authority over this situation. The police and the lawyers had all the real say in what happened next, even if they'd take his recommendations into account. But nonetheless, she felt a little uneasy listening to the cold steel in Kirkeberg's voice.

Skipworth looked down at the map. He traced his finger along a couple of the main trails that ran through the park, orienting himself. His fingers moved up north toward the Verschoor Dam and then jogged off the trail to follow the course of the river for a distance. Finally, he tapped a spot along the river barely a mile from Ranger Station Thirteen.

"There are two camps. This is the bigger of the two, with most of the hunters. There will probably be about twenty men there all told, plus a few scouts and one of Zhang Dong's lieutenants."

"That's practically under our nose," Denise said. Skipworth's finger had stopped over an oxbow curve in the river, indicating that the poachers were just on the far side of the bank.

"The vegetation is real thick right through there. We cleared a section in the middle of it and built up some berms to further hide the tents and trucks. You could probably hide a small army in there, and it would take a while before anyone realized they were there."

"You said there were two camps. Where's the second one?" Kirkeberg asked.

"I can't tell you that."

"Don't test my patience, son."

"I can't tell you because I don't know. The two camps only communicate via a couple of couriers. They and Zhang Dong are the only ones who know where both camps are. The first camp is the hunting party. The second camp is smaller. Zhang Dong, a couple of his enforcers, and our logistics people stay there. If one camp gets broken up, the other one scatters before the authorities can find it."

"Clever," Denise said.

"If the park rangers swoop down on Zhang Dong's camp, it cuts off our supplies and top leadership, but one of his lieutenants will still have a collection of experienced hunters. Shanghai will simply send more people from the organization. If the park rangers hit the hunting camp, we lose all our best shooters and whatever cargo we've collected, but Zhang Dong slips away with the guys who can organize and recruit more hunters locally."

Denise ground her teeth. She wanted to wipe the poachers out too, but they'd set up a clever system. Two cells working together. Eliminate one, and the other would be back with replacements in a couple of weeks.

"This is going to be hard," Denise said. "Will the hunting camp move when they realize something happened to you and Lin?"

"Yeah, they have a lot of areas they move between periodically, depending on where the animals are or when they think things are getting too hot."

"Do you know which one they'd travel to if they get spooked because you're not back?"

"No idea. Zhang's lieutenant decides where they go and when. The park's thousands of square miles, and they have a dozen places. I'm not even sure I know where they all are."

"Hmm. How long until they miss you?"

"Before the end of the day."

"That doesn't give us a whole lot of time. The police units are supposed to arrive in about an hour, and it'll be dark a couple of hours after that."

"They'll be gone by then."

"Dammit," Kirkeberg muttered.

Denise flipped through a couple of scenarios in her head. They needed to come up with some sort of plan before the police got here, something they could use to sweep up both camps as quickly as possible.

The couriers were the system's weakness. They had to carry directions from Zhang to the hunting camp and news from the hunting camp to Zhang. They were the only ones who knew where both parties were at any given time, so that meant that they had to make sure they scooped up at least one courier when they raided the hunting camp.

But knowing who was a courier and who was a hunter would prove difficult without help. No doubt the couriers wouldn't want to snitch out Zhang and would claim they were part of the hunting team. By the time the police sorted out who was who, Zhang would have already realized that the hunting camp had been hit, and he'd be long gone from any location the captured courier could lead the police to.

And that meant they needed to bring Skipworth along on the raid. He could identify which people in the hunting camp were couriers and allow the police to focus all their grilling efforts on them. Anything else would result in the poaching operation's ringleader slipping away and returning with a new team.

Taking her eyes off the map, Denise looked over at Kirkeberg. Given the unhappy expression on his face, he was no doubt making the same calculations. He wanted the doctor out of his hair before the man tried to pin him into giving his word on some sort of leniency. Now Kirkeberg was going to have to ask Skipworth for more help over the coming hours.

Suddenly, someone shouted out in the hallway. A flurry of voices sounded outside. The door burst open, and the same ranger who they met in the hallway earlier. "Mr. Kirkeberg, sir. We found Dr. Thornber. One of the patrols just brought him in."

"Is he alive?"

The ranger looked back into the hallway, and Denise heard a gurney rolling across the floor. When the ranger turned back around, his face had lost a lot of color. "Sir, I honestly hope not at this point, but maybe."

FIVE

POLYCHAETE

Skipworth was quickly shoved back into his cell, and everyone gathered around to look at the shape on the gurney.

"What in the hell happened to him?" Denise asked, looking at Thornber.

"I have no idea, but Matheson and Ritter found him out on one of the trails."

"I thought we'd already checked those areas and had moved on," Kirkeberg said.

"Yes, we had. But Matheson and Ritter were moving out to go look for Crane and De Hoog. They said Dr. Thornber was just lying in the middle of the path next to a couple of dead lionesses."

Cornelia spoke up. "I've seen a lot of injuries in my days, but I don't think lions did that to this man. I don't even know what would leave a body in that sort of condition. If you'd asked me, I would have said it looked like some sort of chemical attack."

"You said maybe he was alive?" Kirkeberg asked. And then the next question, the one everyone was thinking. "How?"

"Matheson and Ritter said he was twitching when they found him. They're still in the motor pool, scrubbing out the back of their car. I'll have them report directly to you as soon as they're done with that." The ranger started to turn around to get clear of the sight on the gurney.

"Wait," Cornelia said. "Did they touch him with their bare hands? Any skin-to-skin contact? I think maybe they might have bigger problems than their car if they touched Dr. Thornber directly."

"No, I don't think so," the ranger said. "They told me they were wearing gloves because…well, I don't think anyone in their right mind would want to get any of that on their hands. I mean, look at him."

"Get this man to the examination room," Kirkeberg said. "Cornelia, you have more medical training than anyone else here. I want you to quickly examine Dr. Thornber to double-check that he's not alive. I'm going to get the visitor center on the radio and ask for them to send us a doctor so we can get a full examination as soon as possible."

"Will do," Cornelia said. "Denise, come with me. I might need a hand while I do this. Help me wheel him to the examination room, too. C'mon, people, clear a path."

Cornelia started to wheel the gurney toward the examination room. The room lay at the far end of the station, not far from the garage. The area served a couple of different purposes. It could be used as a basic medical center, with space for a couple of patients and equipment to care for slight injuries. If someone broke an arm, they could handle the matter at Ranger Station Thirteen. For more serious injuries, the victim would have to be treated at the park's visitor center some thirty miles to the south, with its own complement of medical staff.

The examination room's main purpose was for wildlife autopsies, though. If someone found a dead elephant, it might be hauled back to Station Thirteen and sliced up by an expert to make sure it didn't have any contagious diseases that could be communicated to the rest of the herd. Alternatively, if they knew the cause of death of an exotic animal, either from old age or misadventure, veterinary students would sometimes hold a small symposium while the animal was dissected so they could get some hands-on experience working with something other than pets and farm animals.

The room was covered in green tile and came equipped with different slabs of various sizes for examining both the living and the dead. There were also a few cabinets filled with basic medical equipment and a wall loaded with more exotic tools for the wildlife autopsies. A backup generator and some fuel sat at the far end of the room in case the power failed in the rest of the station.

Looking at Thornber, Denise didn't know how he was ready for anything other than dissection. The rangers who found him must have imagined the twitches they'd seen, because there was absolutely no way that the geologist was still alive.

Some sort of weird black tar, not unlike the stuff they'd found near the entrance at Sulfur Springs, covered his body. Or rather, what was left of his body. Denise could only positively identify Thornber based on the clothes the body was wearing.

The rest of the body had been reduced to something skeletal under all the black slime. Patches of black-caked hair poked up off the skull, but most of the scalp had been eaten away or sloughed off, revealing a layer of grimy bone. Empty eye sockets stared up at the ceiling. Thornber's teeth smiled out from the black mélange, almost the only part of him that wasn't soot-colored.

Parts of his body were more thoroughly covered in the slime than others. From the chest up, there was only a thin layer of the slime. Thornber's arms were covered in a thicker layer of gunk, but they still had a bit of meat on them. The same for his legs.

Denise looked at the slime in fascination. It clung to Thornber's body. In places, it looked like it should have dripped off the cart and onto the floor, but it never did. The dangling black boogers simply continued to hang from his flesh like pendulous ropes. The slime had a strange cohesion to it.

"I wouldn't touch any of that," Cornelia warned her, pointing to the ooze. "I have no idea what it is, but I doubt you want it to come into contact with your bare flesh."

They opened the doors to the examination room and flipped the lights on. Fluorescents hummed to life overhead, chasing the shadows out of the corners.

"Have you ever seen anything like this before?" Denise asked.

"I have seen a lot of sick and injured people in my time. I've seen quite a few dead bodies, too. That being said, I don't think I've ever seen anything quite like this. The closest I can think of is some of the cases of trench foot or other similar problems we'd get during the war. Soldiers were forced to live in watery, muddy holes for a few weeks at a time, could never get their feet dry, and the next thing they knew, they'd be taking their boots off and half the skin on their feet would come off with their socks. This, though? I have no idea what the hell this is."

"What do you need me to do?"

"Here's some gloves. No, here. Take another pair. Double bag it. Like I said, you don't want any of…whatever that is touching your skin. It might be toxic. Or corrosive."

"Do you think Matheson and Ritter were right? Could Thornber have still been alive when they found him? Even like this? They said they saw him twitching."

"No, he couldn't have been alive. Not if he looked like this when they found him. You can see part of Thornber's heart right there, where the flesh peeled off his ribs. Looks like some apes spent an hour slapping it against a brick wall and then dipped it in motor oil. It's not so much rotting as dissolving."

Denise rolled the second pair of gloves on as Cornelia parked the gurney next to a slab meant for animals. She looked down at the body and grimaced. Whatever had happened to Thornber hadn't been pleasant. The parts that hadn't been skeletonized weren't in great condition. He looked like someone had wrapped some bones in seaweed and then dipped the resulting effigy in black paint.

"Help me roll him over onto the slab here," Cornelia said. "You get the legs. I'll work on the shoulders, okay? One good push."

Reluctantly, Denise put her hands on the body. Her fingers sank into the remaining flesh, like pressing down on a damp sponge. The black tar groped at her gloves, instantly sticking to them like it was trying to slurp them off.

Thornber's arm shot straight up in the air so quickly that Denise could hear some of the remaining flesh rip. A tendon inside Thornber's arm groaned as if it were about to snap.

Denise and Cornelia both leapt away from Thornber's body. The arm remained straight up like a flagpole, the fingers spastically clenching and unclenching.

Kirkeberg chose that moment to walk into the examination room. "They can't send us a doctor from the visitor center because someone-- *what the hell is happening*?" He stood there for a second as the door shut behind him with a thud.

"I don't know," Cornelia said, opening up a box of first-aid equipment.

"Is he alive?" Kirkeberg asked.

"No, that's the thing," Cornelia said. "He's stone dead."

"He doesn't look dead," Denise said. "I mean, well, he does, but..."

"I can see inside his damn ribcage. What's left of his heart isn't beating. He doesn't even have any lungs anymore. God alone knows what happened to those."

"Yeah, but..." Denise said.

"It must be some sort of galvanic response or something. Like when biologists run electricity through a pickled frog's body to make it look like it's dancing. The frog's dead, but that doesn't mean it can't do a little soft shoe."

"We're not exactly running electricity through him, though," Kirkeberg said. He moved away from the door and moved around the outer edge of the room, refusing to draw too close to the strange sight. He came to a stop near the station's backup generator.

"No, but sometimes bodies can do strange things. Burp or gasp. Sometimes it's the gas caught inside them."

"This is a lot more than a burp," Denise said.

A second later, the unnatural vivaciousness went out of Thornber's arm. His fingers ceased their frantic scurrying, and his arm fell to his side. The recently active limb laid half on and half off the slab, swaying gently as it settled. Finally, it came to a complete standstill, and Thornber's body looked, if not exactly at peace, at least as dead as the next self-respecting corpse.

"Yeah, this is a little more extreme than anything I've ever seen," Cornelia said. "Sometimes rigor mortis means a body will try to snap back to a prior position. I had a dead guy basically head butt me one time while I was trying to drag him out of the infirmary. He was bent in the middle, and I tried to straighten his legs. He came up at me like I'd stepped on a rake."

"Can you tell me anything about Thornber's condition?" Kirkeberg asked.

"Yeah. He's all sorts of dead."

"I was thinking maybe something a little more specific. Can you tell me how he died? Maybe what that slime covering him is? Did the Triads do that to him? Why is he so, ah, active if he's dead?"

"Frankly, I can't tell you a whole lot. You'd need someone to perform an autopsy to get some of the answers you're looking for, and that's something I'm not qualified for. We'd need someone with more medical training. Speaking of which, you came in here to say something about the doctors at the visitor center?"

"Right. Yes." Kirkeberg seemed to find his footing again. "The park's medical team is out at the southern end of the park. Some nature photographer fell in a crevasse and snapped his legs. They won't be able to send anyone until they've fished him out."

"What about the police?" Cornelia asked. "Could they send someone out with their units before we raid the poacher camp?"

"No, they're already on their way. By the time they could get a qualified doctor out here, it would already be dark, and the camp might start to disband by then. More importantly though, if this is something the Triads did, I want to be able to warn the police beforehand."

"You might want to call off the raid, then. I don't know what any of this stuff is, and I sure don't know if it's something the poachers did. I'd imagine if they could hook up a hose and spray this stuff, the results wouldn't be pretty, though. Judging from the state of the body, I'm guessing it's about as destructive as lye."

"Do you think that's what was happening? The Triads were trying to obliterate evidence so they poured this stuff on Thornber to destroy his corpse?"

"Eh, it might explain why there were a couple of dead lions near the corpse when Matheson and Ritter found it. The cats dug up the body from whatever shallow grave it was buried in, and then this slime poisoned them. But do you want answers or do you want me to just speculate wildly? If it's answers you want, I'm not qualified."

Kirkeberg made a noise deep in the back of his throat. "We don't have anyone else."

"Well, actually, we do," Denise said.

For a moment, Kirkeberg looked at her and then realization dawned on his face. "Surely you don't mean the prisoner? What if he contaminates the body? What if he destroys evidence?"

"He's been cooperative so far. If you actually give him some kind of concrete promise to treat him differently than the rest of the poachers..."

"I don't like it."

"To be honest, I don't especially like it, either. We have a pretty limited number of options here, though. The police will be here soon, and the poacher camp will be moving not long after that. If there's some sort of danger we don't understand, we either need to give the police whatever relevant details we can get, or we need to cancel the raid on the camp."

Denise conjured up the mental image of the police coming up to the camp only to meet a spray of black, flesh-eating slime. The chaos and carnage would be unbelievable.

Kirkeberg closed his eyes, evidently imagining the same scenario in his own mind. He took a breath and let it out slowly as he opened his eyes again.

"Alright, I agree. We need to know as much as we can about what happened. We can't afford to have this turn into some sort of goat rodeo. I'll go get Skipworth, but if we're going to do this the wrong way, we're going to do it the *least* wrong way we can. Cornelia, you'll be helping Skipworth and watching everything he does. Take notes. If he so much as blinks funny during the autopsy, I want you to write it up so we can report it later. We won't give him the chance to tamper with the evidence any more than necessity dictates. If he tries to hide his own complicity in this somehow, we'll have your notes to help screw him to the wall. I'll get Matheson and Ritter, too. Maybe they can shed some light here, and they can also guard Skipworth in case he thinks he can use a scalpel to make a break for it."

Thornber's jaw snapped shut so hard one of his teeth cracked. The sharp clack made Denise cringe. Thornber's jaw flapped back wide, opening further than a human mouth should. Now the tendons in Thornber's jaws were straining, creaking with tension like an old suspension bridge on the verge of catastrophic structural failure. His mouth slammed back shut again with another bear trap crunch.

Cornelia took a step away from the body as the jaw flew open and shut a couple more times, the teeth coming together with a noise like a pair of rotting storm shutters banging in the window of an abandoned house. Soon, they were moving so fast that his teeth were chomping together several times a second. He looked like a cartoon character eating an invisible piece of corn on the cob. After a minute, Thornber's teeth stopped their macabre chattering and went still again.

"Well, then. I'm just going to go ahead and file this one in the 'Hell No' folder," Denise said.

"I could have done without seeing that myself," Cornelia said as Kirkeberg left the examination room to gather Skipworth and the rangers. Denise moved away from the metal slab and stood near the generator and jerry cans.

They were alone in the room with the body now, and Denise could feel the atmosphere crackle around them. She half-expected Thornber to sit up and walk out of the room, but she trusted Cornelia's judgement. The man was dead. Anyone could see he was dead. Somehow, his body just hadn't gotten the message yet.

Denise shuffled her feet as she leaned up against the generator. The air in this corner of the room smelled like gasoline. Even so, that was an improvement over the funk of the air closer to Thornber's body. Near the slab, it smelled of powerful antiseptics, the faint scent of decay, and an undertone of earthy chemical stink that must have been left over from Thornber's descent into Sulfur Springs.

She tried to puzzle out the black ooze covering Thornber's body. They'd found some dried out black goop near the entrance to Sulfur Springs when Thornber, Hartzell, and Planck all went missing. Could the slime have come from somewhere inside the cavern system?

The only people who had gone very deep inside were a surveying crew and Thornber's team. There were thermal vents somewhere deeper in the caves, but that's all she knew of the area below the park.

They'd found some footprints in the dried slime. Could Thornber have gotten covered in the slime and then wandered around for days, avoiding the ranger search parties while the black stuff ate at his flesh?

It seemed unlikely. Even if he was blind from the ooze, he would have stumbled onto one of the paths when he made it out of the cave. The rangers would have found him, then.

Mashing her brains together, Denise tried to come up with some reasonable explanation for how a dead geologist had suddenly appeared on a park path several days after his disappearance, covered in some strange slime and surrounded by a couple of dead lions.

Every answer she could come up with was full of holes. The Triads could have killed Thornber and tried to dispose of his body. That seemed the most likely, but why would they attack a scientific expedition to Sulfur Springs? If Thornber died in some sort of natural accident in the cave, how did he end up lying in the middle of the path? Neither explanation felt quite right, but she wasn't sure what other options there were to explore.

Thornber's toes twitched. They twitched again. Denise waited, but they remained still after that.

Cripes but she didn't like this. She had a dead body on her hands she couldn't adequately explain to herself, and it was doing things she didn't associate with dead bodies. That was a bad combination.

"Why do you think he keeps doing that? Why the jerking and the biting?" Denise asked, as much to hear some human voices in the examination room as to hear Cornelia's thoughts.

"I'd be lying if I said I knew. It might be that whatever that black stuff is, it's chewing its way through Thornber's nerves in such a way that it makes them misfire. They think they're still receiving signals from a living brain. Frankly, though, I wouldn't care to venture a bet one way or another. He doesn't even have much muscle left on that arm that reached up earlier. I wouldn't have thought it was physiologically possible for it to move like that unless you tied strings to him and hired a puppeteer."

Just then, Skipworth walked into the evaluation room. Kirkeberg and the two rangers who had found Thornber followed closely behind.

"Well, that's not a pleasant sight," Skipworth said.

Thornber's whole body arched at the spine, the top of his head and the soles of his feet the only parts of his body touching the slab. The corpse looked like it was locked in the grips of a grand mal seizure. That, or a toe-curling orgasm.

"Now you see why I'm offering to suggest some of the forthcoming charges against you be pardoned off. Tell us why he's doing that, and you have my word I'll make sure the courts hear you were cooperative in bringing the rest of the poachers down," Kirkeberg said. Standing behind him, Matheson and Ritter both made faces, clearly not eager to get anywhere near the body again.

"You're absolutely certain he's dead?" Skipworth asked.

"Oh yeah," Cornelia said. "He's dead alright."

As if remembering he was dead himself, Thornber's body went slack again and collapsed back onto the slab. His head flopped in their direction, his mouth hanging open and dribbling slime where his tongue used to be. Cracked white teeth shone at them under the fluorescents.

"Any idea what that black stuff is or why he keeps doing...that?" Kirkeberg asked.

"No and no," Skipworth said.

"So you're telling me your Triad pals didn't have anything to do with this?"

"Look. First of all, I'm no more friends with them than you are. Second, no. I would know about something like this. It's not their style.

Zhang Dong has killed a few people on park grounds before. The last one a few days ago. They made me watch to prove a point about what would happen if I tried to leave without paying off my debts. But I've never seen this guy before, and I have no idea what happened to him. I can tell you it wasn't the Triads, though. They're real simple. A bullet behind the ear and a deep grave. Not whatever is going on here."

"Hmm," Kirkeberg said.

Denise chewed on the inside of her cheek but didn't say anything. She digested what Skipworth had said, but her brain kept coming back to a particular detail. He said the Triads had killed people right here on park grounds.

And why not? The grounds were vast and open. The odds of the rangers ever stumbling across a fresh grave before the grass grew back over it were next to zilch. Hell, they couldn't even find an entire encampment of poachers without help from Skipworth. Two encampments of poachers. The park was a great place to dispose of unwanted people.

But she'd always thought of the vast open spaces as a place of peace and beauty. This was one of the few places on earth meant to be shielded from mankind's destructive instincts. Knowing that there were murder victims scattered around the park, some of whom would probably never be found and properly laid to rest, spoiled some of her enjoyment. There was a worm wrapped around the apple's core.

"What I can tell you is that I think I've seen this black stuff before," Skipworth said.

"What?"

"On a couple of dead elephants. Lin cut the tusks off them yesterday. He said he'd found them like that, but I wasn't entirely sure whether or not to believe him."

"Details, man. Details. This could be important. Tell me everything you remember about the dead elephants," Kirkeberg said.

"They weren't in very good shape. It looked like somebody had gone after them with a chainsaw. Big chunks were missing out of both their flanks, and they were covered in slashes, some of them right down to the bone. Lin said they were like that when he found them, but I don't know of any animal that can do that to two elephants. I figured he'd simply done that to them out of some macabre curiosity."

"But the slime? What about the black stuff?"

"There was quite a bit of it on the two elephants, especially around their wounds. I didn't know what it was then, and I don't know what it is now. He sawed the tusks off without any problem, but he kept looking around like he wasn't sure what to make of the situation either. I thought maybe he was screwing with me, but nothing ever came of it."

"I think it's time we get to the bottom of some of this, then," Denise said.

"Alright, this isn't going to be pretty," Skipworth said.

"It already wasn't pretty," Cornelia responded.

"Point taken. Can I use these tools over here?" Skipworth pointed toward the collection of items laid out along the far wall. There was a drain in the tiled floor for blood to seep away.

"Be my guest," Kirkeberg said, scowling.

Denise looked at the collection of tools on display on the far wall. To her eyes, they looked like nothing so much as industrial-grade gardening equipment. There were shears and saws and scooping implements that she didn't have a name for. None of them looked particularly pleasant. She made a note to herself to die peacefully in her sleep someday rather than under mysterious circumstances so she wouldn't need an autopsy. There wasn't much dignity in death with strangers pawing through your guts.

Skipworth slapped on some gloves and pulled a small box off the counter, opening it up, and pulling out a scalpel.

"Have you ever performed an autopsy before?" Cornelia asked.

"One. Under a senior doctor's supervision. I've seen several more, though. I understand the basics, even if it's not what I was training to specialize in."

Thornber gave another jerk on the slab.

"Nobody has a shred of experience with whatever's going on here, though." Skipworth looked down at the body like a golfer eyeing a deceptively slanted green. Denise could see him figuring out his approach in his head.

"Is it some sort of disease? Something that could infect the rest of the station?" Kirkeberg asked.

"There might be some sort of pathogen at work," Skipworth said. "But it shouldn't be easily communicable at this point. The patient is dead...ish. He's not breathing. Not sneezing. Not coughing. It's not like you're going to catch anything by just standing in the same room with him. Direct contact could be dangerous, though. So don't touch anything with your bare hands. Don't rub your eyes or touch your mouth. If anything gets on you, wash it off fast. Pretty much the standard rules for handling the dead."

"Peachy," Denise said, settling in near the generator. She knew that if she ventured up to the slab, she'd just be in the way. And maybe violently sick. It wasn't that she'd never seen a dead body before. She'd just never seen one in such a condition.

"Alright, first thing's first," Skipworth said. "Let's see if we can't figure out what this black stuff is. That might at least give us something to start with."

He took a sample jar and used the scalpel to separate off a globule of the slime. The stuff resisted being separated. He'd get some on the side of the blade only for it to slide off before he could stuff it down into the specimen jar. It was almost as if the slime was trying to stay together, the samples always finding their way right back onto the corpse as if by some force of magnetism.

Finally, Skipworth succeeded in scooping some of the ooze off the body and into a little glass specimen jar. He held it up to the light and swirled the gunk around like someone about to sample an expensive brandy.

"Looks like there's a lot of individual particulates suspended in some sort of medium. It's almost like somebody took very fine sand and stirred it into water. The particulates are very small and tend to clump together, though. I'm going to take a look at what's going on under the microscope."

"So is it some sort of chemical, then?" Kirkeberg asked.

"I mean, technically, just about everything is some sort of chemical, but I see what you're asking. I don't think it is in the sense that you mean. This would be very hard to spray or disperse like a normal gas or liquid. Like a chemical weapon. The substance in the liquid would probably clump up too easily and clog whatever mechanism was being used to spread it. I guess someone could have poured this over him with a bucket or something, though. But I don't think it's a weapon or anything like that."

Skipworth turned the light on in the base of the microscope and took out a glass sample slide. Moving slowly, he tried to pour a little of the substance out onto the slide. The black ooze would dangle but refuse drip onto the slide. It stubbornly remained in a single clump inside the jar.

Finally, he managed to dig a smaller sample out and place it on a glass slide. He took another slide and smooshed it over the sludge, flattening it into a thin film. Placing the slides on the microscope, Skipworth stood and adjusted the view until the slime came into focus.

"Anything you can tell us?" Kirkeberg asked.

"Hmm," Skipworth said, gazing down into the microscope. "I thought the particulates in the slime might be rock or metal. Maybe some sort of silicate. But they're organic."

"Meaning what exactly?"

"That sludge covering Thornber is alive. Well, let me rephrase that. The goop actually consists of hundreds of tiny organisms, all of them linked up together. Here, let me show you."

Everyone lined up at the microscope, Kirkeberg looking through the little view holes first. A few minutes later, Denise got her turn to see what was happening on the tiny, flea circus-scale slide below.

Pressing her face to the viewer, she tried to figure out what she was looking at. Black, undulating shapes wriggled below. Their black carapaces glinted in the light as they moved. Each creature was made up of a few banded, armored segments. Tiny filaments that could have been feelers extended off of each creature in every direction, entangling in the feelers of every other creature so that they formed a sort of mat under the slide. They all meshed together like scales on a lizard, creating a shroud of armored bodies. The front end of each animal, Denise couldn't really justify calling any part of it the "head," also bore a set of pincers that would have looked fearsome on anything larger. As it was though, none of the little beasties were much larger than a grain of sand.

"So what exactly are those things?" Cornelia asked.

"If I had to venture a guess, I'd say they were probably some sort of communal polychaete worm."

"A what?"

"Polychaete worms. It's pronounced like polly-keet. They're segmented worms. Think along the lines of a legless centipede. Usually, they're called bristle worms because of the dangly bits coming off them."

"So what's the rest of the ooze made of, then?"

"I'd be speculating, but I'm guessing the worms produce it themselves. Like how a snail or a hagfish will release slime if it's attacked by predators. They're probably releasing the mucus to keep themselves lubricated when they slide against each other. Maybe it's some sort of defensive measure too, though. The only reason I know very much about them is because there's a few parasitic species. But some of them are predatory. You'd have to ask an annelid expert if you wanted to know much more about these guys."

"Have you ever heard of something like this? Worms converging on a human body?"

"Nothing remotely like this. I'm guessing these little guys are probably responsible for shearing most of Thornber's flesh off, though. He wouldn't have decayed this much over just a few days, and it doesn't look like any larger animals tried to eat him."

"Do you think anyone has ever documented this species before?" Denise asked.

"I suppose it's possible. There's about as many different species of bristle worms as you can count. Most of them live in the sea. Some of them even seem to live around hot ocean vents, which means they come up as a topic for study sometimes because we don't really understand how their biology works."

"Ocean vents, you said?" Denise asked.

"Yeah. Again though, we're really pushing the outer limits of my knowledge about things here."

"There's hot spots in Sulfur Springs," Denise said. Everyone else was starting to make the connection as well.

"So did these things attack Thornber or what, then?" Kirkeberg asked, sidling up to the microscope for a second look.

"I doubt they came after him, exactly. Not like one of your lions or some other dangerous park animal, but he may have come into contact with them at some point and they, well, colonized him."

Denise didn't like the sound of that. She pictured Thornber alone out in the wilderness as the worms burrowed into his flesh. Had he scrambled out of the cave only to become so overcome with pain as the worms chewed on his flesh that he became lost and disoriented? She still didn't know exactly how he'd come to rest on the path where Matheson and Ritter found him.

She turned around to look back at Thornber's sad, blackened form. The body wasn't on the slab anymore. It was standing up next to the slab.

SIX

A ROLLS ROYCE ON THE VELDT

Zhang Dong picked up the telephone sitting on the only desk in Ranger Station Two. Unlike some of the ranger stations scattered about the Dracobly Hessler Game Preserve, Ranger Station Two's purpose wasn't to serve as a base for personnel. Ranger Station Two was a glorified storage depot. Far to the east from the next closest outpost, the building contained racks of rifles, gasoline, extra uniforms, replacement parts, and everything else required to keep the park up and running. If for whatever reason, the main ranger outpost at the visitor's center was ever knocked out, Ranger Station Two would be the rallying point for emergency and rescue personnel because they could find everything they needed here.

Of course, that meant that if everything went as planned in the day-to-day operations of the park, Ranger Station Two was almost entirely redundant except when something broke. Redundancy was great for planning but a poor use of staff. Consequently, the large building was only staffed by two men.

The first had a bad knee from the war and three children to feed. Zhang Dong had pictures of the second with a young black girl at a certain establishment outside Johannesburg. The Sun Yee On Triads had a well-hidden financial interest in the establishment, though its value paled in comparison to the revenue brought in by operations at the game preserve. Almost everything else the Sun Yee On Triads did paled in comparison to the profits here at the game preserve.

A little money and a little persuasion gave Zhang Dong access to Ranger Station Two's phone whenever he needed it.

Outside, the two men responsible for inventorying Ranger Station Two's equipment sat on a log, eating lunch. The little unscheduled break wouldn't be noticed, and they weren't about to report it.

Sitting next to them was the most magnificent beast on the preserve, a Rolls Royce Silver Ghost. The touring car was outfitted with special wheels to make its treks across some of the rugged terrain more manageable. The vehicle was one of roughly seven thousand ever made, making it rarer than many of the protected species here in the park.

Occasionally, particularly rich hunters paid the Triads for a surreptitious expedition into the park, bagging whatever animals they wanted regardless of regulations. The Silver Ghost let them know what sort of organization they were dealing with. The place was a park because it had an abundance, nay, an embarrassment of natural beauty. Who would really notice if Zhang Dong and his men took a little off the top?

While he could afford luxuries like the Rolls Royce, the mobile lifestyle his operations demanded meant there were certain necessities that Zhang Dong couldn't otherwise acquire. A telephone was one of them.

He picked up the phone and began the process of dialing out. One operator transferred him. Then another. Then another. After a minute, the circuitous game of hot potato landed him where he wanted to be. There was a click at the opposite end of the line.

"Speak," a voice said.

"Plan A was not successful," Zhang Dong said.

"How did you fail us?"

Zhang Dong made a face that would have gotten him killed if the person at the other end of the line could see it. "The Sun Yee On have not failed you. Your man did not show up at the rendezvous point. We took care of everything before that. The body. The switch. Everything."

"I see," the voice said. "Do you know what happened to our man?"

"We believe he died in the caves."

There was a long pause on the phone. "It must be a bit more...aggressive than we anticipated."

"You sound pleased."

"Believe me, if there's any positive reason to activate Plan B, that would be it. We needed the samples our man was supposed to retrieve. The fact that he failed is disappointing, but it's not a significant setback. Do the local authorities know any of the details?"

"Half the rangers in the park spent the past couple of days beating the bushes out there, but they didn't mount an expedition into the caves."

"That's acceptable. I will have more men there by tonight to ensure that our contingency plan is properly executed."

"We may have more problems than that, though."

Another silence. "Tell me about these problems."

"Some of your samples may have escaped the caves. My men have found a number of dead animals with a strange black substance on their bodies. It's making them nervous."

"Have you explained to them what the substance is?"

"No."

"Good. Then I won't have to pay you extra to kill them. So long as they know to stay away from it, everything will be fine. You still have the equipment we provided you with in case Plan C was necessary?"

"Of course."

"Good. My men will meet you after dark. They will have some additional supplies, given the situation. Plan B will proceed followed by a light cleansing operation."

"Just how light?"

"An environmental purge in the areas where you found those dead animals, mostly. How many park rangers would have come into contact with our man, by the way?"

"Mostly just the ones at the station closest to the cave, number thirteen."

"We will need to find out what they know."

"So you need them alive?"

"For now."

"You're going to be bringing a lot of attention to the park. It will be difficult for me to resume my normal operations again for a long time after this."

"You'll be paid plenty in compensation, I assure you."

"Of course." Zhang Dong stood in the still afternoon air. He placed the phone back down on its cradle. When his contact told him there was a Plan C, he'd written it off as hyperbole. But now that the first plan had run aground, they were one step closer to requiring stronger measures, measures like Plan C.

He regretted ever making this deal with his contact. It had sounded simple at the time. Get the contact's man inside and bring him out once he had the samples. The money was so good Zhang Dong hadn't bothered asking what the samples were or why the contingency plans were so extreme. If they actually needed to arrange Plan C, it would be disastrous for his poaching operations. After all, what could be so dangerous about the samples that they'd need to set the entire park on fire?

SEVEN

VERMIPHOBIA

Thornber wasn't on the slab anymore. He was standing up on shaky, jittering legs. His arms trembled like they were experiencing some terrible chill, and his mouth hung open in a gaping imbecile's leer.

"I think we have a problem," Denise said.

Everyone turned around to see what she was talking about. Skipworth made a sound in his throat. Cornelia cursed softly. Kirkeberg cursed louder.

"I thought you said he was dead," Ritter said.

"He is," Cornelia and Skipworth said at the same time.

Matheson slid along the wall, skirting the far end around the generator to stay as far away as possible from Thornber and the empty slab as he made for the door. He looked like he was about to be sick, so he was making a hasty exit.

"What is happening?" Kirkeberg asked. "How is he on his feet?"

"It must be the worms," Skipworth said, watching the wobbling figure. "The ones on the slide were all hooked together. They must be able to coordinate themselves. With a layer of worms over and inside Thornber's body, they must be able to move him around to some degree. I've never seen anything like it. They're basically using his body as a mobile buffet. That must be what all the twitching was about earlier. It was the worms trying to get control of the body."

"Do you think they could pilot a…living person around like that?" Cornelia asked.

"Maybe. There would need to be a lot of worms, though. And they would be eating into your flesh the whole time. I don't think anyone would survive the process for long."

Denise looked at the thing that used to be Thornber as it stood facing the rear wall, swaying like a drunk. His slime-caked body wobbled where it stood.

"So what are we going to do about this?" Cornelia asked, gesturing toward Thornber.

"More importantly, is this what happened to Hartzell and Planck, too?" Kirkeberg asked. "Are they down in Sulfur Springs somewhere wandering around like this? Skipworth, do you think it's possible to maybe use Thornber's worms to locate my two missing rangers? You said they like to join together. Maybe they would seek each other out."

"I really don't think it works like that. I mean, the distances involved and the--"

Matheson tried to slip around behind Thornber as Skipworth spoke, looking green as he sidled toward the only exit. Thornber jerked once as if someone had run an electrical current through him, and then he lunged at Matheson.

The ranger yelped as a pair of bony hands latched onto him, ripping the fabric on his shirt. Black sludge smeared onto the fabric. Matheson squirmed and wriggled like bait resisting being placed on a hook. Thornber leaned forward, his jaws full of cracked teeth leaning in close to Matheson's throat.

Before the teeth could snap down on Matheson's flesh, Denise drew her revolver and fired a shot. The heavy duty firearm wasn't an elephant rifle, but it was hard hitting and reliable. The gun was meant as a weapon of last resort, something for in case a leopard ever jumped on a park employee and tried to sink its fangs into the person's neck. The ranger could respond by placing the revolver's barrel up against the predator's eye and pulling the trigger. Even from a distance greater than point blank, the gun was designed to blast a mid-sized predator's brains out the back of its skull.

The weapon's roar filled the examination room. The muzzle flash reflected off the tiled floors and walls for a split second. A whiff of smoke turned the air harsh with the scent of warm metal and hot gases.

On the other side of the room, the top of Thornber's head flew off. A pink and black mass the consistency of scrambled eggs splattered against the wall, and the parts of Thornber's brain that were left in his skull started to leak out the hole in his head.

Thornber's corpse stumbled for a second, knocked off balance by the force of the bullet's impact. Then if swiftly righted itself and sank its teeth into Matheson's throat. Matheson screamed, but the noise turned into a wet whistle as his windpipe tore away.

Blood jetted out and splashed across Thornber. The stuff ran in a crimson river down the front of Matheson's shirt. Black slime from Thornber's body marked the edges of the ragged wound.

Matheson kept trying to push Thornber away, even with his throat torn out. He had another few second before his brain started to feel the lack of blood pumping up his arteries. In maybe forty seconds he'd lose consciousness entirely, and soon after that, he'd bleed out and die. The chunk of Matheson's throat fell out of Thornber's teeth and landed on the floor with a plop.

Denise planted three more slugs in Thornber's somehow still-moving corpse, aiming for kill shots. A bullet took off another part of Thornber's head, shattering his right eye socket. The next two found their way square into the center of his chest.

The Thornber thing took two steps backward, dragging Matheson with it. The bullets didn't seem to do much more than keep it off balance. Shouts of surprise rang out elsewhere in Ranger Station Thirteen as the gunfire bellowed out. Matheson made noises like someone trying to drink a milkshake through a straw that was too small.

A claw raked across Matheson's face, obliterating one eye and scraping flesh away as it went. More black discharge secreted onto Matheson.

Firing her last two shots, Denise took Thornber's head entirely off. The bullets smacked into his neck and destroyed his vertebrae and exploded the remaining flesh and tendons. Only about half his lower jaw remained attached to the rest of his body, drooping obscenely where muscle and bone should have held it in place. The revolver clicked on an empty cylinder as Denise pulled the trigger again.

But by then Cornelia, Kirkeberg, and Ritter were firing at the thing, too. More bullets blasted chunks of Thornber's body loose. Shattered ribs poked from his chest. One of his hands flew off, leaving nothing more than a jagged stump of wrist bones. Matheson, no longer moving or thrashing, fell to the ground, Thornber's disembodied hand still clutching his shirt. The cacophony of gunfire and symphony of crackling bones made Denise's ears ring.

Thornber barely slowed down. With Matheson out of his grasp, he came straight toward them. His body didn't even bother to twist around to face them straight on. It sidled sideways, as if the worms hadn't figured out the most efficient means of locomotion for using two legs yet.

Everyone had already unloaded their weapons on the shambling corpse-thing. A barrage of twenty-odd bullets hadn't done much more than slow it down and throw it off balance. Denise looked down and saw Thornber's severed hand scuttle off Matheson's body and start moving toward them, too.

Ritter threw his empty revolver at the thing that used to be Thornber. The weapon smacked into its upper arm with a wet sound and then clattered to the floor. Thornber didn't even react. His feet simply continued their awkward sideways waltz toward them.

One of the other rangers poked his head through the open doorway to see what on earth was happening in the examination room.

"Brady, bring an elephant gun," Kirkeberg called. "We need more firepower."

Brady saw the bullet-riddled form of Thornber up off the slab and moving about. He saw the pool of blood spreading across the floor and pooling around Matheson's still form. He saw the severed hand moving around independently toward the people gathered on the opposite side of the room, cut off from the exit by the moving corpse. Then he did what most sane people would do and slammed the door shut. A second later, Denise heard the lock slide into place.

"Crap."

"Bullets aren't working. We need to chop it up or something," Ritter said, grabbing some sort of circular saw off the wall of autopsy equipment.

Skipworth tried to stop him. "I don't think that's a good--"

Ritter charged forward as the saw blade whirred to life. He moved up to Thornber and raised the snarling saw above his head. The blade glinted for a second under the glare of the florescent lights, and then it arced downward.

Chewing into Thornber's arm that still had a hand attached, the blade spat black slime in every direction. The blade behaved like a bicycle tire rolling fast across a patch of mud. The thick, viscous goo flew back at Ritter and the people standing behind him.

Denise spun away just as a combination of shredded flesh and a ropy strand of ooze landed on her jacket. She squirmed out of the jacket before any of the slime could come into direct contact with her skin.

Most of the slop hit Ritter, though. Red and black spray splattered his face and the front of his clothes. He continued working the saw for another moment before it fell out of his hands, and he tried to lurch away.

Ritter screamed. The worms, too small to see individually but present in the black slime on the man's face, were using their pincers to tear open tiny fissures in the skin and crawl inside. His eyeballs started to hemorrhage where the worms worked their way inside, sending vitreous fluid and blood down his cheeks like red-tinged tears.

Thornber shoved the jagged stump of bone where his hand should have been into Ritter's belly. The sharp bone tore into his stomach and ripped open the flesh, sending streamers of grey-pink intestines spilling onto the floor. Ritter gave a harsh little gasp and grabbed at himself, trying to spool his innards back inside.

Breathing in wet pants, Ritter tried to back away from the bringer of his pain, away from Thornber's moving corpse, but his foot caught around the coil of one of his own intestines. Ritter went down on his knees, accidentally dropping more of his own guts on the floor in the process.

Denise snapped the cylinder shut on her revolver, the chambers freshly loaded with bullets. She emptied the gun into Thornber's center of mass, hoping to somehow kill his rampaging body. Or to at least force it away from Ritter.

Thornber stumbled backward a couple of steps as the bullets slammed into him. Pieces of his body flew off.

But he didn't go down.

Thornber's entire body shuddered for a moment, and Denise could hear the sound of his fractured bones grating together inside his body. Even as she moved to reload again, she realized that bullets alone wouldn't be enough to stop Thornber's corpse. The worms themselves were the real problem, and each bullet she fired could only take out a very small number of them at a given time. There were literally thousands, probably hundreds of thousands of the tiny creatures on Thornber's body, puppeting it across the room.

How were they even supposed to fight something like that?

Raising his severed wrist, Thornber drilled the snapped bones straight through Ritter's eye. Ritter screamed and thrashed, which only caused the sharp stump to gouge deeper into his eye socket. The ranger reached up and pawed at his face, trying to push Thornber away.

Thornber's arm retracted in a quick, efficient motion, pulling what was left of Ritter's eye out like an olive on a cocktail toothpick. All that remained of the eye was a bit of shredded membrane and some dangling optic nerve.

Even as Denise watched, some of the black slime on Thornber's skeletal arm slid off the bones and onto Ritter's face. The effect almost made him look like he'd acquired a black eye in a fistfight, except the black rimming the eye wasn't a bruise, and the eye itself was a gaping red hole.

Denise looked away as Thornber smashed his wrist into Ritter's face again, scraping away most of a cheek. Teeth flashed at her for a second before blood welled up and covered them.

In a few seconds, Thornber would be done with Ritter, and then he'd come after them. Guns weren't going to stop him, at least not their revolvers. Maybe an elephant gun could splatter Thornber's body across so much space that the individual chunks were no longer a threat, but they didn't have any elephant guns.

She needed to think, dammit. Looking around, she tried to put some options together.

Option one. She could grab some sort of cutting tool and start hacking away at Thornber, dismembering him.

Not a real plan. Ritter had tried exactly that, and getting close to Thornber was practically a death sentence. Besides, merely hacking him apart wouldn't make them completely safe, as the hand wandering across the floor toward Ritter's intestines demonstrated.

Alright. Option two. They could try to bash down the door and escape. Brady had shot the deadbolt across the door, but a good solid kick could still smash the door out of its frame. A bullet in the right location could just as easily serve as a skeleton key.

That wasn't a good idea, either. They'd have to get around Thornber to even reach the door, and the walking corpse was as likely to snatch one of them as not as they tried to get past. Second, it would get them out of the examination room, but it would also release Thornber into the rest of the ranger station. Maybe they could end him with an elephant gun before he killed someone else at that point, but maybe not.

And he was spreading his black slime to everyone he killed. If the worms thrived on dead flesh, colonizing more dead bodies would simply create more ghouls like Thornber.

Her eyes fell on something nearby, and a third option popped into Denise's head. Was it a good idea? No. Was it a safe idea? Again, no. But the time for safe ideas passed sometime around when the dead body started to clamber around and it was way back in the dust when that dead body began to murder everyone it could reach.

Denise holstered her revolver and pressed up against the wall. She shimmied along, staying as far away from Thornber as she could. She needed to get to within a few feet, though. Close enough for him to lunge at her.

With the cold, tiled wall at her back, she reached down and grabbed the item she'd spotted. The metal jerry can sloshed as she hefted it up. Maybe a gallon of gasoline was left inside.

Thornber perked up at the sound of the sloshing gasoline. Ritter's face looked like something from a cubist painter's red phase. A thick string of flesh and sinew was the only thing keeping Ritter's head attached to the rest of his body. He fell forward with a splat as Thornber released his grip on him.

Rather than turning around backward to face Denise, Thornber's arms simply repositioned themselves. His shoulders gave a meaty pop as they dislocated themselves. His elbows crunched as they hyperextended backwards. Thornber started walking backward to corner Denise against the wall.

The worms weren't using Thornber's eyes. He didn't even have eyes anymore. They'd eaten them. The worms weren't smart enough to have any sense of human physiology beyond basic propulsion and grabbing. They probably couldn't even understand a body shape that wasn't radially symmetrical. They manipulated his body like a blind child playing with the limbs of a stuffed doll.

Denise darted out of the way as Thornber jabbed his wrist bones against the wall. The bloody bones made a noise like a steam shovel biting into rock as they scratched across the tile. The thing that had been Thornber pivoted and walked backward toward them, swaying and jittering as the worms sheathing his body fought to control speed and balance.

Denise's fingers scrabbled at the jerry can's cap, trying to unscrew it as the ghoul drew closer. Too late.

Thornber shot out his arm again, trying to excavate a hole in Denise's chest cavity. She threw the can up like a shield.

Slicing through the air, Thornber's exposed arm bones struck the can, puncturing the metal and denting it inward. The examination room filled with the stifling scent of gasoline, blocking out even the overpowering odors of antiseptic and fresh, coppery blood.

Thornber wrenched his spear-like arm backward, ripping the jerry can out of Denise's grip. Gasoline splashed across the floor, across Thornber, across Ritter's still form. More liquid glugged out of the can onto Thornber's legs as he raised his arm to strike again. The can was still stuck to the end of his arm like some half-assed robot hand.

Denise fumbled in her pocket for a lighter, her fingers trying to extract it from a fold in the cloth. Thornber drew his arm back and jackhammered her with the jerry can. The metal canister smashed into her chest like a battering ram, knocking her off her feet and sending her sprawling on the ground. If the can hadn't been stuck on Thornber's arm, his wrist bones would have chewed a divot out of her.

That didn't mean the impact didn't hurt like hell, though. The air went out of her lungs and she had to lay on the tile for a second. She could feel the outline of the jerry can where it had struck as a burning rectangle of pain. She tried to suck some air back in but almost gagged at the scent of gasoline.

Thornber stood directly over her. His body was a mass of bones and black slime. Kirkeberg and Cornelia unloaded another volley from their revolvers into Thornber, but his headless corpse did little more than shudder with each bullet impact.

Denise squirmed backwards as gasoline trickled in her direction. Thornber took a step forward.

She reached a hand into her pocket, the pain flaring up in her chest as she moved her arms. Thornber took another step forward, his foot landing squarely in the stream of gasoline. The jerry can was still stuck to his hand, though the flow of gas from its ruptured side had slowed to a trickle.

Her fingers closed around the edges of the lighter, gripping it tight. Thornber stood directly over her now, his broken, twisted form blocking out the florescent light directly overhead.

Tearing the lighter out of her pocket, Denise flicked the starter. Thornber reached down toward her with his black, skeletal hand.

A tiny flame sprang to life at Denise's fingertips, and she tossed the lighter at Thornber's feet. The effect was instantaneous.

The lighter's little flame hit the gasoline fumes and billowed up into a sudden fireball. Denise scurried away as the tiled floor near her boots turned into a sea of blue and yellow fire. The flames spread across half the floor in a second, leaping up toward the ceiling.

Thornber virtually exploded. The worms on his legs had been splashed with gasoline too, and they went up in the instant inferno. As the worms on his legs disentangled themselves from each other in a desperate bid to escape the burning fuel, the rest of the worms on his body lost their cohesion.

Like a nervous system sensing pain and sending signals out across the body, every worm attached to Thornber's corpse instantly knew that a substantial portion of their legion were in trouble. They panicked and tried to jettison off their burning host. The process was like watching Thornber disintegrate as all the thousands of worms fell off his bones at once.

There was nowhere for them to go, though. They plunged off Thornber's body and plummeted straight into the roaring flames like the souls of the damned into Hell. Individual patches of slime writhed and bubbled as the worms died and sizzled by the thousands.

Now free of worms, Thornber's skeletal remains collapsed into the flames as a collection of lifeless bones and shreds of moldering flesh.

Denise pulled herself to her feet. Cornelia grabbed a fire extinguisher off the wall before the whole building could catch on fire.

"Now then," Denise said. Thornber's hand scuttled past on the floor and she punted it into the flames. "I think the park might have a problem."

EIGHT

SHIMMERS IN THE DISTANCE

Denise lay on her stomach in the tall grass. She could still feel where the jerry can hit her in the chest, but it didn't hurt as much as it did an hour ago.

"Okay, we're in luck. There's two couriers in the camp right now," Skipworth said, handing her binoculars back to Denise.

"Which ones?" She pressed the binoculars up to her own eyes. The poacher camp below sprang into focus. About two dozen men went about their work below. Some of them cooked. One of them had the hood popped open on a truck and was fishing around inside. Several more stood near the out edges of the encampment, rifles slung over their shoulders. Drab-colored tents hid more of the poachers. From ground level, it would be almost impossible to spot the camp behind the berms and vegetation until someone stumbled directly into it.

"See the guy toward the back of the camp with the crewcut and safari vest?" Skipworth pointed. "That's Hu."

Denise tracked her binoculars around until she spotted the Chinese man. He sat on a log, whittling a stick with an oversized knife. A pistol lay within easy reach next to him.

"The other one is Chen." Skipworth pointed and Denise tracked it with her binoculars. "He's the one in shorts smoking his pipe."

Denise zeroed in on the second man.

"Hey, can I ask you a question?" Skipworth said.

"Now may not be the best time ever."

Skipworth barreled ahead anyway. "Your boss, Kirkeberg, will he actually help me when all this is said and done?"

Denise took a breath. "What did he tell you he was going to do?"

"When he came back to my holding cell and asked me to help with the autopsy, I asked him to make me a firmer promise about what would happen to me."

"Did he make it?"

"Yeah, although he wasn't very happy about it. I'm just worried that he'll try to renege on his promise later."

"I didn't necessarily like you at first, either," Denise said.

"Have you at least changed your mind?"

"I'm still making it up. On the one hand, you seem like you mean well, and you're helping us. That, I like. On the other hand, you've been helping to destroy something I love. I hit a rough patch in my life before finding my way here to this park, and keeping it pristine for the rest of my life and for future generations is very important to me."

"I didn't want to help Zhang Dong."

"I know. You did it to get out of trouble with the Triads. Now you're helping us to get out of the trouble we landed you in. That's not to say I don't appreciate that you're giving us a hand with your former colleagues. And with the incident involving Thornber. I do. I genuinely do."

"But?"

"But so far most of the things I know about you, you've done because you were trying to squirm out from under some trouble or another." Denise looked down the opposite side of the hill and watched the police vehicles draw closer, moving slow and steady. "I haven't really gotten to know you at all. The real you. I suspect you want to do good, but part of me wonders. If the shoe were on the other foot, and Zhang Dong and his cronies captured the two of us and said all would be forgiven if you shot me in the head, I don't know what you'd do. So far, you've sided with everyone who gains leverage over you. It's not a feeling that builds trust."

"That's not exactly fair."

"No, no it's not. Maybe under other circumstances, we'd be firm friends. Under other circumstances, we'd probably never meet, and neither of us would have a worry here. But the world isn't fair. You can count on a few things, though. If Gunder Kirkeberg said he'd promise to help you, he'll help you. He may not always be fair, but he keeps his word."

Denise thought back to her meeting just a few days ago when she learned Kirkeberg had thrown out her application to join the anti-poaching team he was putting together. God, but that seemed like an eternity ago. If she hadn't become upset and requested Hartzell and Planck accompany Thornber, she'd have gone down into Sulfur Springs on that expedition.

Now, she was here. That one request had probably changed the trajectory of her life. Instead of being dead in a pit somewhere, she was dismantling the poaching operation in the park and dealing with the aftermath of Thornber's expedition. Who thought that the world turned on such little things?

"So just how *did* you end up here?" Skipworth asked.

"Hmm? Sorry, I went wool gathering for a moment."

"You said earlier that you went through some rough times before you landed here. What happened?"

Looking down the hill again, Denise saw the police vehicles were still a good distance off. Their shapes swayed and quivered in the heat rising off the ground. "I used to be the best hunter in Cape Town. Big game enthusiasts would hire me, and I would take them out where they could find their desired prizes."

"Seems a bit odd that you would end up here, then. You almost had more in common with Zhang Dong's men, it sounds like."

"No, not really. At least, I don't see it that way. Down there, they're just interested in the profit from killing the animals and selling their parts on the black market. I was in it for the sport. Before I took over the business, my father was Cape Town's premier hunter. After my mother died, he more or less raised me out on the game trails. I was handling rifles as soon as I was old enough to understand how they worked, and I loved it.

"My formal education mostly consisted of reading books and lessons under a tent during downtime on the hunt. The rest of the time I was out with my father, learning the tricks of the trade. I learned everything there was to know about the animals I was helping to hunt. I knew how to track them. I knew their migration routes. I knew what scents would attract them into a trap. I knew their inner anatomy so I could aim for their hearts and other vital organs so I could bring them down quick.

"But it was all a very shallow understanding. I understood how the animals worked on a mechanical level, but I didn't really understand the animals. Intellectually, I knew they were living things, and that was what made the hunt so glorious. There is no greater thrill than tracking a wily and dangerous beast through the brush and landing the perfect shot to bring it down. Pitting all your skill and gumption against a worthy opponent and coming out on top is always satisfying.

"The reason the hunt was so amazing was because the animals were these living creatures. They were crafty and hard to sneak up on because they were afraid. Afraid of death and pain and suffering. The dangerous herbivores were dangerous because they were defending themselves against creatures that had come to inflict suffering on them. The dangerous predators were dangerous because as they were afraid and hungry. I'm not trying to equate the feelings of animals with those of people, but they're driven by some of the very same things that make humans tick. There's some basic symmetry there. A congruity.

"I didn't really learn that until it was too late. I'd been hired by a group for a hunt. A bunch of Belgian dentists who had formed a hunting club. They were on their big, yearly vacation, and they wanted to hunt elephants. I'd been on plenty of elephant hunts, so I didn't really think very much of it. Pretty typical request, really.

"I took them out to a place not all that far from the park, actually. I had managed to locate a herd of elephants that was suitable. There was an older female they could shoot. I set us up near the watering hole and waited. I'd pointed out the older female to them and made sure they understood what they were supposed to do.

"After a few hours of waiting, the whole herd came past us to drink. I don't know exactly what happened. The dentists must have made a plan with each other when I wasn't listening. The next thing I knew, they'd all leapt up and started firing. I started yelling at them to stop, but I couldn't even hear myself over the ringing in my ears.

"A bunch of the elephants went down. Some of them dead, some of them dying. I could actually feel the ground shift as they collapsed all at once. The survivors trumpeted and started to run away, moving as fast as they could away from the watering hole, and that's when the dentists started reloading. I realized that they planned to wipe out the entire herd, to each take a trophy, even if it meant they had to kill every elephant they saw.

"The herds of elephants and rhinos had already dwindled just since I was a little girl. A lot of it was due to poachers killing unsustainable numbers of animals. A lot of it was also due to habitat loss and human settlements encroaching ever deeper into the wilderness. I hadn't really seen such wholesale slaughter so close up before, though.

"That's when I saw one of the baby elephants, probably no more than a few months old. One of its ears had been blown off in the initial fusillade, and it was standing next to one of the dead elephants, nudging it with its trunk. Trying to get its dead mother to stand up again. I think that's when everything hit me, and it hit me hard.

"I kept yelling at the hunters to stop, but they didn't pay any attention to me. I punched one of them, knocked one of his teeth out, as a matter of fact. Knocked him to the ground. It didn't make any difference, though. The rest of them shot the remaining elephants."

"What happened to the young one, the one trying to wake its dead mother?" Skipworth asked.

"Shot," Denise said. "I couldn't save any of them. I wasn't sure what to do with myself after that for a long time. I couldn't hunt anymore. It gave me the cold sweats, and I couldn't get that baby elephant out of my mind any time there was something in my sights."

"And now you're here."

"And now I'm here. I took some detours on the way. Ran the old hunting business into the ground because I didn't know what to do. Got suckered into a bad deal working with Yersinia Bioresearch to procure some biological samples. It didn't go well. But I'm here now. I don't think it's any sort of grand repent-for-your-past-sins kind of thing. I get to be out in the wild where I'm happy, and I get to help with something I believe in. On paper, it's a pretty good idea."

"On paper? It sounds like a great fit for someone like you, even off paper."

"Yeah, well, things haven't always gone the way I thought they would. You're not the only person here that sometimes butts heads with Gunder Kirkeberg. He told me the other day that I was only here because I had connections with one of his friends."

"That's a rather harsh thing to say."

"He's at least a little correct. I have lots of skills the park needs, but myself and Cornelia wouldn't have been hired if not for her father. Sometimes, the world works the way it does, not the way we think it should. Kirkeberg is one of those people who will tell you whatever he thinks, whether you want to hear it or not, he'll assume it's objective fact, and he's smart enough to be right most of the time but dumb enough to think he's right *all* the time."

"You could transfer to a different part of the park. Work at the visitor center where you don't have to deal with him."

"It's not so much Kirkeberg that's the problem. I can deal with the likes of him, even if he managed to punch me right in the ego the other day. No, I've been thinking about more recent events. You said your boss, Zhang Dong, has killed people in the park?"

"Quite a few. More than you might expect. The Triads like to make lessons of people they think have wronged them, and they think that about a lot of people. I don't even know how many people he's ordered killed on park grounds."

"See, that's part of the problem. This place was becoming a sort of home for me, and finding out something like that bothers me. If I told someone that there were more murder victims than they might expect buried in their basement, it would bother them. One murder victim buried there would bother people. The idea that there might be a lot more is a thought with hooks attached, and it'll get stuck in your mind and refuse to dislodge itself."

"I guess I can see your point, there."

"And this incident with Thornber."

"Hey, if you hadn't set him on fire, we'd probably both be dead right now."

"Oh, no. You mistake me. I'm not sorry I set him on fire. I'm not a stranger to violence for the sake of survival. I'd have set him on fire in front of a bunch of screaming school children and then roasted wienies over the corpse and not felt bad about that. He was a killing machine at that point. If you get infested with worms and come after me, I'm setting you on fire too, and I won't feel the least bit bad about it."

"Point taken."

"My problem is that I was supposed to be with Thornber when…whatever it is that happened to him happened to him. It happened to a couple of other rangers instead, and we still don't know where they are. They might be wandering around the park like Thornber was. They might be dead underground somewhere. We may never know. I just keep wondering if there wasn't something I could have done to help. Maybe things could have been different if I was there."

"I saw this sometimes with former soldiers who survived experiences where they survived and others didn't. An artillery shell would go off and kill the man next to them while they were unscathed. Freak chance like that. They felt like they should have been the ones. Like maybe they didn't deserve to still be here."

"It's not like that. Well, maybe there's a little of that. I still haven't been able to sort out all my feelings over the past few days. But that's not what I'm really getting at. There's more to it. I'm here helping the park, and that's good. It's a good thing, but it's a static thing. I'm just trying to preserve something while it gets chipped away at. Sometimes, it's something like Zhang Dong and his poaching operation. We might wrap that up today, but there will be more like him. It's like clutching a fistful of sand; some of it's always going to sift through your fingers. Maybe you can hold onto it for a long time, but eventually, most of it is going to disappear. And that's just with problems like the poachers coming around and killing unsustainable numbers of animals. Now we have to deal with problems like whatever the hell happened to Thornber. I just feel like there's something more proactive I should be doing."

"We're getting rid of the Triads. That's proactive."

"Yes, but something will come along to replace them eventually. Maybe some homegrown poachers who can take over in the vacuum left by the Triads. We might already have a bigger problem now, though. You said you saw a couple of elephant carcasses covered in black goop the other day?"

"Yeah. Not to the degree Thornber was, but around the wounds."

"There's already something out there, something that we don't know about. It doesn't sound like those elephants were killed by human beings."

"After you burned Thornber, Kirkeberg said the rangers could quarantine this part of the park."

"Yes, we're planning to call in everyone we can and block the area around Verschoor Dam and Sulfur Springs off, everything Ranger Station Thirteen normally oversees. It's a start, but it's only a start."

"You think Kirkeberg isn't taking this seriously?"

"Not seriously enough. We don't even totally understand what we're dealing with here, but it's already created a bigger problem than the poachers by themselves. Matheson and Ritter are both dead. They went out searching for Crane and De Hoog, who still haven't reported back, and the two rangers that were with Thornber are still missing, too. I'm not holding out much hope for Hartzell or Planck at this point. We could be down up by six rangers already before we even know what we're up against. Speaking of which, have you been able to figure out much more about these worms?"

"I have a whole lot more speculation than facts at this point."

"Hit me with it."

"Alright, we'll start with something I do understand. Have you ever seen ants try to survive a flood? Once the waters start to rise, the workers will all scramble into a single mass and link their legs together, using their mandibles to clamp themselves into a big, interlocking mat. They put the queen and the eggs in the center of the mat, and when the waters rise high enough, they float. They basically become a raft, carried away to safety.

"I think the worms are doing something similar, albeit more sophisticated. They entangle their bristles together and use their pincers to lock into a solid sheet, not so different from the ants. The primary difference seems to be the scale on which they're organized. Ants can rapidly form a simple raft. These worms are using their bodies to move something as complex as a human corpse around. They don't get it quite right, but the mere fact that they can coordinate their flexing and squirming to achieve that sort of result is pretty remarkable."

"Any other thoughts?"

"Well, I was thinking about when Thornber was first found and brought to the ranger station. He wasn't up and ambulatory yet. All he was doing were those weird, random movements. I'm starting to think I understand why. At least to some extent."

"So what are you thinking?"

"I can't exactly prove it, but do you remember how their slime works? It's really two different components. One part is the worms themselves. Their black bodies are what make the stuff so dark. The rest of it is some sort of secretion they're creating, some sort of mucus. At first, I thought it was purely defensive in nature, and that might be part of it. I think it has a couple of other uses, though.

"First, I suspect it makes the environment they're colonizing more amenable. If these things came from inside a poisonous cave, the surface world is probably something of a shock to their systems. Emitting chemicals into their slime makes it more livable while they make due eating the host and breaking down its body. It's sort of like settlers building a new town next to a swamp. The first thing they're going to do is drain the marshes. Except in this case, the worms are doing their best to bring the marshes with them because that's what they like.

"The second is a little less pleasant to contemplate. In addition to protecting the worms and helping them survive, the slime is probably awash in reproductive fluids."

"Lovely."

"I scrapped a couple of small samples off the walls of the examination room. The ones that didn't burn with Thornber. I dropped a little meat into a couple of the samples. By the time we left to help the police efforts here, the worm population had roughly doubled in size. The worms can breed quite rapidly if they have a source of food."

"How does that explain why Thornber was twitching rather than up and walking about when we found him?"

"Well, consider this. The men who found him said they also discovered a couple of dead lions nearby. I don't know who attacked who. Maybe the lions made a mistake and thought Thornber looked like easy prey. Maybe he went after them. The worms aren't exactly friendly, after all.

"Either way, I bet if I could examine those lions right now, I would find a considerable amount of black slime on their bodies. I suspect the worms, how shall I say, overexerted themselves by colonizing both animals. There weren't enough individuals left on Thornber's body to assume full control of his limbs. They had to brew up a new generation of worms to completely control him again. The best they could do up until then was move single limbs or cause the body to flop around a bit. That's what we were seeing when Thornber was brought in. Sometime after that, they were able to completely take control again."

"So when you say the worms are colonizing the lions…"

"Eventually, what happened with Thornber will probably happen to those lions. They'll get up again, and they'll start spreading their own worms."

"Jesus, we don't know where all Thornber has been the past few days. He could have infected dozens of animals by now. Double or triple that if Hartzell and Planck are out there somewhere."

"Indeed, I told the same thing to Kirkeberg before he sent us ahead to identify Zhang Dong's couriers."

"Good. What did he say?"

"He said he'd look into it."

"That's all?"

"That's all he said."

"These things could be a real threat, though. He saw what just Thornber was able to do all by himself to Matheson and Ritter. And now you're telling me that there will probably be a couple of lions with the same infection loose in the park soon?"

"It's possible they'll die out in an environment they're not used to. This could be a fairly brief episode."

"It's possible, yeah, but you were just the one telling me that you could only speculate about how they worked. Maybe they'll adapt. Maybe we'll be neck deep in black slime by the end of the week."

"That is another distinct possibility. I raised a similar point with him, but he stuck to his position. Something about dealing with problems as they arose. I think he wants to nail Zhang and his crew before he starts worrying about something he doesn't understand."

"Okay, but we need to make sure we have our priorities straight here. Zhang Dong is a problem, but this could turn into something worse fast. The poachers aren't good for the park, but you don't have to set them on fire to make them stop."

"I don't know. I think I'm with Kirkeberg on this one. I wouldn't mind taking Zhang Dong off the board first. Sooner or later, he's going to figure out that I've been helping you, and if he learns that before he's behind bars, I'm going to be in a rough spot."

"Let me try to frame this in terms you'll understand: saving your own skin. If, a week from now, you find yourself trapped in the ranger station while a hundred of those worm monsters are pounding down the doors, you might wish Zhang Dong found you instead."

"Terms I understand? Yeah, I spend a lot of time trying to save my own skin, as you put it. But I'm doing what I can to help, here. I've made mistakes, and I've taken my lumps for them. Now I don't want to end up dead or in prison for the rest of my life because of it."

"Alright, alright. Fine. I'm just a bit on edge because a dead guy being controlled by a bunch of worms tried to kill me earlier and came way too close to succeeding."

"Yeah, I hate it when that happens, too," Skipworth said, trying to smile.

"But here's part of my problem. This thing is getting worse while we're not watching. Take those dead elephants with the black slime you found, right? All gouged up?"

Skipworth nodded.

Denise pursed her lips. "So they might very well be up and about right now. Maybe those lions, too. And they're going to go try to spread the worms to something else, too. Think about it, though. Do you have any idea what killed those elephants?"

"Frankly, no."

"Right. Thornber, covered in worms or not, couldn't have ripped them down to the bone the way you described. So he didn't do it."

"Well, maybe something Thornber killed did it."

"I mean, maybe, but what? It would have to be something big, and that brings us straight back to the problem that Thornber might have trouble doing that all on his own. I mean, maybe he could spread it to a lion, and the lion spreads it to a water buffalo, and the water buffalo spreads it to a rhino, and the rhino spreads it to those elephants you found, but that seems awfully fast. That's a very rapid rate of contagion, but I don't know what could kill two elephants in the way you described other than maybe a very determined rhino."

"So…what, exactly? You think there's something else out there?"

"Something big? Like, really big? I don't know. Maybe. There's a lot of things none of us understand at play here, but that's bothering me. Even if there's nothing out there aside from infected wildlife, I think we need to do a hell of a lot more than Kirkeberg is doing. When we get done with these poachers, I need to light a fire under Kirkeberg's ass."

"Do you really think there's something big out there? I mean something genuinely different from what we've seen before?"

"I don't know."

"I personally doubt it. The worms only seem to attach themselves to available, articulated bodies. If they could take collections of objects and aggregate themselves into some sort of slime golem, we could have a problem. I don't know what killed those elephants, but I doubt it was some sort of giant monster."

Denise didn't say anything for a moment. She looked back down the hill. Below, the police vans had resolved themselves into distinct shapes as they drew closer. They'd be here in just a moment with Kirkeberg, a few other rangers, and a mess of police.

"So what would you do if you were in charge?"

"Easy. I'd get the Army out here. Get them to bring all their flamethrowers with them. Set up a few tanks in reserve for the big animals that had been infected, like the elephants. If there's something big enough to kill elephants out there, surround it with everything we have, set it on fire, and shovel the ashes over with dirt. Then set up a perimeter and sweep it back and forth a few times. This isn't something we should pussyfoot around."

"Heh. You sound like you know what you're doing. With your skills, maybe you should be a professional monster hunter if you decide not to stick with the game preserve."

"Hmm."

"I was joking," Skipworth said.

"I know," Denise said as the police vans pulled to a halt at the base of the hill, hidden from view of the poacher camp by the ridge.

Just as the police vehicles had resolved themselves out of shimmers in the distance, an honest-to-goodness idea had resolved itself out of Denise's half-understood emotions.

Denise DeMarco. Professional monster hunter.

It had a certain ring to it.

NINE

SHOOT THE MESSENGERS

Denise stood behind the police vans with the other rangers as the police swept around the perimeter of the poacher camp. With the tall grass swaying in the breeze, the police commandos were almost impossible to track as they crawled into position.

The camp backed up to the river, the water stemming down across the plain from the Verschoor Dam. There was already a police unit crouched down on the opposite shore in case anyone was brave enough to risk crocodiles and hippos and try to swim across. All around the other sides of the camp, the police were moving into place, preparing the raid.

Denise was happy to leave the initial business to them. She was skilled in subduing animals, not people. She knew her way around a fight, but she wasn't trained in controlling a situation the way the police commandos were. If things went haywire, she would be the wrong person to have in the middle of it all.

Cornelia, Kirkeberg, and Skipworth stood nearby, watching the proceedings unfold. No one said anything, lest the breeze carry their words over to the poacher camp and alert them that someone was nearby. Denise and Skipworth had told the police that not one but two couriers were present in the camp, exactly who they needed to interrogate to learn where Zhang Dong was holed up.

The breeze went still for a moment, and Denise couldn't see anything of the police commandos hiding in the grass. She waited, hoping to catch some glimpse of what was going on.

Suddenly, a blazing red flare shot up into the sky and several dozen men all popped up from the grass all at once and dashed into the green labyrinth that the camp lay hidden in. Shouts in English and Afrikaans told the Triads to freeze and drop their weapons. Denise didn't know if any of the Triads spoke either of those languages, but the message was plenty clear from just watching the police swarm in from all sides at once with shotguns and pistols.

One of the Triad sentries burst out of the tree line, his rifle bouncing against his back as he sprinted away. He looked back, and a police commando shot out of the same gap in the vegetation and crash tackled the man, knocking him to the dirt. The tall grass blocked most of her view, but Denise saw the rifle tossed away and the police officer dig out a set of handcuffs. A few seconds later, he hauled the sentry to his feet and dragged him back in the direction of the camp.

It was all over in less than a minute. Calls of all clear filtered out of the camp, and Denise and the other rangers walked out from behind the police vans and rounded the ridge.

Denise parted some of the greenery at the camp's periphery and walked into the center of the poaching operation. Several tents had been trampled in the sudden chaos. Personal effects lay in the mud. Half-eaten plates of food sat on a table.

A couple of Triads lay on their stomachs, their hands cuffed behind their backs. One of them kept mumbling something in Mandarin, and a police commando nudged him with the side of his boot. Denise couldn't tell if the man was praying or quietly cursing the police.

The rest of Zhang Dong's hunters stood in a row with their hands in the air while the police searched them one at a time and placed cuffs on their wrists. Some of them looked scared. Others annoyed. Most of the Triads looked carefully indifferent.

Then Skipworth walked through the foliage into the camp. The collection of Triads turned their heads to look at him, realizing that he wasn't on their side anymore. A variety of sneers appeared, and a couple of the poachers started to curse him out in a mixture of languages.

Most of the poachers were Asians, Triad regulars, but there was some local talent, too. There were two Boers who looked like they were probably brothers, a black woman with a bandolier full of brass, a black man with an eye patch, and an Indian with sunglasses and slicked back hair.

A tall man with sharp, handsome features walked up to the rangers. "I'm Captain Blenavis. I'm in charge here." Blenavis had the sort of face that would have looked good stamped on ancient currency. Assured and commanding. "I'm told we need to separate out a couple of our prisoners and interrogate them first to find another camp."

"That's correct," Kirkeberg said.

"Time is ticking here. It's only a matter of time one way or the other until the ringleader knows his camp was hit. Who do we need to speak to about finding this other camp?"

Skipworth raised his hand. "You'll need those two, right there." He pointed to Hu and then Chen. Hu's safari jacket had gotten all muddy, and Chen had lost the stick he was whittling, but Denise recognized them both from her earlier reconnaissance with Skipworth.

"Alright. Take those two back to the vans and start sweating them through the translators. Find out where that other camp is."

Denise smiled to herself. Even if she still wanted the problems surrounding the black slime dealt with, it was still nice to make some progress on another issue plaguing the park. Knowing she'd helped drag Zhang Dong down was worth a certain amount of satisfaction.

Two big police commandos grabbed each of the couriers and started to take them away. The rest of the poachers suddenly realized what the game was. Skipworth hadn't just betrayed them to the police, he'd timed it so they could chop the head off the snake soon after. Shouts erupted from the prisoners, and the couriers struggled and wiggled in their captors' grasps.

The police hadn't finished searching and cuffing all the Triads yet. One of them pushed the commando searching him away and pulled out a knife, lunging after Hu as he walked past.

The entire camp exploded in that second. Police commandos reached for their guns. Triads broke from their frozen poses and went for weapons hidden on their persons or stashed nearby.

The man with the knife jabbed it into Hu's neck. Blood instantly welled out and ran down the front of his ruined safari jacket. Back splatter squirted across the police hauling Hu away, and a fine red mist colored the attacker's face. A second later, a third officer clubbed the man in the stomach with a shotgun butt and knocked the knife out of his hand. The Triad went down on the ground.

Hu, the front of his shirt and jacket now completely red, thrashed in the grasp of the officers like a fish dragged onto the deck of a boat. The two police commandos threw him on the ground and immediately started trying to pinch the squirting arteries shut and apply enough pressure to save the man's life.

Even put back on her heels by the sudden violence, Denise could tell that the man wouldn't make it. Hu would be dead in the mud before they could even load him into a vehicle.

The man who had killed Hu would go to jail for a very long time, but the Triad leadership would hear of his loyalty in protecting Zhang Dong. In the future, he would be an important part of the organization in South Africa.

That left only Chen with the knowledge of where Zhang Dong was, and several Triads had made the same calculation as the one currently being swarmed by police commandos. Now the mission was clear to the remaining Triads. Kill Chen before he could squeal.

A Triad charged out of the tent next to Denise, a pistol in his hand. He raised the weapon in Chen's general direction as the commandos tried to drag the courier out of the sudden combat zone.

No more than a few feet away from her, one of the commandos fired his rifle. The gun let loose a giant crack that cut through the yelling and shouting.

The Triad with the pistol jumped as if he'd been stung by a bee. His weapon flew out of his hand. When his feet touched down on the ground again, his legs crumpled under him and he went down in an ungainly sprawl. A red stain started to spread on the back of his shirt as he thrashed in the dirt.

Denise grabbed her own revolver with one hand and Cornelia's arm with the other. She wasn't afraid to defend herself, but she didn't want to get caught in the middle of a firefight. Kirkeberg, Skipworth, and the other rangers retreated into the relative safety behind the curtain of greenery outside the camp.

Denise and Cornelia had been standing closer to the center of things, and simply fading away wasn't an option. "There." Denise pointed at the truck she'd spied a Triad trying to repair earlier through her binoculars. The metal body would give them some sort of cover as things heated up.

"Why can't anything ever be easy?" Cornelia muttered to herself, drawing her own revolver. Another gunshot rang out in the middle of the camp. Denise couldn't tell if the shot was fired by a poacher or a police officer.

A Triad with a knife suddenly dashed around to their side of the truck, apparently also thinking that it would provide good cover. He skidded around when he saw them, surprised but spotting an opportunity. He charged straight for Denise from no more than a few feet away, the knife in his hand gleaming in the muted sunlight.

The man aimed a clumsy blow at Denise as he darted forward. Denise pivoted to the side, grabbed his knife hand and used his own momentum to swing him face-first into the side of the truck. He slammed into one of the doors, leaving a big dent and a greasy smear on the metal. He collapsed on the ground, and Denise brought a boot down directly on top of his already mashed face. The Triad made a noise like a surprised dog and curled up into a ball.

Denise scraped some teeth off the bottom of her boot. Cornelia dropped to one knee to make sure the dazed Triad didn't choke on any of the loose teeth in his mouth in case he fell unconscious. She picked up his knife and tucked it into her own belt first, though.

With the space now to themselves, Denise poked her head up above the hood of the truck to see what was going on. The camp was a mad house.

The Triads handcuffed on the ground were trying to work their way to their feet to run away. Denise didn't know where they thought they would be going with their hands chained behind their backs. If the rangers and police didn't pick them up, they were as likely to be eaten by wild animals as not. Or eaten by something else loose in the park. But several of them seemed determined to escape, if they could.

Maybe some of them would even succeed in making it out of the camp. The police commandos had their hands full with the Triads trying to assassinate Chen.

One Triad emerged from a tent with a long rifle only to find himself staring down the barrel of three police shotguns. He dropped the weapon and sent his hands skyward again.

Meanwhile, three more Triads made a break straight for Chen and the two police commandos trying to drag him away. Only one of the Triads had a gun, a grungy-looking pistol that probably hadn't been cleaned in a long time.

The police commandos dropped their grip on Chen and brought their own weapons up, but the Triads were already on top of them. Denise couldn't do anything from this distance without possibly hitting Chen or one of the police officers.

Shouting for the Triads to drop their weapons, the officer on the left tried to convince them to surrender. The officer on the right simply drew his own gun and shot the pistol-wielding Triad in the leg. The poacher went down with a shriek, the grimy weapon spilling out of his hands onto the dirt.

One of the poachers stabbed the second police commando in the arm with a knife only to be clubbed across the jaw by the first officer. The Triad went down in a heap, his jaw clearly broken.

The last of the three Triads also had a knife. He lunged forward toward the uninjured commando. Most of the other poachers had already been subdued again after their brief mass assassination attempt. More of the police commandos were running over to assist their brother with the last poacher.

Denise watched the commandos converge on the final Triad, but then she noticed some movement behind them. Chen took two steps over, picked up the grimy pistol, inserted it into his mouth, and pulled the trigger.

The gunshot was slightly muffled but still louder than a car crash. Part of Chen's head jutted up like a tiny creature was trying to hatch out of his skull, and a squirt of red shot out. Chen's feet went out from under him like a drunk who had wandered onto a patch of ice, and then the last poacher gave up his struggle and allowed himself to be tackled by the onslaught of police commandos.

Denise's mouth went dry. Both Chen and Hu were dead. They were the only ones who knew how to reach Zhang Dong. Without them, Zhang's group would soon discover this camp had been routed, and then they'd pick up stakes and disappear for a couple of months, only to return with more hunters. That meant this whole process would have to repeat itself, assuming the rangers could even catch another break and find the Triads again once they returned.

Damnit.

Damnit, damnit, damnit.

Chen had evidently decided that he knew the cards on the table. If he was the only courier captured and the police later raided Zhang Dong's camp, the Triad leadership would quickly figure out where the weak link lay. No doubt something unpleasant would have happened to him in due course. Given the thing's Skipworth had mentioned seeing the Triads do to people they didn't like, the quick, neat suicide might have been Chen's best option. Even if he clammed up and didn't tell the police anything, the Triads would no doubt consider him of suspect trustworthiness after that. He'd be damaged goods, and therefore, he probably wouldn't last long at all.

After a few minutes, the commandos rounded the remaining Triads up, finished frisking them and dragged them off toward the police vans. Captain Blenavis picked up the unconscious man Denise had smashed into the side of the truck and handed him to two waiting commandos.

"Is your man with the stab wound alright?" Cornelia asked. "I could take a look at him if you want."

"He'll be fine. He just needs some stitches and to take it easy for a little while. The poachers who tried to fight got the worst of the encounter. We'll be taking them to the visitor center's medical station and then hauling everyone else away."

Skipworth approached from around the far side of the truck. "What about the dead couriers?"

"We'll take them with us, make sure they're properly identified, and then notify any next of kin. Assuming we can find them, of course. That can get tricky with foreign nationals."

"No, I mean, were you able to get any information out of them before they died?"

"We only had them in our custody for a couple of minutes. We hadn't even asked either of them a single question yet. So, no, we don't have anything to go on at this point."

"That's not good. One way or the other, Zhang Dong is going to hear that this camp was raided. He'll know he can't stay in place after that. There's no way we'll be able to find him after twenty-four hours."

"Maybe. Maybe not," Blenavis said. "There's a few types of people I have to deal with on a regular basis. There's the ones that don't plan ahead. Sometimes, it's because they're dumb and bad at being criminals. Sometimes, it's because they weren't planning to commit a crime until it happened. Normal people in a moment of rage or jealousy or drunkenness. They're all pretty easy to track down. They leave a trail that's not hard to follow. The smaller group of people I deal with are the organized ones. They're thinking ahead. It sounds like this Zhang Dong fellow is one of those planning-types. The thing that makes my job a lot easier is that even the smart ones get complacent or make mistakes. Once all the suspects are loaded into the vans, my men are going to turn this camp upside down and look for something to figure out where that other camp is. Care to help us? Another few sets of eyes won't hurt."

"Sure," Denise said. "I think we'd all like to see this wrapped up rather than have things get away from us. We know the game preserve pretty well. Maybe some of the stuff around here will help us narrow down where the couriers have been lately." Cornelia and Skipworth nodded.

A few minutes later, they were pawing around the perimeter of the camp. "So, any idea what we're actually looking for?" Cornelia asked.

"Well, a map with a great big red X on it to mark Zhang's camp would be ideal, but I don't think we're going to be lucky enough to get that. Even something simple to start with would be a help. Tire tracks leading out in a specific direction. Written instructions from Zhang Dong or his lieutenants. Pieces of plants that only grow in a particular section of the park. Something."

She looked inside the tents rimming the camp and saw dirty clothing and guns. Nothing immediately leapt out at her. If they found nothing, she'd let the police go over everything with a fine-toothed comb, but she wanted to survey the whole camp first.

Toward the rear of the camp, she found a collection of the poachers' prizes. Elephant and rhino ivory. Lion and leopard skins. Antelope horns. Pebbled crocodile leather. The items filled up several large, open crates. Each of the crates was sorted by individual contents.

Denise stepped closer and laid her hand on a small horn. She recognized the little lump of ivory as a baby rhinoceros horn, no more than a few inches tall and wide. It looked like it had been sawed off close to the base. The underside of the horn was coated in old blood. No doubt, the animal it belonged to was no longer alive. More horns of various sizes sat in the crate, some from adults and others from juveniles.

"How long would it take to amass this many horns?" Denise asked Skipworth.

"Probably about a couple of weeks. Less if the hunters managed to corner a whole herd of rhinos and shoot them all at once. They get lucky like that sometimes."

"Where is all this stuff going?"

"Some of it will go into making jewelry and other luxury goods. That sort of thing."

"And the rest?"

"Traditional medicines. Ground up rhino horn is very popular in parts of Asia. Some people think it can cure liver disease or hangovers. Others ascribe miraculous qualities to it. A lot of the very rich simply like to mix it into their drinks as a status symbol. If you're eating lunch with a businessman and he sprinkles a little powdered rhino horn into his beverage, it's a subtle way of telling you that he can buy you, use you to feed his hunting dogs, and then buy your entire extended family for the same purpose."

"Does the rhino horn actually cure anything?"

"Of course not. It's basically made from the same stuff as your fingernails. It doesn't do a thing, but persistent folktales have a way of making the stuff much sought after, regardless. Plus, it's difficult to find reliable medicine in some areas. There may be a lack of doctors or necessary equipment. People who are critically ill might find it easier to use all their savings on some poached rhino horn rather than send it away and hope a doctor arrives in time. Zhang Dong and the Triads are happy to fill that void, peddling the equivalent of snake oil to the hopeless for outrageous prices. Having two markets, the luxury good route and the quack medicine route, means there's always a massive demand. They just have to find the highest bidder."

"What if they kill off all the rhinos in this area?"

"Great for them. It simply makes the resource that much rarer. Simple economics. Less supply amid constant demand means they can charge higher prices. All they have to do is find a new supply of rhinos somewhere else to hunt to extinction. Set up camp there. Wash, rinse, and repeat. They simply repeat the process *ad infinitum*."

"Yeah, well, there aren't exactly *infinitum* rhinos out there in the world. You can only repeat the process so many times before you run out of rhinos. Did they ever think of that?" Denise could feel her blood pressure doing interesting things.

"I guess they just figure they're going to ride this gravy train for as long as they possibly can, poaching and killing until they can't poach and kill anymore. After that, there's still plenty of opportunities to make money. There's always the old standbys. Extortion. Racketeering. Other forms of contraband."

"Surely the demand will start to dry up once the animals become scarcer and scarcer?" Cornelia asked.

"Maybe the market will dry up to some extent as the crank medicine people are priced out. But, hell, the guys who are buying it specifically because it's hard to get and distinguishes them? They're going to want it even more. They'll throw down a fortune and ask Zhang Dong to wipe out the last rhinos on earth just so long as they get the last horns. They're buying this stuff because they want it, not because it's any sort of good idea to actually have it."

"So what do you think they'll do once this stuff becomes truly rare, not just hard to get?"

"I know Zhang Dong has some associates in the big cities. If somebody breaks into a hunter's house and steals any mounted rhino heads, he'll give them a good price for them. It's sort of a standing bounty. Thieves get a better price for sawing off the horn and giving it to Zhang Dong than they would trying to just fence the mounted rhino head. They probably just throw the head away after they saw the horn off," Skipworth said.

"Yeah, but at some point, they'll even run out of mounted rhino heads. What do they do once they've finally scraped the bottom of the barrel?" Cornelia asked.

"They're not going to scrape the bottom of the barrel. We're going to figure out better ways to keep track of the animals at the game preserve and stop the poachers before it gets to that," Denise said, still looking at the crate of rhino horns in front of her. Looking at the evidence in front of her, she wasn't entirely sure she believed it herself.

"Hard to say," Skipworth said, ignoring Denise's comment. "Zhang Dong and his people are movers and shakers. I doubt they'd just let a valuable market dry up simply because they'd used up all the supply. I think they'd just turn to the next best thing. Maybe that would be fraud, which would be a little easier. Tell people you're selling some of the very last rhino horn powder on earth when it's really fingernail clippings ground up with a couple of herbs and spices.

"The other way to do it, and what they're just as likely to do, is start some other ridiculous miracle cure and start whipping up demand for it. Panda teeth. Walrus ovaries. Tiger tongues. Whatever they think it is that will match the same level of scarcity with the high levels of demand."

"That's...rather depressing," Cornelia said.

"Yup," Skipworth agreed. "I should know. They were using me to help them ship this stuff out of the game preserve and into the market."

"There's a sealed crate here," Denise said. "Any idea what they were keeping inside? It's a lot bigger than the others." Denise pointed out the crate.

"I have no idea," Skipworth said. "That arrived a little while ago. Normally, we're the ones shipping things out, noting taking deliveries."

"Who sent it?"

"Again, I have no idea. Zhang Dong had me and a couple of his lieutenants pick it up from a drop point they use occasionally. Then we carted it back here."

"Did he say what it was for?"

"He just said it was in case things went wrong. I don't know what he meant by that, and I know better than to ask questions when I probably don't want to know the answer."

"Let's open this bad boy up, then," Denise said. "Maybe it'll tell us something about where it came from, and we can use that to figure out some of Zhang Dong's favorite haunts."

"It's a start," Cornelia said as they all grabbed tools and started prying the wooden crate open.

The wood groaned and whined as Denise wedged a crowbar between two corner slats and pried at the edges. One by one, the nails popped free. After a couple of minutes of effort, the side fell off the crate and allowed them to see what was inside.

Denise wasn't sure what she was expecting, but it wasn't this. "It's...some kind of bomb?" She rubbed her chin.

Cornelia leaned in close to get a better look at the thing. "It's an old Mark Six naval mine. American. Somebody's done some tinkering with it, though."

"Tinkered with it?" Skipworth asked.

"I know a good bit about explosives. Side effect of dating a bomb technician for a while. Yeah, this thing looks like it's been refitted to jam more explosives inside. Somebody didn't care if it floated anymore or not, so they packed even more power into the thing. Not sure why they would need to, though. A regular one can already punch through the hull of a submarine or a warship. The Navy laid about two hundred thousand of them off the coast of Britain to try to keep the German U-boats in check. Took five months to clear them out again. I guess a few must have gone missing."

"So what exactly are we looking at here?"

"Pretty standard naval mine. About three feet across and more or less spherical. Aside from the extra payload, it looks like somebody did a few things to the fuses. See these nubs on the upper half of the bomb? Normally, those would float a bit under the surface of the water. They're called Hertz horns. They're supposed to have a little glass ampule inside. A lot of people think that naval mines explode just because a ship bumps them and disturbs the explosives inside, but it's a little more complicated than that. With a contact mine like this, you have to bend the horns, which breaks the glass ampule. The contents of the ampule then connect an open circuit and blow the whole shebang sky high."

"So it sounds like if you just bump into them, there's a decent chance your ship might be able to survive," Skipworth said.

"Not something I'd like to test out. If the mine gets jarred while it's floating, it will probably spin around and the ship will bend one of those horns. There's actually a second detonation method, though. See this divot at the top of the mine? When it was deployed, there would be a little buoy and a copper wire. Basically, if a ship's metal hull touched the copper wire, it would work like a battery. Along with the seawater, it would create a circuit, and that would trigger the explosives just as easily. Technically, the ship doesn't even have to touch the mine itself to activate the bomb, which makes it especially dangerous. Even what would otherwise be a near miss sets everything off."

"But you said somebody had messed with everything. I'm guessing the poachers didn't plan to mine the river. All they'd do is blast some poor hippopotamus across half the park and attract attention to themselves."

"Right. This mine isn't even set up to be used in the water anymore. It's loaded with so much extra explosive that it won't float anymore. Normally, a naval mine like this is switched 'on' by dumping it in the water. It should have safety switches held open by salt pellets. The pellets dissolve in water, so once they're gone, the mine is armed. Somebody ripped the whole system out and replaced it with a manual primer and some kind of timer. Instead of an instant boom, now you have to press this switch and wait a little bit. Probably a couple minutes to get a safe distance."

"What would be a safe distance for one of these?" Skipworth asked.

"With all this extra explosive material added? Really far away."

"Why would a bunch of poachers need something like this?" Denise asked.

"I honestly have no idea. If it was part of some grand master plan by Zhang Dong in case everything went awry, maybe he thought he could blow up a ranger station with this. Create a diversion. Or revenge.

Or just go out in a blaze of glory and take everyone with him. I don't know."

"Could you really level one of the ranger stations with this thing?"

"Level it? Pfft. There wouldn't be anything level about what was left. This much explosive would simply leave a big old crater. They'd be finding bits and pieces of the structure spread around the area for years. Forget about anyone inside at the time. Aside from a few chunks of bone or whatever. They could bury whatever was left of you in a matchbox."

"I'm not sure I care for the idea that a bunch of gangsters were able to get their mitts on this," Denise said.

"Zhang Dong's operation brings in a lot of money. A lot. He could have probably gotten this encrusted in diamonds, if he wanted," Skipworth replied.

"Not exactly reassuring." Denise eyed the mine, noticing for the first time that it was sitting on some sort of wheeled jack for easy transportation. Somebody had thought of everything.

"What is that?" Captain Blenavis asked as he walked around a set of tents toward them.

"Modified Mark Six naval mine," Cornelia said as if this was a patently obvious fact.

"I see," the police captain said, missing a beat. He gave Cornelia a *how did you know what that thing is* look and then glanced back at the mine. "This might be a problem."

"How big of a problem?" Kirkeberg asked, appearing behind Blenavis.

"We brought vehicles and translators, but we don't have any explosive experts with us. I don't want that thing riding with us all the way back to Pretoria."

"So what exactly are you going to do with it, then? You can't just leave it here. Somebody might come pick it up."

"No, you're right. I'm definitely not just leaving it here. It's evidence. There's probably about three more charges we can write up for Zhang Dong and his men over this thing. Just to poke a stick in their eye."

"We have to find Zhang Dong first before you can stick any parking tickets to his windshield," Kirkeberg said.

"Right. But I don't want this thing rattling around in the back of a van for miles and miles. We'll drop it off at your ranger station for safe keeping and to keep the chain of custody clean. Then we'll send somebody back with the right training to deal with it and bring it back to the evidence lock-up in Pretoria."

"It has to be triggered manually. It should be safe to take back with you whenever you want," Cornelia said.

"'Should be safe' is not a standard I want to promote. Especially when the item in question looks like that," Blenavis said, pointing in the direction of the jury-rigged naval mine.

Denise couldn't blame him. But she also didn't like the idea of having the thing sit around Ranger Station Thirteen. Not after what Cornelia said it could do to the building if it went off.

Apparently, Kirkeberg didn't fancy the idea, either. "Are you sure you should move it at all? Keeping it at the station doesn't exactly appeal to me."

"Yes, we have to keep it somewhere."

Cornelia spoke up. "Oh for Pete's sake. I'll take care of it. So long as nobody touches that button, we won't have a problem. You have to treat explosives with respect, not like cursed idols. You won't have any problems so long as you let me handle things."

The answer seemed to settle things for Captain Blenavis. Kirkeberg looked like he'd just received bad news at the dentist office. Mixed resignation and unhappiness. Denise knew the feeling.

"Sir! Sir." One of the police commandos rounded the corner and spotted Blenavis.

"Yes, what is it?"

"We've found a body, sir."

"I'll be right over. Any idea who it is?"

"Not sure yet. He's probably only been dead for a few days, so he's is pretty good condition overall, though."

"Alright, take us to him." The police commando made a walk-this-way gesture and Blenavis set off after him. Denise and her group decided to set off after them.

"Skipworth, any idea who this body might belong to? Think it could help us identify where Zhang Dong is?"

"It's possible. One of the couriers came back with a big box about four days ago. He said there was a body inside and we needed to bury it. I had to help dig the hole."

"Any idea what that was all about?"

"None at all. If Zhang Dong wants to provide an object lesson, usually he or one of his lieutenants will execute the person in front of everyone. It has a way of discouraging snitching. This fellow was dead on arrival, though. He was some white guy, maybe in his mid-fifties. Probably a business associate who tried to renege on a deal."

Kirkeberg scowled. "You know, any assistance in a murder makes you an accessory to the crime."

"What, you think I was thrilled about this? Believe me, I wasn't. This was all done under duress. I was a little bit valuable to them, and that's why they didn't kill me straight off months ago to terrorize some other schmuck into paying up. I wasn't *that* valuable, though. If I suddenly decided I had my druthers and I wasn't going to help with digging the grave, I'd be going straight in there on top of the box. No thanks."

"Well, aren't you just the martyr," Kirkeberg said.

"Don't get all holier-than-thou on me. I made mistakes. I made a lot of mistakes. Believe me, I'd rather be scuttling off to try to set my life straight again rather than showing my face around here anymore. But I'm trying to make things at least a little bit right."

"Trying to save your own skin is more like it," Kirkeberg said.

"Oh, shut up, the both of you," Cornelia said. "Boss, you're right. The good doctor here is kind of a sleaze for helping out with this operation, but you promised to help him when it comes time for the police to determine responsibility. Skipworth, you're also right. You didn't do any of this stuff because you wanted to, and by helping us, you're showing responsibility and helping to set things back together, but you're still a bit of a sleaze for getting your ass in this crack. There? Everyone on the same page? Now lay off each other for five minutes."

Kirkeberg and Skipworth looked both scowled but stopped sniping at each other. They arrived at the pile of excavated dirt where the body lay. The grave was shallow and muddy. Wild dogs or other animals would have probably dug it up about five minutes after the poachers moved to their next camp.

The police had opened up the box and were dragging a dead man out of it. His body was stiff, his joints bent into place. Two officers had to grunt and pull just to get the figure out of the hole in the ground.

"So who do we have here? He got anything on him that might tell us where he's been?" Captain Blenavis asked.

The cops patted the body down, searching for anything on his person. Aside from the bullet hole in the middle of the man's forehead, it would have looked like they were a couple of movers trying to manhandle a particularly realistic statue into place. A fly buzzed over to the body, landed next to the little hole in the man's forehead, and then crawled inside his skull.

"Found a wallet," one of the commandos said, prying it out of one of the corpse's pockets.

"Show me," Blenavis said, holding out his hand. The wallet appeared in his palm, and he flipped it open. There were a few American dollars in the back flap. Not many, but they were there. Evidently, Zhang

Dong hadn't cared about the small sum enough to rob the man after he was dead. Denise was more interested in the fact that it was American money rather than South African pounds or British sterling.

Blenavis closed the back pocket and searched through the items in the front flaps. A second later, his fingers plucked a driver's license out of one of the front pockets.

Denise caught the briefest glimpse of a picture, the man smiling for the motor vehicles office.

The fly crawled back out of the hole in the body's head and rubbed its legs together in apparent anticipation. Time to stake a claim. There was gold in them thar' hills.

"Let's see here," Blenavis said. "Registered in New York City. The picture matches the body. Looks like the name is one Albert Neville Thornber. That mean anything to you?"

TEN

AND ALL THE AMMO YOU CAN CARRY

The tiled walls and floor of the examination room had seen better days. The walls had been carefully scrubbed of slime and ooze, and the other remnants of the battle that took place there earlier had been incinerated. A large, dark stain in the center of the floor indicated where the flames had consumed the worms earlier that day. Darker stains that couldn't be attributed to burning alone splattered other parts of the floor.

Despite being hosed out and blasted with heavy-duty cleaning solutions, the room still smelled like fire and burning flesh. The room's entire interior would probably have to be torn out and replaced before the place would smell anything less than revolting.

This was the last place Denise wanted to find herself in again as the sun set over the rolling plains. She'd much rather be outside, watching the sunset turn the river to sparkling diamonds and casting the dam in purple shadows.

Instead, she was in a small room that stank of gasoline and burning death and the harshest chemical cleaners available. Right now, it was more important to pour over Thornber's equipment and see what she could discover, though.

Or rather, the equipment belonging to the man she had believed was Thornber. Now she had no idea whose corpse got up off the slab and tried to kill them earlier. She had no idea who led Hartzell and Planck into Sulfur Springs and accidentally brought something awful back with him.

Now, there was a new body on the slab. The paperwork found with him identified *him* as Dr. Thornber of the United States Geological Survey. There couldn't be two Thornbers. One of them was an imposter.

All things told, Denise figured the body they had right now was more likely to be the real Thornber. The driver's license they'd found looked legitimate and untampered with, and the picture attached to it was certainly the dead man.

But that meant they'd be needing Skipworth's services one more time tonight. Blenavis and the police commandos had already dropped off the naval mine at Ranger Station Thirteen, and now they were driving toward the park's visitor center so they could patch up the injured and process the Triads back in Pretoria.

Denise and Cornelia would be poring over the items left behind by the fake Dr. Thornber to see if they could figure out anything about his real identity while Skipworth performed the autopsy on the new body. If Denise and Cornelia couldn't come up with anything, maybe Skipworth could at least tell them something about what happened to Thornber, the real Thornber, before he died. It was a long shot, but maybe they could use that to figure out where Zhang Dong was hiding out, and the police commandos could come back for a second raid in the morning. And maybe jolly old St. Nick would stop by and bring them each a pony while they were all wishing for things.

Skipworth walked into the examination room and donned a set of gloves as Denise started to look over the unused expedition supplies. At least the medical examiner's tools mounted on the wall hadn't been damaged by the fire earlier today.

Kirkeberg walked in behind Skipworth, dark rings starting to form under his eyes. He looked about ten years older than he had a few days ago. The scars running down the sides of his face were white streaks through his stubble. He'd agreed to spot for Skipworth during the autopsy and ensure that any evidence was properly handled before being handed off to Captain Blenavis.

"Alright, let's try this again," Skipworth said. "We're going to be examining one Dr. Albert Neville Thornber of the United States Geological Survey. The real one this time. Hopefully. Kirkeberg, I'm going to need you to take that camera and notebook. I want all the documentation I can get on this."

"In a second," Kirkeberg said. "Cornelia, would you and the doc here mind leaving the room? I want to speak to Denise in private for a minute."

"Sure thing," Cornelia said, putting down the tool she was using to examine the rejiggered naval mine.

"And no blowing us all up," Kirkeberg said with the tone of a beleaguered father fighting a losing battle to corral rambunctious children. Cornelia nodded and left the room with Skipworth.

"How are you holding up?" Kirkeberg asked.

"It hasn't exactly been a fun day. Got attacked by a dead guy and had to set him on fire. A member of an organized criminal syndicate tried to stab me, and I had to smash his face into a truck. Some of my friends are missing or dead, and now we've got our second autopsy of the day. So, yeah, keeping busy. How about yourself? This hasn't exactly been a walk in the park for you either," Denise said, noting how tired Kirkeberg looked.

"No, it hasn't. Given what I've seen today, I have to assume that Hartzell and Planck are dead. Regular dead, hopefully. Not 'dead but up and about.' I don't want to be there if we find them up and walking around somewhere. We still don't know what happened to Crane and De Hoog, and that's not a good sign, all things considered. Plus, we lost Matheson and Ritter. Added onto that, we still weren't able to wipe out the poachers. It has been a," Kirkeberg took a deep breath as he tried to come up with the right word, "taxing day. You seem to have done a good job of keeping your wits about you despite everything. That's partly why I wanted to talk to you."

"I'd like to think that when Cornelia's father recommended me for this job it wasn't just as a favor. I've seen my share of troubles, and I learned how to handle myself."

"Yes, I can see that. The rangers we lost over the past couple of days keep weighing on me, though. They were good people."

"Yeah. But don't blame yourself too much. You didn't know what we were dealing with, though. No one did until it was too late. We didn't have any idea what was happening in the park until a dead body got up in the middle of its autopsy earlier today. It's not like anybody is going to pop up to give you a 'told you so.' Polychaete worms driving dead bodies around like skin taxis wasn't something any of us expected to be dealing with when we woke up this morning."

"Fair enough. That doesn't mean I won't always wonder if there isn't something else I should have done on the day Hartzell and Planck disappeared."

Denise thought about the conversation she'd had with Skipworth earlier. She thought about the dead elephants and about whatever it was that killed them.

"Listen. I've been talking to Skipworth, and some of the things he's said worry me. I think there might be something else out there. Something big."

"You mean something in addition to the worms?"

"I don't know. Something connected to them at the very least." She explained about the two elephants Skipworth had discovered, black goo seeping from their deep and deadly wounds. Wounds that would require something awful to inflict them.

"So what do you think is responsible?" Kirkeberg asked.

"I don't know. I'm just worried that the worms are steering something big around. Like, really big."

"Bigger than the elephants? We don't have anything bigger than elephants in the park. Nobody does."

"I don't know what else could take down two elephants so close together with just teeth and claws. That sends alarm bells off in my head."

"I'll be organizing a sweep of this section of the park tomorrow. Elephant rifles and kerosene. We'll get every available ranger we can from the other stations and eliminate whatever crawled out of that cave before it can spread too far. That's not what I wanted to talk to you about anyway, though."

Denise wanted to say something else, but she mashed down the words. Kirkeberg had a look on his face that said whatever he was about to say wouldn't be easy.

"I was wrong, earlier. I pulled your file again and added your name to the list of candidates for the anti-poaching squad they're putting together. You've handled yourself well, given the circumstances. With my report on the matter to headquarters, you'll have your spot on the squad. All you have to do is ask for it."

"I...well...that is to say, I'll have to think about it," Denise said.

"I thought that was what you wanted."

"It was. I just need to think about it. That's all." Skipworth's comment that she should become a professional monster hunter had been bouncing around inside her head. The very idea was preposterous. Silly. Ridiculous. This time a year ago, she'd never even believed monsters existed.

Except now she did. Just this very afternoon, she'd killed a walking corpse. If that wasn't a monster, she didn't know what qualified. Before this was over, she expected to see a few more similar beasties, too.

She couldn't hunt for sport anymore. Putting some creature in her sights while it grazed peacefully on the grassland made her stomach roil with queasy acid. Killing something like what the imposter Thornber had become, something hell-bent on slaughtering as many people as it could, didn't affect her, though.

With all her time in the field, she'd heard stories. Stories about remote villages terrorized by creatures in the night. Stories about entire hunting parties wiped out by things cunning and unnatural. Stories about ruins haunted by things uncategorized by science.

In the past, she'd always chalked them up to superstitions and misidentifying perfectly normal animals. People exploring an unfamiliar place attributing a leopard's unearthly yowl as something ghastly.

Her more recent experiences had taught her that sometimes there were monsters out in the night, though. There were things that killed without remorse, things that posed unique threats to the people who encountered them.

In one sense, something like the worms that came from Sulfur Springs weren't so very different from any other animal trying to survive. They had needs, and they saw to those needs in the only way they knew how. Presumably, they were too dumb for malevolence, but they understood hunger just fine, that basic common denominator that connected both mankind and the tiniest zooplankton floating in the sea.

In another sense, they were anything but normal creatures. The worms were abominations that destroyed everything they touched. They left husks and ghouls in their wake. If they spread too far into the game preserve, they'd cause more damage than the poachers ever did.

Denise tried to imagine what would happen if a few of the walking shells the worms used to feed and transport themselves made it to a population center. There would be utter bedlam. Shambling, slimy masses devouring people in the streets, constantly making more of themselves, spreading and spreading until they were a black blot on the landscape.

No, something separated the worms from other mere animals, pushing them into the shadowy category of monsters. Millions and millions of years of evolution inside that poisonous cave had turned them into something separate and apart from the rest of the natural order. They had no place in any other environment. On the map of life, they were somewhere off the traveled routes, in the areas labeled 'Here be Dragons.' Introducing them anywhere else on the planet would only lead to destruction and suffering.

The Dracobly Hessler Game Preserve had many qualified and enthusiastic people dedicated to keeping the park pristine. There would always be people ready to ensure the fate Skipworth talked about regarding the rhinos would never come. Surely, it would never come, would it?

Even without her, the game preserve would continue its important mission. She didn't really know of anyone else who had her kind of experience investigating the dark corners of the frontier, though.

Was it better to stay here doing something she thought was important but where she wasn't entirely necessary, or was it better to go out and help people with something maybe only she had the experience to assist with? Could she even make a living doing something like that?

She tried to picture a storefront sign or a business card with what she was thinking about. *Denise DeMarco: Monster Hunter*. She honestly couldn't tell if the idea was the craziest thing she'd ever heard or if it was just right for her. Maybe both.

"I'll think about it," she said.

Kirkeberg nodded and opened the examination room's door again. "Alright, you two can come back inside. We talked about what we needed to talk about. Cornelia, you and Denise go over the stuff our fake Thornber left behind. Maybe there's something we overlooked when we didn't think there was anything to be suspicious about. Check it top to bottom. Everybody leaves something behind. Skipworth, you're with me. We're going to see what we can find out from the real Dr. Thornber."

"Let's get to it, then," Skipworth said. "I'll need pictures from a couple of angles before we begin, and then you'll hand me that scalpel there. No, not that one. The big one. There it is. That's right."

Denise turned away before things got gross over on the makeshift morgue slab. She turned her attention to the piles of stuff the fake Thornber had brought along with him and never gotten an opportunity to use. Some of it was marked with stamps from the United States Geological Survey. Denise figured that the fake Thornber had probably gotten that from his real counterpart, whose documents showed he really was a member of the USGS.

The way Denise figured it, the real Thornber must have made it to South Africa. The park had checked all his papers when he applied to study Sulfur Springs, and everything had checked out at the time. No one had asked for a picture of the geologist, so no one in South Africa would know if someone else showed up with Thornber's papers and equipment.

Obviously, whoever the fake Thornber was, he had been working with Zhang Dong and the poachers. Zhang's men intercepted the real Thornber sometime before he made it to the park, killed him, buried him, and then the fake Thornber assumed the scientist's identity. Had he made it out of Sulfur Springs alive, no one would have been the wiser until the United States Geological Survey reported that the real Thornber hadn't returned.

But the relationship still seemed weird. Why would Zhang Dong help the fake Thornber? The poachers' business wasn't common murder and identity fraud. The Americans would inevitably find out something had happened to their scientist, and that would bring additional attention to the park and create extra risks for the poachers. Zhang wouldn't want to endanger his primary business over just any old thing. Obviously, the fake Thornber had access to money. Lots and lots of money. Denise didn't see what else would convince Zhang Dong to get involved with a scheme so far out of his usual bailiwick.

Money implied some sort of organization, though. It would be strange if some rich kook decided he was going to murder and replace a

USGS scientist all on his own. Presumably, some group wanted one of their own agents investigating Sulfur Springs so they could reap some perceived benefit from the cave.

But why the hell would anyone want what was down there? Obviously, whoever sent the fake Thornber had some inkling about what to expect below the surface. Only one group had ever sent an expedition down there before, and they'd returned to the surface just fine. Denise had skimmed the report that survey team issued, but she would have remembered if they wrote up a section about killer worms. Something like that would have gotten the park's attention.

Behind her, she heard the rasp of cold metal on colder flesh. Skipworth had finished his initial examination of Thornber's body and was now getting into the full autopsy. Denise didn't turn around. She didn't need to spectate as the man was pulled apart a little at a time.

She dove into the pile of supplies, starting with the weirdest thing in the bunch. A full dive suit, complete with helmet and air hoses, sat in one box. Denise ran her fingers over the sealed, waterproof fabric. The bulbous metal helmet, with its glass portholes so the diver could see out, looked like something out of a science fiction pulp magazine about little green men invading from distant planets.

Denise pulled the dive suit out of the box and checked all the equipment pockets. She held it up and ran her hands along the inside just in case there was some secret pocket hidden somewhere. Nothing. The dive suit was just that, with no additional mysteries to be solved.

Evidently, Thornber had assumed there was some sort of body of water inside Sulfur Springs. Maybe that made some sense. She seemed to recall the report from the prior expedition saying there was some sort of lake down there, trapped under the rock.

It was hard to tell which supplies belonged to which Thornber. Had the real one or the imposter wanted to bring the dive suit? Which supplies were just those of a well-prepared geologist and which belonged to a collaborator in that geologist's murder? Being able to sort the two from each other would tell them more about the fake Thornber's plans.

Inside the next box was a harpoon gun, something someone would probably only bring along if they expected trouble. That had to belong to the imposter Thornber. The real Thornber was only here to study the geology of the place, not to tangle with the subterranean wildlife.

Frowning, Denise turned to the collection of seismographs that lay in a number of small crates nearby. The boxes were each stamped, labeling them as the property of the USGS. She wasn't sure if the fake Thornber had even opened the boxes, but she was here to look for any clue she could find. If the fake Thornber had squirreled some secret away somewhere, he might very well leave it with the technical equipment, which was less likely to be searched or scrutinized by customs agents reluctant to damage anything potentially sensitive or expensive. She checked each one, one right after the other.

Behind her, she heard the crackle of bone. The noise sounded like someone breaking a waterlogged branch over their knee. Crisp yet squelchy. Skipworth had started shearing his way through the ribcage to get at the organs.

Denise opened a new crate of supplies and found a carefully folded tent and ropes. She dragged the ropes out and performed a quick inspection, making sure that there wasn't anything bound up inside the coils.

She was starting to feel a certain futility about the search. How carefully would the fake Thornber have hidden anything? Was there even anything to find? Maybe she was simply pawing through a dead man's things, looking for something that wasn't even there.

Moving onto the tent, she dragged the fabric out of the crate, intending to flatten it out on the ground and search for any hidden pockets. A couple of handguns clattered out onto the floor.

Denise stopped and stared at the well-oiled weapons. Gunmetal gleamed under the fluorescent lighting. The barrels lay pointed toward her in a silent threat, like a couple of lazy snakes. One of the weapons was a large revolver not so very different from the ones the park rangers carried. The other was a Colt M1911, the same type of sidearm used by the United States Army.

"What do we have there?" Cornelia asked. She stepped away from the luggage and personal effects she'd been rooting through to examine the guns.

Grabbing some gloves, Denise picked up the revolver by the barrel. The weapon was a mean-looking thing, meant for close-up, dirty fighting. The Army pistol was a hardy weapon that could survive a fair amount of mistreatment if it had to.

"I doubt the United States Geological Survey hands these out as standard issue," Denise said.

"Put them aside and we'll get them to Captain Blenavis tomorrow," Kirkeberg said, looking up from the notepad where he was recording everything that Skipworth noted about the condition of the body.

"Great Scott of Scoot," Cornelia said, examining some of the spare ammunition. "Looks like our friend knew his business. Check this out. Dumdum rounds for the revolver."

Dumdums were bullets with a hollow tip. Instead of shooting through the target's soft tissues, they expanded on impact to cause as much damage as possible. The tips flattened out into a jagged metal flower as they sheared their way through the target's innards. Whereas normal bullets cut a mostly straight line through muscle and tissue before exiting the body, these entered and more or less exploded.

The park service used them for their own weapons because they were meant to stop very large animals. A charging water buffalo wasn't a pleasant creature. When most sensible animals found themselves punched through with holes of various sizes, they would lay down and die. Not so with water buffaloes and some of the other larger beasts of the park. Anything short of an internal Titanic disaster wouldn't stop them. Most people didn't expect to face down an enraged African animal in their day-to-day lives. Hunters, hitmen, and the people obsessed with self-defense were the primary market for such bullets. Whoever the fake Thornber was, he was obviously familiar with the use of deadly weapons.

Setting the guns aside, Denise returned to her work of trying to tease out any more clues from the supplies. Where there was one find, there were likely to be more. Now that she knew there were actually things to find, she felt like an archeologist discovering a single potsherd. Perhaps there were more hidden nearby just waiting to be excavated. All she had to do was dredge them up. Maybe if she found enough, she could learn what she wanted to know.

Behind her, Skipworth had gotten into Thornber's stomach contents, seeing if he could identify anything that might be linked to a particular region of the park. Maybe Zhang Dong's men had kept Thornber alive long enough to feed him a meal. They were grasping at straws at this point, but Denise didn't know what else they had to go on. Either way, she did her best to tune out Skipworth's dry and clinical observations.

She didn't want to think about what was happening only a few feet behind her. People who needed an autopsy wouldn't find much dignity in death, not when they were being turned inside out and having their skin pulled off to see what lay underneath. Denise knew that pretty soon, Skipworth would peel Thornber's scalp off and yank his face away from his skull so he could saw his way down to the brain and fish the bullet out.

Denise would rather succumb somewhere out in the wilderness and be picked over by the vultures than be autopsied. Buzzards, for all their ugliness, were remarkable birds. Nature gave them bald necks so that when they crammed their heads up the dead, decaying anus of some miserable roadkill, they wouldn't have to worry about the effluvia sticking to their feathers. Very efficiently designed animals, those buzzards. Plus, they ate all the tidbits from rotting corpses that would normally sit around festering and spreading disease. Denise would prefer to provide a meal for the vultures over an autopsy. At least then somebody would get a full belly and glow of contentment out of the situation.

Cornelia overturned a bag of personal items. Clothing of every nature tumbled out onto the floor in a heap. She sorted through it, checking pockets as she went. All she came up with was some spare change, a bit of lint, and a punch card for a New York sandwich shop.

She took the empty bag and started to push it to the side. Something crinkled inside the bag. Cornelia stopped and patted the bag with her hands again. The crinkling noise, like someone sitting on a folded newspaper, came again.

Grabbing the bag, she held it up and flipped it upside down. Nothing spilled onto the floor. She shook the bag. Still nothing. Flipping it back over, Cornelia looked inside again.

Cornelia stuck a hand inside the bag and felt around. A second later, the crinkling noise came again. She pulled out a utility knife and flicked the blade out.

"Did you find something?" Denise asked.

"I'm not entirely sure yet. It could just be a poorly made travel bag, or…" She stuck the knife into the bottom of the bag and started working the blade back and forth along one of the internal seams.

A few seconds later, she'd created a big enough hole to reach inside. She returned the knife to her belt and poked her fingers inside the new hole. They emerged clasped around a plain manila envelope. A set of keys fell out and plopped into her hand, too.

"A false bottom," Cornelia said. "When all the clothes are packed in there tight, nothing can shift around too much to make noise. Not bad."

She undid the clasp on the envelope and emptied the contents onto a table. The first thing to fall out was a brick of South African pounds and American dollars. Cornelia laid the keys next to the carefully stacked money.

"Travel expenses," Denise said.

"Also good for a quick spot of bribery if you land in some trouble."

"Who doesn't enjoy a quick spot of bribery now and then? What else is in there?" Denise bit the insides of her cheeks as Cornelia pulled a thick sheath of papers out of the envelope. This had to be what they were looking for. This would explain what had happened. A surge of hope filled Denise.

Cornelia flipped the papers over to see what they were. She laid it down on the table beside the money and the keys.

"It's a copy of the report from the last expedition that went down into Sulfur Springs," Cornelia said.

Denise felt the sudden rush of hope building inside her wither up and die. "We have a copy of that on file somewhere. It's nothing new."

Cornelia flipped the report open. Various points had been highlighted. Some sections were underlined in red pen with notes off to the sides. Most of the notes seemed to serve as a checklist for the kind of equipment that would be required to mount another expedition into the cavern system.

A few pages later, the report ended by noting that there was some sort of body of water deep inside the main passage, and it was probably heated by geothermal vents. Like hot springs. A red-lettered note next to the paragraphs about the lake read, *"Diving suit required for further study??? Maybe harpoons."*

That was the end of the report that the game preserve had on file. They'd received it a couple of months after the surveyors and geologists crawled back out of the hole, and that had been the end of the matter as far as Denise knew.

This report had several more pages tacked onto the back, though. Information that hadn't been passed along.

Denise read along with Cornelia as they thumbed through the pages. The first team had discovered some sort of weird red moss or lichen that was never mentioned in the report that was passed along to the game preserve. More pen marks left extensive notes in the margins about the red plant life. *"Chemosynthetic? Thermosynthetic? Entirely unknown? How does it survive in poisonous darkness?"*

Maybe the pen strokes came from the fake Dr. Thornber himself. Some of the comments read like the author intended to visit the cave at some point.

"Chemosynthetic? Not to sound dumb here, but what is that?" Cornelia asked.

Denise nodded. "Yeah. It's easier to explain it by contrasting it with something we're familiar with. So, we know roughly how photosynthesis works. The short and skinny of it is that there's energy in sunlight. Plants use that energy to fuel their growth. Specialized parts in their cells drink in the sunlight and use it to survive. Our whole ecosystem is based off photosynthesis. The plants take energy in from the sun. Then an herbivore eats the plants, and it uses the energy from the plants. Then a carnivore eats the herbivore, and it gets energy from the herbivore, which got it from the plants. And so on and so forth on up the food chain. It all starts with plants taking what they can get from the sunlight, though.

"So, the proposal with chemosynthesis is that it's based on something other than sunlight. After all, there are lots of compounds out there that can be used to produce energy. Methane. Hydrogen gas. Hydrogen sulfide. Theoretically, you could have an organism that doesn't need sunlight to survive so long as it had a source of the right kind of chemicals. That way the plants or animals don't actually need any sunlight to survive. They basically just need raw materials. Thermosynthesis is a related idea, except life would take energy directly from heat. That's my understanding of it anyway. Someone with a degree in biology could give you a better rundown and explain everything better."

"No, that helps. Basically, this cave might have the right mix of chemicals that weird stuff can grow there even when it's been sealed away for millions of years."

"Yup. The thermal vents are probably supplying the matter required for these things to live down there."

They went back to the text. It spent a few more paragraphs describing the unusual lichen and theorizing about it. Another paragraph went to insisting that another team be immediately sent down for additional studies. The small number of samples the team was able to take wouldn't be enough to properly study the ecosystem down there. Whoever the author was, Denise could tell they were practically ebullient about the discovery, even behind the dry scientific language.

The next section of the text dealt more with the lake. The report began with the theorized geology beneath the lake. Apparently, the scientists on the expedition believed that the lake had formed over a trench. The rock beneath the lake would be a thin layer of basalt and igneous intrusions above an active magma chamber. In a few particularly thin places, the superheated gases and chemicals from the magma chamber below spewed out across the lake bed. Not surprising, given that the report's author also believed the creatures down there were chemosynthetic organisms.

Denise looked over the report's closing paragraphs. "Son of a bitch," she muttered.

The team had taken samples from the black lake and discovered it was teeming with tiny organisms. At the time of the report, the creatures hadn't been thoroughly studied yet, but the author bubbled with excitement over the possibilities regarding the nearly microscopic creatures, which they'd tentatively identified as polychaete worms. The final sentences promised a follow-up report once the samples were taken back to Chicago for a more thorough study.

There was only one more thing in the packet of papers, a newspaper clipping stapled to the back of the report. Denise checked the headline. *Tragedy: Researchers Killed in Mysterious Laboratory Fire*. The article was dated a few months prior.

A police lieutenant named Sam Black was quoted extensively in the paper. Apparently, the police believed the fire was set intentionally from inside the laboratory. They'd found four dead bodies inside the lab, all of them scorched down to the bone. All the samples and work had been destroyed in the sudden fire too, leaving the police at a loss for what sort of work was occurring in the laboratory. Perhaps strangest of all, the positions of the charred bodies made it appear that they were fighting each other when they died.

The report listed the names, and Denise checked them against the names of the expedition members who first went into Sulfur Springs and wrote the report. They were the same men.

Denise could picture the scene all too clearly. They'd been testing the samples when there was some sort of containment breach. They hadn't realized the trouble they were in until it was too late. By then, the laboratory had a situation like the one that had occurred in the examination room earlier that day. A couple of scientists had been turned into thralls for the worms, and the others weren't able to escape.

But obviously someone had an idea of what happened. Someone had given the fake Thornber the scientists' full report and sent him out to hijack the real Thornber's expedition. Someone stood to gain from all this.

"I don't like this. I don't like it at all," Denise said.

"Agreed," Cornelia said.

"Somebody knew what happened in Chicago, knew about the worms and the deaths, and they said to themselves, '*Whoa, I need to get involved with something like that.*'"

"Yeah, I figure they're probably not somebody I'd care to be dealing with myself. That's why they tried to disguise their guy as Dr. Thornber. The real Thornber was on some unrelated scientific study that we authorized, so they simply took the real Thornber out of the equation and inserted their own man in a way that was hard for us to find out about. Whoever the fake Thornber was, he was clearly supposed to finish up on the work from the secret part of the first report. The part that we weren't supposed to know about."

"So that obviously asks the question, just who the hell was our fake Thornber, and who sent him?"

"Which was square one."

"Which was square one. Maybe we can get to square one and a half, though." Denise picked up the keys that had been hidden with the money and the reports.

A key fob hung off the jangling keys. *Shandor Apartments. Room 292.* The fob also included a phone number for the apartment building.

"It's getting on in the hours here, but it should be, what, mid-afternoon in New York City? Let's see if the Shandor Apartments can tell us anything about our fake Dr. Thornber," Denise said.

"They probably have some sort of privacy policy. They won't just tell you all about him."

"Maybe. It might depend on just how we ask." Denise picked up the phone and started dialing. The process of dialing out to a different continent and hemisphere required going through a couple of different operators and several connections, but after a few minutes of patient waiting, the phone started to ring at the front desk of Shandor Apartments.

"You've reached Shandor Apartments. How may I help you today?"

"Yes, hello. This is Denise DeMarco, at the Dracobly Hessler Game Preserve in South Africa."

"Oh, uh, we don't get many calls from that far away. Why do you need to contact us?"

"I'm a park ranger. One of your residents was on a business trip down here, and he seems to have left his keys with us. He was part of a group touring the park, some sort of corporate retreat. Unfortunately, we don't have his name or where he's staying. Could you possibly give us a hand? We know he's staying somewhere in Pretoria. If we could learn who he is, we could get him his keys back before he leaves for the United States again."

"Oh, I see. I'm really not supposed to give out--"

"I would really appreciate it. And I'm sure your resident would, as well. We could just drive down and give him his keys at his hotel, if we knew who to contact, and I'm sure he'd appreciate it, too."

"I see. Yes, I suppose that's reasonable. What's the room number?"

Denise gave the clerk the room number and winked at Cornelia. She heard some shuffling around and there was a pause.

The voice from half a world away came back a second later. "That room belongs to Dr. Francis Caputo. He's been having us hold his mail for a little while, so I knew he was gone. South Africa though, huh? He didn't tell us he was vacationing there. Sounds nice."

"Well, I certainly think so," Denise said, doing her best to sound pleasant through the inanities. "I don't suppose there's any chance you have any additional contact information for him? He was here on some sort of corporate retreat, but they booked through a travel company. His office should be able to contact him. I don't suppose you have any idea who he worked for?"

"We're not really supposed to give out information about our residents."

"I'm sure it would save him a lot of hassle if he could simply head straight to his room after that long flight back to New York. I don't know about you, but I wouldn't be very happy if my landlord refused to help me get my keys back I'd complain to the management, myself. Besides, we have a few other things of his as well. Some sort of official-looking report that looks work-related. It would be easier to return it to him while he's in the country rather than mail everything to New York."

"I suppose you're right. I've got his mail right here. Looks like his paycheck is from Yersinia Bioresearch."

"Oh...I see. Thank you. We'll contact them next to, uh, figure out where he's staying right now." Denise almost dropped the phone as she tried to put it back on the cradle.

"That was pretty slick. What did they tell you?"

Denise repeated what she'd learned.

"They're that company that's been in trouble for trying to develop new types of weapons. The League of Nations just tried to ensure none of its members contract with them anymore. You and my father had that run in with them."

"Yeah. That's them. Publically, they're very interested in researching medicines and whatnot. They also like to dabble in biological warfare too, though. Smallpox blankets for the brave new world of the twentieth century."

"I'm starting to see why Sulfur Springs might tickle their fancy," Cornelia said, eyeing the spot where they'd burned Caputo's body in the middle of the examination room.

"Yeah, I'm guessing they want to study those worms for themselves, but they don't necessarily want other people to know they have them. Or that they even exist."

"And I'm also guessing they don't want to study them so they can come up with a marketable alternative to kids' ant farms."

Kirkeberg put his pad of paper down and motioned for Skipworth to stop the autopsy. He walked over and grabbed the phone. "We need to tell Captain Blenavis and the police about this. They should still be at the visitor center before returning to Pretoria to process everyone. We can still catch them there and tell them what they need to know."

He lifted the phone and dialed the number for the administration section of the visitor's center. Speaking into the phone for a minute, he looked up and then set the speaker back down on the cradle.

"Blenavis and his men haven't made it to the visitor center yet."

"What? How? It's only thirty miles away. They left quite a while ago. They should have been there…" Cornelia checked her watch.

"I don't like this," Denise said.

"They're a police convoy. Their vans have more armor than a small tank. Most likely, they just broke down. One of them threw an axle or something. A flat tire. They decided to huddle up and fix it on the road rather than separating," Skipworth said, stripping off his gloves. Not even he sounded terribly convinced.

"Get the cars," Kirkeberg said.

"And the elephant guns," Cornelia added.

"And all the ammo you can carry," Denise said.

ELEVEN

WORM BLOODED

Denise drove the game preserve car along the dusty track leading to the visitor center. Dirt and gravel kicked up against the undercarriage as she sped along, headlights bobbing in the night. Her tires hummed as they moved over the hard-packed earth.

Beside her, Cornelia sat with a .577 Nitro Express in her hands, ready for use. Another one lay on the back seat along with several boxes of ammunition and a couple of full canisters of gasoline.

The long grass whipped past on either side of them, fading away into darkness beyond the reach of their headlights. Only a few silver strands of moonlight revealed the details beyond their little bubble of artificial light.

There could be anything out in the darkness. Anything at all. Denise pressed the gas pedal a little harder as the path rose up in a gentle slope. Kirkeberg and Skipworth drove behind her, their headlights dimmed by the plumes of dust Denise was kicking up.

With luck, they would drive straight to the visitor center and find Blenavis and the rest of the police commandos already there, delayed after some small problem. With a little less luck, they would run into Blenavis on the road, one of his vehicles broken down or mired in some hazard.

Denise knew there were other options, though. Somewhere out there, there were probably a couple of lions, their dead bodies subject to the tyranny of the worms. Maybe Hartzell and Planck and Crane and De Hoog, too. And a couple of elephants.

And whatever it was that killed those elephants.

She still had no idea what could bring down a couple of full-grown pachyderms with just teeth and claws. Whatever it was, it was out there somewhere in the darkness. Amongst the deepest shadows of all.

In some ways, the entire veldt had become like the interior of Sulfur Springs. The darkness was vast and uncompromising. The sliver of moon overhead was like a half-seen entrance to some distant surface world. And all around her there was wriggling. The grass moved and swayed in a mesmerizing dance more felt than truly seen.

"See anything out there?" She asked Cornelia for the third time.

"Nothing yet," Cornelia answered, her grip tight around the elephant gun's stock. She was trying to peer through the darkness just the same as Denise.

They reached the top of the incline, and the grassland opened up in front of them on the other side. Suddenly, Denise saw it.

A lone pair of headlights sat in the middle of the road perhaps a mile ahead, facing away from them. It was the only other source of light anywhere amid the suffocating blackness.

Denise let off the accelerator slightly, trying to figure out what was going on up ahead. She could only see the single vehicle, a lone police car, sitting in the middle of the road, seemingly idling.

"Where are the other vehicles?" Cornelia asked.

Rather than answering, Denise slowed further, giving Kirkeberg and Skipworth time to catch up and see what lay ahead.

Now that she was a little closer, she could see something lying in the police car's beams. Whatever it was, it sat in the very edge of the light, not moving.

"Maybe they had engine problems," Denise said, the words sounding hollow and lame even to her own ears.

She pulled up behind the stopped police car and slowed down to a crawl. Sliding up next to the parked car, she looked inside.

Nothing. The police car was empty. She'd feared the inside would be torn up or the driver would be injured or dead. Instead, the car was simply abandoned, the keys sitting in the ignition and the engine purring.

Denise pulled to a stop a bit behind the police car. Putting the ranger car in park, she left her keys in too, just in case they needed to take off fast again. She reached into the back and grabbed an elephant gun of her own before stepping out of the car. Kirkeberg and Skipworth pulled up and stopped directly behind the cop car.

Pulling out her flashlight, Denise shone it on the thing at the edge of her vision, where the headlights started to trail off. It was a dead hyena. The creature looked like it had probably been hit by several vehicles before someone emptied a few dozen shotgun rounds at it. There wasn't much left of the creature, and Denise's main clue as to its species were the few patches of shaggy brown fur that weren't covered in black slime.

"Hey, remember that good thing we saw that one time?" Cornelia asked. "Because this is pretty much the opposite of that."

The hyena didn't move, even as Denise took a few tentative steps closer. Apparently, a combination of massive bodily trauma and gunfire had rendered its body so damaged that not even an armature of hungry worms could drag it along any further. Now it was simply a meal for the worms rather than another method of transporting themselves and infecting more of the landscape. They couldn't make the hyena get up and walk around any more than they could a sack of broken glass.

Brass shells littered the ground at the edge of the road. Denise crouched down and examined them. Pistols and shotguns. The police didn't have anything in their arsenal as large as the Nitro Express elephant guns. Maybe it wouldn't have made a difference either way.

She spotted dark spot in the dirt near the spent casings. At first, Denise thought it was more black slime, but then she realized it was blood. The droplet hadn't even completely sunk into the dirt yet, and it was still wet.

"This happened recently," she said.

"We should check if there are any survivors and then get out of here," Kirkeberg said.

Denise nodded. They had to make sure no one was still stranded out here, but the longer they were out here, the better chance they'd run into whatever did this in the first place.

If they could find any of the other vehicles in the police convoy, that would be the place to start. She shone her flashlight down on the dirt track. The brightness of the headlights gathered around the scene threw every groove and rut into sharp relief. Every pebble cast a dark shadow across the bleached-out earth.

Denise spotted what she was looking for. Tire tracks. Their edges were still crisp in the dirt, so they were recent. The wind hadn't eroded them away. No more than a few hours old. Those probably belonged to the other vehicles in the police convoy.

If there were tracks heading toward the visitor center, that probably meant the police car they'd already found had been toward the rear of the pack. The rest had driven further on first. That meant they were somewhere up ahead, somewhere in the darkness, somewhere in the heart of the night.

The grass whispered. Denise looked up every couple of seconds to check her surroundings and make sure there weren't any empty eye sockets watching her from the swaying grass. Every scuff of her feet sounded unnaturally loud. The low growl of the cars rumbled like a brood of angry flies.

She stepped closer to the dead hyena, keeping a few feet of distance between herself and the shredded corpse. Slime bubbled and oozed out of its countless wounds and spilled onto the dirt. The goop was already drying around the edges. If the worms didn't find somewhere else to go soon, they'd die there on the ground.

There wasn't enough light beyond the corpse. Denise walked back to her own car, moving with purpose. She opened the door and pulled out a canister of gasoline and some matches. Walking back to the dead hyena, she poured some of the gasoline over its corpse. Striking a match, she lit the dead body on fire.

The sudden poof of flame lit up more of the landscape beyond the headlights. She took a step around the flaming, crackling carcass and tried not to inhale any of the fumes.

She found a side mirror a few feet into the darkness. It lay in the dirt, ripped off some vehicle or another. Beyond that, she saw footprints.

There were a lot of them. Most of them were wearing matching boots, and they were all moving in the direction of the parked police car before swerving off into the grass. More shell casings lay around the footprints.

The matching boots were no doubt the police. The few footprints with a different tread were most likely some of the Triad prisoners.

There were other footprints too, though. Footprints rimmed with dried black ooze sloughed off the feet of the walking dead. Most of them were paw prints of varying sizes. Denise could tell at least six animals had gone after the fleeing group of police, including what appeared to be a couple of lions.

Another set of black footprints were distinctly human. One foot was bare, and the other was wearing a boot. The tread on the boot didn't match the tread on the police boots. That meant it probably belonged to one of the missing rangers.

Denise shone her light further out, trying to see where the footsteps were leading. Her light reflected off a hulk of crumpled metal. The shattered glass and smashed chassis of the ruined police van cast weird gleams of light back at her.

Huge, jagged rents ran down the sides of the police van, leaving thick gashes in the armor. More of the thick steel plating had simply been torn off entirely, cast away into the darkness.

The tears in the metal were all several inches long. They usually came in sets, several all next to each other as they ran down the length of the crushed and smashed van. Simply because of their size, it took Denise a moment to realize they were claw marks. The biggest claw marks she'd ever seen. Far bigger than anything that lived in the game preserve.

Likewise, it was obvious that the van hadn't driven into the field. It had been flipped and rolled and overturned like it drove off a cliff. The dirt track was smooth and even around here. Even if the driver sped off the road into the grass, the van wouldn't have spun out of control like that. It looked like a wrecking ball hit the van and sent it careening end over end into the night.

Maybe a rhino or an elephant could smash a van like that if they were going at a full charge. Maybe they could flip it right off the road and bat it around like a toy. Maybe they could do that, but neither a rhino nor an elephant had claws that could bite into steel like that.

Denise opened one of the pockets on her vest and pulled out a few rounds for the Nitro Express, just to have them in her hand and at the ready. A light breeze rolled over the plains and brought with it a coppery scent.

Shining her light further out, Denise could see more wreckage. Apparently, the entire police convoy had been wiped out. The vehicles were crumpled up like paper cups or flipped over and smashed into the ground.

She wanted to walk out into the knee-high grass and investigate, but she stayed away. There could be anything lurking in the grass. Maybe there was nothing, but maybe there was something like the hyena, mostly immobilized but still capable of latching onto her leg the second she stepped too close.

"Good Lord," Skipworth said from behind her, surveying the scene. "What could have done this?"

"I don't know," Denise said. "But I'm guessing it's the same thing that killed those elephants you saw a couple days ago."

"Do you think it got everyone? All the police? The Triads they were escorting?"

Denise looked back at the footprints in the road. The police and Triads had run off into the grass. A motley horde of creatures had pursued them. There weren't any places to make a last stand out there. No good defensive positions for miles.

"I think we're on our own out here. Even if there were someplace good to hole up out there, most of them wouldn't reach it. We've seen these things in action when the worms turned that Yersinia agent into one of their playthings. They can move fast. About as fast as when they were alive. See those tracks?" She pointed toward the footprints.

"Yeah."

"Lions. A couple more hyenas. An antelope. Probably a water buffalo. And that's just what crossed the road right there. If we look around more, there's probably more prints elsewhere. More creatures turned into ghouls by those worms. And that's not even counting whatever wrecked the convoy itself."

Denise tried to imagine some giant beast smashing the vehicles, trying to get at the screaming men inside like someone trying to knock a snack out of a vending machine. Her mind couldn't quite conjure up what the abomination would look like, try as she might.

"All those animals are faster than a human being. Even if the worms aren't coordinated enough to make the corpses run at full speed, they'd still run a person down in short order. And whatever crushed those vans was presumably able to catch up to a vehicle trying to speed away. Whatever that thing is, shotguns and pistols aren't even going to slow it down. Our elephant guns probably won't even slow that thing down."

She held one of the bullets in her hand up in her fingers. The brass shell looked more like a round for an artillery piece in a Lilliputian army than a standard bullet. Even one round was the size of a cocktail weenie.

Denise turned her head. She thought she'd heard something. Maybe not heard, precisely, but it was as if there was some subsonic vibration from somewhere nearby, a sound too low to be heard with the ears. She strained her ears, listening for the sound to come again.

"Did you hear that?" she asked.

"Hear what?" Skipworth looked around.

On the other side of the road, Kirkeberg and Cornelia were looking for any signs of survivors, too. Kirkeberg's head suddenly whipped around. Cornelia continued to shine her light around, stopping it on one piece of wreckage or another.

Denise locked eyes with Kirkeberg for a second. Cornelia was smart and quick, but she hadn't grown up in the bush. She had never made her living as a hunter. She wasn't as familiar with the subtle rhythms of the veldt that spoke to Denise. Kirkeberg had been a hunter before he joined the game preserve. He was just as attuned to the environment as Denise.

The vibration came again, actually slightly audible this time. It was a low boom, like the first roll of thunder from a distant storm.

"We should get back to the cars," Denise said. Kirkeberg nodded.

"Why, what's happening?" Skipworth asked, his voice lowering to a whisper.

"There's something coming," Kirkeberg said.

Once again, the vibration hit Denise. Now it was clearly audible, a heavy thump. If they weren't in the park's grassland, she would think that a large tree had just fallen over and hit the ground somewhere. But it wasn't a tree. There weren't any trees around here.

Denise spun around and walked back toward the cars without waiting for Skipworth. Kirkeberg did the same. Skipworth, the only one not holding an elephant gun, stuck so close to Denise that she could hear his breath growing quick, nearly hyperventilating.

The car headlights, which had helped them see just a few seconds before, were now blinding as they walked directly toward them. Behind them, the burning hyena corpse had begun to gutter out, leaving the lights ahead as the only source of illumination again. Denise chose to squint against the lights rather than take a hand off her elephant gun to shield her eyes. Even so, the lights were transfixing, pinning them on the road like actors on a darkened stage of the macabre.

That sound came again. Denise strained her ears, trying to tell just how far away it was. Depending on how big the thing making it was, it could be far away, or it could be all too close.

The ghouls reached out of the darkness and grabbed Kirkeberg. Slime-coated claws latched onto his arms and shoulders and ripped him off the road and into the grass. With the lights in their eyes, Denise never even saw the revenants approaching.

Kirkeberg screamed and tried to club the oozing figures away with the butt of his elephant gun. Denise raised her own weapon and blew the ghoul that used to be Blenavis away. The former police captain blew apart from the chest up, scattering globules of red and black meat into the field. Cornelia fired too, blasting the legs out from another monster.

But it was too late.

Hungry hands grabbed Kirkeberg and pulled him away into the grass. Teeth flashed in the night as Denise broke open the elephant rifle and popped another shell inside.

She raised the rifle to her shoulder and fired again, ripping a ghoul in half. Bone and viscera spewed away from the impact, but the monstrous figure barely seemed to notice. Its upper half started crawling toward Denise and Cornelia, and the lower half kicked and writhed. Cornelia hit the man's torso with her next shot, turning him into little more than a pair of arms astride a puddle of black pulp.

Kirkeberg was down in the grass, six or seven of the things piling on top of him. A hand shot up into the air like a drowning man going under for the final time. His thumb had been bitten off, and splashes of black slime covered the skin on his arm.

A shape moved in the darkness behind the human figures, a huge black lion emerging from the grass. Its one remaining eye glittered in the diffuse light at the edge of the road. Denise could see more shapes moving behind the lion, too. A lot more shapes. Hundreds. All of them moving and writhing closer.

That wasn't even Denise's biggest concern at that point, though. During the muzzle flash from her last shot, she'd seen something moving up behind the cars. She couldn't see it anymore because of the glare of the headlights, but the brief glimpse she caught of it was enough.

The fierce flash of gunfire revealed teeth. An ungodly number of teeth. The teeth were somewhere high up above Denise's head, floating perhaps twenty feet up in the air amid a towering stain of slime.

Denise ran over to the parked ranger vehicle and hurled open the driver door. She knew what those booming noises they'd all heard earlier were. They were footsteps drawing closer and closer as the titanic beast marched toward them.

Grabbing Skipworth, Denise threw him into the backseat and hopped behind the wheel. Cornelia dashed over a few steps behind her, the mass of dribbling figures following fast behind them.

Throwing the ranger car into gear, Denise didn't even wait until Cornelia's door was closed and her butt in the seat until she jammed the accelerator to the floor. Behind her, the stars were blotted out in the sky by the black mass behind them.

Suddenly, the headlights of Kirkeberg's parked car went spiraling off the road as the vehicle was launched sideways. The massive creature simply knocked the car aside as it crashed forward, lunging after Denise's accelerating vehicle. The parked police car went next, almost snapping in half as a foot crashed down on top of it.

There was nothing they could do for Kirkeberg, but maybe they could still save themselves. A slime-coated figure grabbed onto the side of the car's frame as Denise sped away. She thought she recognized the half-devoured face of the Triad she'd smashed into the side of the truck earlier that day.

"Cornelia, I could use a hand here," she said.

"Watch your head," Cornelia said, maneuvering her elephant gun around until the barrel was only a couple of inches away from Denise's nose.

The Triad bashed his free hand against the window, leaving black smears on the glass. A second later, he arched his head back and smashed it against the side of the window. The glass didn't shatter, but a spider web of cracks appears where his head impacted.

Denise nearly lost control of the car as the blast from the elephant gun tore the dead Triad off the side of the vehicle. It also filled the car with the smell of gunpowder and a roar like Krakatoa erupting. The only thing Denise could hear was a high-pitched ringing, and a flashbulb aftereffect was tattooed on her eyes from the muzzle blast. She guided the car more by feel than sight for a couple of seconds until she could see again.

"Reload," Cornelia said, tossing the elephant gun back to Skipworth. He dug a round out of one of the boxes in the back and jammed it into the breech, handing the weapon back up to the front of the car.

Denise glanced in the mirror again. "They're following us," she said.

Behind them, hundreds of figures of every shape and size had amassed on the road, cavorting toward them under the moonlight. Towering above them all was the massive creature that Denise couldn't identify. The monster was still coming toward them, but it was losing ground.

Things were worse than she thought. The horde of dead things must have moved through the park away from Sulfur Springs, gaining bodies as it went. Like a hurricane gathering strength over the ocean. They were sweeping across the game preserve, sucking in everything unfortunate to cross their path, and they had some sort of massive monster amid their ranks.

"What in the world is that thing?" Denise asked, more to herself than because she expected any sort of answer.

"I didn't get a very good look at it, but I think it was a dinosaur," Cornelia said.

"A dinosaur? I wasn't aware the Dracobly Hessler Game Preserve had any dinosaurs," Skipworth said, still breathing far too fast. "I mean, that's crazy."

"You know what else is crazy? Almost getting surrounded and torn apart by a bunch of dead guys," Cornelia shot back. "But why not? Sulfur Springs has been sealed away for millions of years. It could be that a dinosaur fell in there at some point before the system was completely closed off, probably even before the worms evolved into such vicious bastards. Now they have the dinosaur's ossified bones to play with."

"Great," Denise said. "Any idea what kind of dinosaur, assuming it even is a dinosaur?"

"I didn't get a very good look at it in the darkness. It has a long snout, kind of like a crocodile."

"And way too many teeth."

"I couldn't tell, but it looked like there were some elongated vertebrae sticking out of its back, too. I'm guessing it was probably something related to a *Spinosaurus*."

Ahead of them, Denise saw the visitor center's lights. The park was closed for the night, so the only people there should be park rangers and support staff. Thank God. Trying to evacuate hundreds of tourists from the park would be a logistical nightmare with the army of the dead only a few miles away.

"Dinosaurs or no dinosaurs, what are we going to do?" Skipworth asked. "I mean, how do you even deal with something size? Something that isn't even alive? I have no idea how you're supposed to deal with something like that."

"Fire. Lots and lots of fire," Denise said.

"I hope you're not thinking we can deal with that thing on our own," Cornelia said.

"No, not entirely. We'll hit the visitor center and tell them what happened. We need to get the word out to evacuate the park and bring the military in." Denise started to slow the car down.

"But it will take time to get the Army out here," Skipworth said.

"We can buy a little time," Denise said, pulling the car to a halt in the middle of the dirt track. "Hand me that can of gasoline."

Skipworth gave her the canister and she stepped out of the car. A few seconds later, she sprayed a stinking wave of petrochemicals over the grass to the right side of the road. She repeated the process on the left. She lit a match and tossed it into the grass. Almost immediately, the night lit up with a merry orange glow.

Hopefully, the fire would spread fast enough to block off part of the route to the visitor center before the worm freaks could arrive. If they were really lucky, the winds would brew the flames up into a firestorm and sweep them straight toward the ghouls, devouring them until there were none left. If they were really unlucky, the winds would shift and that same firestorm would come sweeping straight toward the visitors center.

She got back in the car and continued driving toward the only shelter for miles.

TWELVE

WYRM

Denise swerved out of the way as a couple of fire trucks charged out of the visitor center's garage. Their bells clanging, they flew straight up the road. Waving and gesturing, Denise tried to call them back, but no one saw her. Or no one cared.

The big, red trucks zoomed past, leaving rooster tails of dust in their wake. Denise pulled back onto the road and sped up to the entrance. She triple parked directly in front of the doors. Ripping the keys out of the ignition, she tumbled out with Cornelia and Skipworth.

Bursting through the doors, she near smacked into a repair technician. The man gave her an odd look as he stepped outside and donned a floppy, shapeless hat. He stopped for a moment to look at the flames further up the road, and Cornelia and Skipworth nearly bowled him over.

"Hey, you three can grab a step stool and jump up my butt. You know that? Get out of here," the repairman said.

"Get inside before they get here," Cornelia called over her shoulder. The man waved a dismissive hand at her and continued outside to watch the fire.

Inside, Denise pushed her way through the press of park rangers and other staff who had gathered around to watch the flames. Even though it was after the hours when the general public were allowed into the park, there were still plenty of employees at the visitor center. Rangers, security staff, janitors, and a couple of staff biologists were all still on park grounds.

"Everybody needs to start making an orderly evacuation," Denise shouted. "There's a big problem, and it's coming this way. C'mon, people, get going. It's time to move. You won't be safe here."

Her warning was met with a low rumble of concern and confusion. A couple of people lobbed questions at her. She heard somebody stage whisper to another person. "She's hysterical."

She realized she probably cut quite a sight through the crowd. Powder marks on her hands and face. Reeking of gasoline. Carrying an oversized rifle. She didn't care, though. A hand grabbed Denise at the elbow, and she jerked away, bringing her elephant rifle around. Archimedes Prescott, the park director, jumped away from her.

Forty years ago, Prescott had been one of the generation of renowned British explorers, crisscrossing the continent, living in the bush, and encountering places and peoples. Now he was a slightly pudgy man with a snowy white goatee and bifocals who looked like, and probably was, someone's favorite grandfather.

Denise dropped the elephant gun to her side. "Sorry, but we need to get out of here, Mr. Prescott. This place is about to get hit. We need to get on the phone first, though. Call up the Army."

Archimedes Prescott eyed her for a second with a look of concern. Finally, he pushed his glasses up on the bridge of his nose. "Are you alright?"

"Yeah, just a little rattled. We came from Ranger Station Thirteen. Everything's gone to hell between here and there, though."

"Station Thirteen? Ah, that means you're under Gunder Kirkeberg. I think I've heard of you. Ms. DeMarco, I presume?"

"Yeah. That's me. Now c'mon. We don't have a lot of time."

"Is Mr. Kirkeberg with you?" Prescott eyed Cornelia and Skipworth, evidently wondering what this ragged band wanted of him.

It dawned on Denise that Director Prescott didn't know what was going on. Kirkeberg must not have told him exactly what was happening, maybe thinking he could still take care of the situation himself. By the time it became clear just how bad things had gotten, he'd been just as wrapped up as the rest of them to make a full report to Prescott and the other higher ups. Prescott barely even knew who they were, let alone the scale of the disaster coming toward them.

"Kirkeberg...didn't make it. Listen, it's very important that everyone--"

"Perhaps we should speak in my office," the director said.

"But we have to get out of here before--"

"In. My. Office." Archimedes Prescott started off toward the administrative section of the building and waved them along, brokering no argument.

"Everybody needs to leave," Denise said one last time before taking off after the park director. Cornelia and Skipworth followed behind her.

A minute later, they reached Prescott's office and stepped inside, he shut the door behind them. "Now, I know Gunder gets some odd notions sometimes, hiring a couple of female rangers, and all that. But he has some good ideas too, from time to time. That poaching squad business of his, for instance. However, I simply cannot fathom why he would have allowed you three to travel out here and create this disturbance. Explain yourselves."

Denise closed her eyes and imagined throwing Prescott through the large window on the far side of his office. She opened them again and tried to keep her voice even. "I don't have time to explain everything, but you need to recall those fire trucks and start evacuating the park. Kirkeberg is dead. The police commandos who helped with that poaching raid are dead. The Triads they captured are dead. And we're all going to be dead if we don't get our butts in gear."

"What? Gunder can't be...I just spoke to him yesterday about his two missing rangers. What happened?"

"There are things coming down the road. We ran into them earlier, and now they're probably following us. They'll be here soon. We went out to investigate why the police convoy was late, and we found it destroyed. They got Kirkeberg before we could get away. We set the fire to slow them down."

"I see," Prescott said in a way that indicated that he clearly didn't see. "We were expecting that convoy to get here some time ago, but I'm sure there's a perfectly reasonable explanation. You said you started that fire? That's against all our regulations. We can only have controlled burns when--"

"Director Prescott, there isn't a perfectly reasonable explanation. I just told you the completely unreasonable, goat shit insane reason, but it's the real one. There's a horde of dead creatures, including a damn dinosaur, coming this way as we speak, and they are going to kill everything in their path and just keep moving. We need to start getting people out of here. Right now."

"A dinosaur now is it?" Prescott nodded. "I see. Yes, well, that changes everything." He smiled at them as his finger moved over to his intercom button on his desk. Pressing the button, he leaned forward and buzzed out. "Samantha, could you get security to my office? Now, please." His finger came off the button and he leaned back in his chair, still smiling affably. Prescott thought he was dealing with crazy people.

This was not what Denise needed. Hell was fast approaching, and they were wasting time. She raised her hands in a placatory gesture.

"Look, I know you think I'm out of my tree, but I'm just asking you to help. You don't have to believe me; just order a general evacuation and put in a call for the Army. We're going to need tanks and flamethrowers."

"I appreciate your concern. Dinosaurs are serious business, after all. However, I'm afraid I couldn't do that even if I wanted to. Our phone lines went down about fifteen minutes ago. I sent someone out to repair them, but we're cut off from outside the park. One of the wires must have gone down." Prescott spoke slowly and calmly to the frazzled, heavily armed woman standing in his office talking about zombie dinosaurs.

The frazzled, heavily armed woman jerked forward. "What?"

"The phones are down. We can't contact anyone from here. I'm sure it will all be fixed soon, though."

"Oh God. Okay, we need to get somewhere with a working phone. This place won't last long once they get here."

Archimedes Prescott rubbed his brow. "Maybe you three should just stay here for a little while. You can rest down in the infirmary. How about that, hmm?"

"I'm a doctor, and she's a nurse," Skipworth said, pointing toward Cornelia. "We don't need rest right now. We need you to start getting people out of here. We're wasting time talking about this."

Prescott eyed Skipworth's torn clothes and too-wide eyes. He sighed.

A second later, the doors to the office opened up. Several security officers and a couple of park rangers stood in the opening, looks of concern etched on their faces.

"Could you come with us please, ma'am?" one of the security officers beckoned.

Denise looked out the window. The fire had died out near the road and was now spreading in opposite directions away from the path. She could barely make out the rectangular notches where the fire trucks were parked in front of the flames. From this distance, it almost looked like some sort of shadow puppet theater.

"Ma'am? Come along."

Denise's mind raced. No one was listening to her, and the phone lines were down, cutting them off from outside communications.

How in the world had the phone lines gone down? There weren't any storms in the area that could knock them down. The leading edge of the monster army hadn't reached the lines yet. There shouldn't be any maintenance scheduled this late at night, so it was unlikely a worker had accidentally turned something off he shouldn't have.

"Ma'am, I need you to come with me right now." A hand reached out to grab her shoulder.

"Look," Cornelia said, pointing out the window.

Denise tried to follow her friend's finger, but the outside world was nothing but darkness and distant flames. It was difficult to make anything out.

Suddenly, she saw it. A shape drifted across the screen of fire. With bulky legs and a long tail, it was perhaps forty feet long, as long as the fire trucks. A lengthy, crocodile-like head bobbed as it walked. Huge spines jutted out of its back to create a shape like an old-fashioned lady's fan.

"What is that?" Archimedes Prescott asked.

"It's about thirty tons of told-you-so. We need to get people out of here."

One of the fire trucks started to move, trying to speed away from the massive shadow approaching it. The creature's arms shot out, claws at the ready. Grabbing the truck before it could gather much speed, the dinosaur arrested its forward movement. Locked in the monster's grip, the truck jittered and bounced as its tires chewed futilely at the dirt, unable to move forward.

Dipping its head down, the dinosaur chomped down on the truck's roof. Ripping the metal away, the *Spinosaurus* tossed the crumpled metal away like a hungry man about to tear into a tin of potted meat. The monster dropped its head again, this time rearing back up with something squirming between its jaws. Throwing back its head, the wriggling thing disappeared.

Denise didn't think the *Spinosaurus* actually "ate" the fire truck driver. After all, it was just an amalgamation of bones and writhing worm bodies. The bones didn't need to eat. No, the worms were simply covering the unfortunate man in more of themselves by stuffing him down into the dinosaur's belly. The worms would eat him a little at a time once he was dead and they had control of his body. He just had to be slathered in slime first.

In a few minutes, the man would no doubt reappear as a member of the ravenous horde, another vector and source of food for the worms. A walking brood factory.

Smaller shapes, some of them walking on two legs, most of them on four, swarmed the other truck. The entire scene played out in crackling orange and black silhouettes. There was no sound from this distance, leaving everyone to fill in the screams of terrified men and the crumpling of metal with their own imagination.

The director's finger moved over to a different button on his intercom. "This is Director Prescott. Everyone in the facility should immediately grab a weapon and assemble outside the building's north entrance. I repeat, the north entrance. Large caliber weapons are recommended."

"What in the blazing blue hell are you doing?" Denise asked.

"I'm saving this park from...from whatever those are out there. I will not allow a bunch of animals to chase me away from our mission here."

"Those things aren't animals. At least not anymore they aren't. They aren't even alive anymore."

"Nonsense. I can see them moving out there. Of course they're alive," Prescott said, standing up from his posh leather chair. He shrugged a coat on.

"No, I assure you, they're dead bodies being controlled by polychaete worms," Skipworth said.

"Poppycock," Prescott responded, walking over to the far wall. He reached up and pulled an old black powder elephant gun off the wall, the sort of thing that was fading from the business when Denise was only a little girl. "If it's moving, it's alive, and if it's alive, we can kill it. I don't care how big it is. Old Charlotte here has enough stopping power to knock a freight train off its tracks."

Denise knew her weapons, and she knew that wasn't true. The old rifle was powerful, maybe even on par with her .577 Nitro Express, but it wasn't designed to take down anything as large as a *Spinosaurus* or whatever that abomination was. Even if the monster was alive instead of just a collection of rattling bones held together with biological voodoo, Prescott would need a perfect shot to bring that monster down. "Old Charlotte" wasn't designed for dinosaur hunting. They'd need an anti-tank rifle for that. Or better yet, a howitzer.

"What we need to do is leave," Denise said. "You can't fight these things. They took out a whole police convoy."

"I am not about to abandon this place to a bunch of filthy animals simply because they've gone rabid or got worms or whatever the problem is. We need to deal with this issue here and now, or it will only get worse."

Prescott was right that things were going to get worse if they weren't dealt with. He was just wrong about how to deal with the problem.

"Let's get out of here. We need to warn people and get the Army out here," Denise said. She started to walk out of the office, leaving Prescott and the security officers behind.

"Where do you think you're going?" Prescott asked.

"We're going to gather whatever back-up we can. We need to find a working phone line somewhere so we can get the military out here."

"No need. Just stick with us. We'll need the extra hands around here. Tell me. You there, lad. Do you know how to shoot?"

"Not particularly well," Skipworth said.

"Ah, well. I imagine you'll have learned by the end of the night. The ladies there can hand you one of their rifles, and they'll help reload along with the secretarial staff while we form a firing line along the north side of the building."

"Uh, sir. Mr. Prescott. These things don't go down that easy. Even hitting a vital organ won't bring them down. I've seen it with my own eyes. You have to expend a small arsenal's worth of bullets just to deal with one of these things, to make it so its body literally can't function as a mobile thing anymore. And even then, fire works a lot better."

"Bah," Prescott said. "Security, see to it that these three come along and grab some serious weapons for yourselves. I'll show them how it was done back in the old days, by Jove."

"This is not how you want to be doing this," Denise said, but there were already hands on her arms, guiding her out the doors after the park director.

Most of the staff were already outside, holding weapons. Some of them shuffled around. Others murmured amongst themselves. Some of them had seen what had happened to the fire trucks, but they didn't know how to interpret the strange, phantasmagorical silhouettes they'd seen.

Prescott stood with some of the rangers, slapping backs and spraying pep talk. Many of the people here were perfectly good shots and very capable in their own right, but they still didn't know what was coming toward them.

Denise tried to explain that they needed to escape to some of the staff people, who didn't look like they knew what they were doing with their rifles. They were as likely as not to injure themselves or have the big guns fly straight out of their hands the first time they tried to fire one of the things. One of the security men dragged her away, and the staff only looked at her strangely when she tried to explain that they were all about to be attacked by a bunch of moving carcasses being controlled by worms. It was not a message that went down easily, she had to admit.

In the distance, the fires were spreading away from the visitor center, moving up over the hill. In a few minutes, all they'd be able to see outside the building grounds would be a thin film of wavering light beyond the horizon, like dawn was trying to launch an early surprise attack from the wrong side of the sky. With the flickering of the flames, it almost looked like a distant battle was taking place. There was nothing but darkness between the ragged line of park rangers and the fire, though.

The minutes dragged by like dogs scooting their butts across the carpet. Slowly. Uncomfortably. Anticipating worms.

Denise gripped the Nitro Express tight and kept her eyes peeled. Cornelia and Skipworth stood in silence. She would club Prescott over the head and order everyone to leave herself, but the security men were hanging off her like remoras, apparently eager for some kind of stand-up fight.

Suddenly, she heard it. Or rather, she felt it as much as she heard it. There was a rattle in her bones, as if the ground was vibrating ever so slightly beneath her feet. The impact came again, slightly more intense this time.

She had ammo. Lots of ammo. She could feel the weight of the giant slugs in her jacket pockets, shifting and clinking each time she made a movement. The problem wasn't ammunition.

Another impact. Audible this time. A few of the rangers and staff looked at each other, suddenly more uneasy than a few minutes before. Another impact and another. They were clearly audible now. Loud enough to be heard as well as felt.

Boom.

Boom.

Boom.

Prescott stood at the front of the makeshift firing line, the look of enjoyment sapping off his face. It was one thing to mentally relive the glory days and try for one last ride. It was quite another to hear it approaching with thunderous footfalls, realizing that this was something bigger than anything seen during the glory days. This was an entirely different scale. The look on the park director's face cast itself into a mold halfway between steadfast determination and frightful anticipation.

The first wave of ghouls lurched into the lights. Wild dogs. Hyenas. A three-legged crocodile. Antelopes. Dead Triads and police commandos. They all came forward in a surge of black slime. Claws and teeth and bones gleamed in the moonlight.

A dozen elephant guns all went off at once. Denise aimed at an oozing skeleton that had once been a leopard. The blast smashed the creatures off their feet, blowing them back in a tidal wave of ooze and ruined meat. Limbs tore off. Rib cages imploded inward. Heads disintegrated.

Then the creatures got right back up, the wave of monsters that had built up behind them already rushing in like a hungry tide.

The line of rangers and staff recoiled as if they had been the ones struck by the bullets. Denise broke open her Nitro Express and jammed a fresh round inside. The leopard she'd been aiming at was now in several pieces, but each piece was still crawling forward on its own.

The station's meager defensive line wasn't enough. There were dozens of creatures dripping with black slime just in their sights. Denise knew there were dozens more, maybe even hundreds more, behind those.

They needed something other than guns, even powerful guns. Denise ran around the corner of the building to the car she'd arrived in. Throwing open the door, she considered just driving off, driving away as fast as she could into the night to go find a working phone.

She tossed the idea aside for now. If she left right now, she'd simply be leaving everyone here to die. Maybe, just maybe, they could pull this off right and most of the people would be able to escape instead.

Reaching around to the back seat, she grabbed one of the gasoline canisters they'd filled up at Ranger Station Thirteen. So far, fire was their most effective weapon. The worms might be able to survive near a thermal vent, but they couldn't take an open flame.

Lugging the canister back toward the north side of the building, Denise kept her Nitro Express ready as more gunfire boomed out. The sound of a large number of elephant guns all firing in short order was like the world splitting itself apart and the earth's plates grinding against each other.

A flicker of concern over going prematurely deaf flitted through Denise's brain and just as quickly flitted out. She had to survive the night before she started worrying too much about what lay down the road for her. There were monsters to deal with first.

She arrived back around the side of the building just as the park staff started falling back. It wasn't a full-blown retreat, but the creatures were drawing closer and closer. The hammer blows from the elephant guns were blasting them into smaller and smaller pieces, but new creatures kept coming up to replace the ones that were completely obliterated. The space in front of the visitor center looked like a Chicago slaughterhouse had an abortion. Bit by bit, the building's defenders were being pushed back toward the entrance.

Denise lobbed the gasoline canister underhanded into the writhing center of the mass of bodies. Leveling her Nitro Express, she aimed and fired. The recoil from the elephant gun hit her a second before the wave of blast furnace heat.

Yellow and blue fire shot out, spraying the nearest creatures with burning liquid. Everywhere the fire touched, the worms fell away to try to save themselves. If one section of worms sloughed off a body to get away from the flames, it usually caused a chain reaction where the carefully coordinated invertebrates suddenly lost their cohesion and spilled off their host. For some of the smaller creatures, it looked like they had been dunked in acid as the worms fell off their skeletal forms and the bones fell to the ground.

Some of the bigger animals could shrug off small patches of fire, though. The burning worms fell to the ground and died, but the survivors simply spread out more and took their place.

But it was still progress. She'd blasted a huge hole in the monsters' frontline. Maybe with more gasoline bombs, they actually stood a chance of holding the unnatural ghouls back long enough to escape. Maybe they had a real shot at this.

The *Spinosaurus* lumbered forward, its right foot smashing down directly on top of Archimedes Prescott. A huge claw swept out and tore across the line of park employees. One of the rangers spun away screaming, his guts hanging from his torn shirtfront. Another fell to the ground, his face a red and black ruin. More creatures immediately set upon the fallen, vomiting black sludge onto the bodies.

In just a few minutes, Denise knew those dead park rangers could be up and on their feet and coming after her. The bigger problem was the dinosaur, though. They didn't have anything that could stop it.

Cornelia fired her elephant gun again and fought her way over to Denise. "We have to go. Right now," she yelled.

In front of them, the line of defense broke and gave way. First, a few individuals ran back for the relative safety of the building's interior. Then, the *Spinosaurus* bit a secretary in half as she tried to reload a rifle. A few more people ran, and that triggered the collapse of the entire line. Sensing their comrades scrambling away, the other rangers and staff bolted. A few stayed planted where they were, determined to hold their ground. They died almost immediately.

"Get to the car," Denise yelled. They spun around to run to the parked vehicle for more ammo and a quick escape.

The creatures had already cut them off, swinging wide around the edge of the building. Denise took two steps before she realized the darkness ahead of them wasn't just the night. It was a flailing mass of hungry bodies wrapped in liquid ebony.

"Never mind. Inside." She pivoted and launched herself through the open doors to the visitor center. Skipworth and Cornelia ran in directly behind her.

Denise slammed the doors shut. The strong metal doors were reinforced in case any rogue animals tried attacking the visitor center, but they were designed to prevent a single animal from forcing itself inside. She had no idea if they'd be able to keep a cemetery's worth of the dead out.

The door rattled in its frame a couple of seconds after Denise shot the bolt through the lock. Fists and paws beat against the cool metal from the other side. Claws and horns scraped at its surface, but it was holding.

With a little luck, the door would stand long enough for them to get everyone out a different entrance.

The wall next to the door exploded inward in a shower of wooden beams and drywall, and a massive claw groped inside. Cornelia leapt away from the huge talons as they pawed around for human flesh. The arm withdrew and then bashed its way through another section of the structure.

A snout pressed its way through the holes. Teeth snapped and clacked as the *Spinosaurus* tried to get at them like a pig rooting for truffles. After a few seconds of useless flailing, the snout pulled out of the gap, and the dead stormed inside.

The first creature to enter was De Hoog, one of the rangers from Station Thirteen who had gone missing while searching for the fake Thornber's ill-fated expedition. Denise cut him down with a blast from her Nitro Express. De Hoog blew backwards out through the side of the building, leaving behind nothing but streamers of sludge. More creatures immediately filled the gap.

"We have to get out of here. Those things are going to tear this place right out from under us," Cornelia said, firing her own gun at the next creature to squeeze through the hole in the wall.

As if on cue, the dinosaur's massive claws latched onto the sides of the ragged breach and started pulling and scratching. More supports gave way, and the gap grew wider.

"Right. This place has a garage. I don't think we can get back to our car anymore at this point." Denise paused to fire her Nitro Express again. Her shoulder throbbed like someone had taken a baseball bat to it. The gun's barrel was hot to the touch as she snapped the weapon open and reloaded again. "Maybe we can still get out of here with a different vehicle, though."

Behind them, the remaining rangers and staff assembled hasty barricades out of desks and chairs and anything else that looked sturdy. Denise, Cornelia, and Skipworth ran down the hallway. The creatures would tear this place apart sooner or later. With the help of the gigantic, undead dinosaur, Denise was betting on sooner rather than later.

They needed to get to the far side of the building, to the maintenance and repair areas that weren't open to the public. There would be vehicles there. At least, Denise hoped there would be vehicles there. From there, their best bet would be to drive straight out of the park and get some help.

At this point, they might need some bombers to fly over and drop incendiaries over this section of the park. Nothing short of fire or truly massive body trauma seemed to have any effect at all on the creatures.

The wall behind them ripped away completely, and the building shuddered in protest. Stomping its massive feet, the *Spinosaurus* simply waded through the structure, tearing at the roof and support pillars as it went. Rubble rained down from overhead, and the dead streamed inside.

Denise didn't try to stand and fight them back. She'd already seen what would happen. The barricades the park staff had set up might give them an extra minute of time, but there were too many ghouls, and they were too hard to kill. Add a rampaging dinosaur into the ranks of the dead, and the living never stood a chance.

Another set of security doors stood directly ahead. Denise dashed through them as a volley of gunfire erupted behind them. Then the screaming started.

Perhaps the most unearthly thing about the scene behind them was the silence of the undead. They didn't growl or roar, snarl, or moan. Why would they? They were just dead bodies being piloted along by creatures not much larger than plankton. The only noise they made was the squelch of their feet shuffling forward or their bones clacking together as they moved. Otherwise, the killing was done silently, almost with the quiet, solemn air of a priest sacrificing an animal to some unknown god. The people made all the noise as they shouted and panicked and died.

Denise found herself in a long hallway. The floor was done in cheap tiling, and the walls were painted a shade of vaguely seasick green. This was a work area, not open to the public. Off to her left lay the visitor center's infirmary. The garage lay directly ahead.

The infirmary's wall exploded inward as an elephant, matted with black tar, blasted through the barrier. Its trunk was in danger of falling off like a precariously balanced scoop of ice cream starting to melt. The elephant had no tusks, just a pair of bloody stumps jutting out from the sides of its skull. This must be one of the elephants the Triads found dead. Now it was effectively back for revenge against Skipworth and those who failed to protect it in the first place.

Cots and medical supplies flew everywhere as the elephant tried to push the rest of the way into the building. Bottles of pills and medicines spilled out of the overturned cabinets and shattered on the floor. The elephant pushed and squeezed itself inward, still partially caught in the half-demolished wall.

Denise ran past the open door, not bothering to fire at the monster. So long as it was stuck just a little bit longer, that would be more effective than trying to stop it with her Nitro Express.

Part of the roof caved in behind them as they raced down the corridor toward the garage. The *Spinosaurus*, that hateful dragon that probably killed the elephant now chasing them, knocked over a barricade of desks and snapped its jaws down over one of the park's security agents.

The door to the garage was closed. Denise kicked it open and dashed through. They had their choice of a few cars, a couple of big cargo trucks, and a lone garbage truck. A key to each vehicle rested on a pegboard on the wall.

Denise decided to take one of the cars. They would be fastest, even if they didn't offer as much protection. She reached out for a set of keys.

The wall blew inward as the dead elephant from the infirmary rammed its way through. A chunk of broken cinderblock slammed into Denise and knocked her down. A tongue of white hot pain lashed her where the block struck.

She had other problems to worry about, though. The keys on the pegboard had scattered when the wall collapsed. Some of them slid away across the floor and others lay buried under the pile of rubble. Directly in front of her, the elephant used its mass to smash the rest of the way into the garage. Down the hall, a pack of undead wildlife stormed toward them like a black tsunami.

There was no time for anything else. Denise grabbed the only set of keys within easy reach, the ones to the garbage truck, and hauled herself to her feet. She pointed to the huge, bulky vehicle, and Cornelia and Skipworth started running toward it.

Denise clambered inside just as the elephant in the room finally smashed the rest of the way through the wall and came charging forward. Jamming the key into the ignition, Denise punched the truck's accelerator. Time to get out of here.

The truck crept forward. A massive impact sent them slewing sideways as the elephant rammed into the side of the truck. They met with a crunch of metal and a meaty smack.

For a horrible second, Denise thought the truck would tip over onto its side, but then it rocked back onto its center of gravity, the engine muttering and grumbling. Antelopes, hyenas, and former park employees plowed into the side of the truck, clawing at the metal, trying to get a hold on the sides.

Denise poured power back onto the accelerator and worked the gears, forcing the truck forward like a buggy driver cracking the whip. A few seconds later, she smashed straight through the garage doors, scraping the stragglers off the sides of the truck.

She started to turn toward the park exit, but the path was blocked by dozens of ghastly forms. Upon sensing her, they moved away from the sides of the visitor center and started to come after the truck.

That route was out. Denise swerved back onto the southern road, the only path that wasn't blocked by the dead. She gently touched the spot where she'd been struck by the cinder block and hissed. In a couple of days, she'd have a bruise that practically extended off her body, but it didn't feel like anything was broken or fractured.

"We need to find a route out of the game preserve," Denise said. She checked her mirrors. The creatures had taken notice of her escape as she rumbled away from the visitor center, and they were following her. The *Spinosaurus* pounded after them, each footfall kicking up a plume of dust.

"We're heading south, right?" Cornelia asked.

"Yeah."

"If we leave the park, those things are just going to follow us," she said. "There's villages between here and the next town. Little places without electricity or means of transport. They don't have phones, so we'd just have to drive straight through."

"And we'd be leading the creatures right to them," Skipworth said.

Denise sat for a moment. She hadn't thought of that. The villages weren't big, just little subsistence farming hamlets that had sprung up. Probably only a few hundred people each. Cornelia was right. Leading the ghouls through there would create a massacre.

"So what are we going to do?" Denise asked.

"I might have a plan," Cornelia said.

Behind her, a few more shots rang out from the interior of the visitor center, and then everything went quiet.

THIRTEEN

A FATEFUL MEETING

"Alright, we won't have a ton of time to prepare," Cornelia said as Ranger Station Two crept into view. The supply depot provided spare parts and emergency backup reserves for most of the park. "So, let's go over it again. Pop quiz. What are you doing once we arrive?" Cornelia pointed to Skipworth.

"Gathering fuel and anything else you can use," he said.

"Correct on the first try. You can give yourself a gold star sticker when we get done with this. Gasoline. Heating oil. Greasy rags. Whatever you can find. I'm going to put together a little something to turn it into a fire bomb. It'll be a bit crude, but with enough combustible material, it shouldn't matter. Now then, Denise, what are you doing once we get there?"

"Getting on the phone. They have their own lines out of there. Maybe they're still connected to the outside world. If not, they have a certain amount of radio equipment. One way or the other, I'll be able to get ahold of somebody out there," she said as the depot bounced closer.

"Hey, gold stars for everybody today. Apple juice and animal crackers for recess."

"Do you think it'll work? The bomb, I mean," Skipworth asked.

"Well, there's no guarantee I can get all of them at once with the blast, if that's what you mean. Hopefully, the initial explosion will take out a lot of them, and the flames will spread out fast enough to trap the rest and burn them up. There might be some stragglers, but these things seem to travel in a big group."

"Probably because the worms themselves are communal. They naturally flock together," Skipworth said.

"Yeah, and that's going to be our best chance to get them. I'm going to take some gasoline and pour it out in lines radiating away from the depot. That'll help the fire spread out faster."

"It sounds like a good plan," Denise said. The creatures were still following her garbage truck. She'd been driving slowly, only a little faster than the creatures could run, leading them out like the Pied Piper. That would keep the creatures interested in them instead of leaving the park and attacking the nearby villages.

"I agree," Skipworth said. "Everybody is lucky to have the two of you here. Prescott got all his people killed when he actually had an opportunity to help fix this, and Kirkeberg never totally understood the severity of what was going on. If this works, you might just be saving a lot of people."

"Flatterer," Cornelia said.

"Well, thanks," Denise said. "You know, we're lucky to have you in our own right. Without you, we wouldn't really understand how these creatures work. We wouldn't know about the worms themselves. Knowing what they are will help us get rid of them. Besides, you didn't have to come out here with us. You could have stayed at the ranger station when we went to look for the police convoy."

"There could have been people hurt. I thought maybe I could do more out there than just sitting around."

"You've done a lot to help us," Denise said, pulling up next to Ranger Station Two and parking the truck. "Above and beyond what you needed to do just to get help from Kirkeberg. You helped me sort some things out for myself, too." She opened her door and hopped out.

"Oh, like what?"

"I was thinking of one of the comments you made earlier. I think I might not stay with the park service too much longer. Maybe I'll open up a little business myself. Sort of a niche market. Not sure it'll pan out, but I think I'd be good at it. Maybe do something that nobody else can handle. Cornelia, when this is all over, I'd be looking for someone to help me out with a job like that. Maybe you'll be interested. You, too," she said, turning toward Skipworth.

A set of hands grabbed Denise as she walked around the back of the truck toward the depot's entrance. She tried to spin around and reach for her revolver, but the hands seemed to expect that. They slammed her into the side of the truck. The place where the cinder block hit her exploded in roaring pain.

Before she could recover, the hands stripped her revolver out of its holster bashed her upside the head. The world went fuzzy around the edges for a second, and she had to fight to stand up. Her Nitro Express was ripped out of her hands, and then a boot to the back of the knees sent her to the ground.

Instead of the warning she tried to shout, she said, "Boof." She tried to roll over, but a boot caught her squarely in the ribs.

A few feet away, Skipworth and Cornelia were also down on the ground. All Denise could see of their captors were several sets of boots.

"Let us up. We're not infected," Denise said.

"Well, obviously," a voice said from above her. "Might I ask who you are, though?"

"I'm one of the park rangers. Let us up."

"Again, it's obvious that you're a park ranger. You're wearing the uniform. I'm not blind. Details, please."

"I'm Denise DeMarco."

"Ah, from the ranger station near the dam. How splendid to make your acquaintance. Now, I know Dr. Skipworth over there. Fancy running into you here, Lyndon. Small world, isn't it? But who are you?"

"Cornelia van Rensburg."

"Ah, yes. You're that famous hunter's daughter. Here to try to forge something in common with your father. And, Denise, I hope you don't mind if I call you Denise? We're all going to know each other rather well soon enough. You have quite the reputation as well. I hope you don't mind that I read your files? I decided to study up on the personnel at Ranger Station Thirteen after you found my good friend Dr. Thornber."

"Are you with the game preserve?"

"No. Very much no. Pardon me a moment. Oh, Dr. D'Arnot? Will you be needing all three of them for questioning? Is two an acceptable number?"

"We don't have a lot of time to work. Two is plenty," a voice said from further away.

"Ah, splendid." The speaker, still holding Denise's revolver, walked over to Skipworth and shot him in the back of the head. Skipworth jumped once and then went still. He barely moved at all when the second bullet smashed into the back of his skull.

Denise and Cornelia screamed and thrashed as blood pooled out of Skipworth's head and across the dusty ground. The boots on their backs prevented them from squirming too much, though.

"Now then," the voice said as several sets of hands hauled Denise and Cornelia to their feet. The speaker turned to them. "I haven't properly introduced myself. My name is Zhang Dong. Perhaps you've heard of me?"

FOURTEEN

YOU ASKED

"You son of a bitch," Denise said.

"No, the pleasure is mine. Now that the initial pleasantries are out of the way, I would rather like to have a discussion with the two of you."

"You didn't have to do that," Cornelia said.

"I assure you, it was completely necessary. The good Dr. Skipworth was a dog, and when a dog turns on you, you put it down. It's as simple as that."

"He wasn't. He was a good man, and you basically turned him into an indentured servant. You could have released him from his debt after he'd worked for you for a while."

"Believe me. He was a dog. The worst kind of dog, in fact. One that does not even know that he is a dog. I can already tell he told you the story where he worked his way into debt at some illicit gambling house or another. It's quite true. You would be amazed by the depth of the pit the good doctor dug for himself. But he told you the debt was to the Sun Yee On Triads, didn't he?"

"Well, yes. But that doesn't change the fact that--"

"He actually came to us for help. Skipworth never carried a debt with us. We turned him away because it was obvious we wouldn't see any returns from someone like him. He was blacklisted from the establishments we operate early on. There are always other places, though. He just went down the food chain. A few months later, he came back to us. He told us that some loan sharks were out to kill him. He said he would do anything, absolutely anything, if we would protect him. They sent him to me, and I laid out the terms. There was no fine print. No tricks. It was a simple contract. He would provide services for us, and we would protect him. He even knew what kind of work he'd be used for. And the price for disloyalty? Well, you just saw it. He knew about it when he agreed.

"Skipworth's problem was that he never believed he was to blame for anything. He never took the time to reflect on how he got himself into his predicaments, because he believed he was always on the side of the angles. The fact that we had him in a situation he did not enjoy meant that the facts soon transmuted themselves for him. We became his oppressors rather than his protectors in his eyes. He didn't like the facts as they were, so he started telling people that it was the Triads he owed money to, not petty, jumped-up local gangsters. Then it sounded like *we* were the ones who wronged *him*. I think maybe he even convinced himself everything he said was true. The facts are what they are, though. This was simply the logical conclusion to a breach of contract."

"You can't just treat everything like a business contract. You just killed a man."

"Oh, you noticed? What keen observation skills you must have. And I most certainly will treat my contracts as contracts. They are a personal agreement between two individuals, and they will be upheld; I will see to it. Even the ones I do not particularly care for, such as my agreement with Dr. D'Arnot, here." A pair of hands turned Denise around.

D'Arnot was a scrawny man with sunken cheeks and a slight stoop. He could have been anything from thirty-five to fifty years old, though it was hard to tell. With his gaunt face, he looked like a well-preserved mummy.

He was standing in front of a row of armored vehicles parked along the far side of the building, mostly obscured by bushes and the structure itself. A large number of men with close-cropped hair and machine pistols stood by the vehicles.

The men were wearing strange, mostly black uniforms. Denise would have been able to tell they weren't with the military even if they weren't with D'Arnot. The uniforms were thick and padded, completely different from anything used by any standard army. She recognized the idea, though.

The uniforms were designed like ancient medieval padded armor. Back then, the thick stuffing was meant to stop arrows from piercing the wearer, and glancing sword blows wouldn't penetrate down to the flesh. It was a cheaper alternative to chainmail and plate metal for the peasant armies of feuding fiefdoms. Gunpowder and the advent of more powerful firearms meant the padded armor went out the window with the chainmail and the armored knights, though.

These men weren't expecting to be accosted with pitchforks and swords or even guns. They were wearing the armor to protect against teeth and claws. In addition to the machine pistols, about every third man carried a flamethrower. They'd come prepared.

This must be the backup for Francis Caputo, the man who died imitating Dr. Thornber. The man whose body she had to set fire to only this afternoon. God, but it seemed like a long time ago now.

This must be Yersinia Bioresearch's cleanup crew. Denise swallowed hard.

Dr. D'Arnot stepped forward. "Hello, Ms. DeMarco. Ms. Van Rensburg. While I realize that what happened to your colleague was no doubt upsetting, I can assure you that I have no interest in harming you."

Denise didn't need a degree in psychology to tell that was a big, fat, hairy lie. Now it was perfectly clear what had happened. Yersinia Bioresearch wanted to quietly study Sulfur Springs after that laboratory in Chicago burned down. They didn't want to be seen doing it, given that they were already under a cloud of sanctions, so they hijacked the next innocent expedition that went down there by replacing the scientist with one of their own men. Zhang Dong was their man on the ground to make sure the replacement process went off correctly. Since their man mucked everything up and brought a plague of the undead up from the bowels of the earth, Yersinia still had to work with Zhang Dong long enough to square everything away and erase all their fingerprints from the incident.

That meant destroying the evidence, destroying the monsters, and destroying the witnesses. Given what Denise knew about how the company operated though, they'd no doubt try to keep one of the monsters so they had a usable sample of the worms. It wouldn't do if the entire expedition was for naught, obviously.

There wouldn't be any room for leaving Denise and Cornelia around in that scenario. A cold sweat broke out on Denise's brow. Zhang Dong and his Triad lieutenants had stripped them of their weapons, and Yersinia had about forty men. Denise kept doing calculations in her head, and the numbers kept coming up as zeroes. They were screwed.

"All I would like is some information, and then you will be free to go," Dr. D'Arnot said. "First of all, since the incident with Dr. Thornber, have you seen anything unusual at all in the park?"

Denise stared at the Yersinia scientist. The question seemed absurd after everything she'd seen tonight. The night had zoomed right past unusual and straight into weird shit a long time ago.

But then she realized that Dr. D'Arnot and his band of merry men must not have been in the park for very long. Putting this collection of men and material together must have taken a little while after Yersinia realized their original plan had crumbled and was in danger of being exposed.

D'Arnot was fishing. He didn't know what she knew. He didn't know she already knew about Yersinia's involvement. He didn't know the visitor center had already been destroyed. He didn't know there was a horde of monsters bearing down on them.

Maybe, just maybe, if she played her cards right, they'd get out of this alive.

"Anything unusual? We've had unusual out the--" Cornelia started to say.

Denise cut her off. "Oh thank goodness you're here. Did the Army send you? Please, you have to arrest these men. They're poachers. They just killed an innocent man. Help us," Denise said. This would work better if they thought she was clueless and forthcoming. If they realized too early that she knew too much, the questions would get pointed, and she wouldn't survive long after they figured out how to get answers out of her.

"The Army? Err, yes. We are a sort of...liaison for the military. Biological containment. We're here to help you. We'll arrest these men if your story checks out, of course. But you have to tell us everything before we can help." Dr. D'Arnot gave a smile that was supposed to be reassuring. By being the friendly one after Zhang Dong killed Skipworth, D'Arnot thought they'd spill their guts to him. Reassurance. Safety. All very promising after something as traumatic as their friend's death.

He thought he was playing the tune, but Denise already had him making assumptions that weren't true. So long as he thought he was getting the information he wanted, D'Arnot could be more helpful than he realized.

"Yes, of course. There's something loose in the park. We'll need your help," Denise said.

Cornelia gave her an odd look and then started to look over her shoulder, in the direction the undead horde would be approaching from. Then she caught on, too. Her expression morphed into something halfway between afraid and simpering.

Right now, D'Arnot thought he had all the aces. He had the guns, and he had them captive. What he didn't know, and what Denise wasn't about to tell him was, in about ten minutes, he was going to have problems. Big, big problems. Something was coming for them out of the darkness, and when it came, Dr. D'Arnot and his "biological containment" team wouldn't have time to deal with Denise and Cornelia. They'd be too busy fighting for their lives.

"Something in the park? As in, one creature? Or many?"

"Uh, we think there's a group of them. Probably."

"If I were to show you a map of the park, do you think you could pinpoint just where these creatures are?" D'Arnot asked.

That was the kill question. He needed to mop up after his dead agent and collect a specimen. That was his endgame here. If Denise could tell him where the creatures were, D'Arnot wouldn't need her anymore, and she didn't think she'd last more than two seconds after D'Arnot had what he needed to know. She wouldn't last much more than two seconds if he found out too early just how close the creatures were, either.

"Well, we know where they've been. We were tracking them, but no, we don't know where they are right now."

"If you'll excuse me for a moment, Dr. D'Arnot, may I interrupt with a few questions of my own?" Zhang Dong asked. "Something seems off about this."

Denise bit down on her tongue. Dammit. She'd had D'Arnot on the hook. Time to dig in her heels.

"Oh, no. I don't want to speak to you. You killed my friend. D'Arnot, get rid of him."

Zhang Dong smiled. All charm and polish. "I assure you, it will only take a moment to assuage some of my troubling suspicions. You said you were tracking these, shall we say, anomalous creatures. What are you doing out here? We've been here for some time, and we haven't seen anything. You can believe it when I tell you we would have noticed if the creatures you're looking for were here."

"D'Arnot, get this man away from me."

Dr. D'Arnot held up a hand, thinking for a moment. "No, it will be alright. Just answer the question. I will protect you."

Dammit all over hither and yon and back.

"We decided we needed to stock up on ammunition and some other supplies from the depot here." Denise just needed to improvise her story for a few minutes longer. She needed to keep her lies straight and not become tripped up. Seemingly forthcoming and honest. Any other impression would lead to a swift death.

"Mm-hmm. Of course. And I couldn't help but notice the vehicle you arrived in. I drive a Silver Ghost, myself. Rolls Royce. Very comfortable. You, on the other hand, drove up in this garbage scow. An interesting choice. Not something I would choose myself. The game preserve has a large fleet of cars for the rangers. Why aren't you driving one of those?"

"We found a wrecked ranger car at one point. It didn't have the rangers in it. Just some black slime," Denise lied. "We wanted something that was bigger and could take more damage." She watched D'Arnot perk up. Leading the conversation back toward the creatures would get his attention, and start him asking the questions again. It would be better if she could get him back in charge of the questioning. He was smug and complacent. He thought just because he had the upper hand now, things couldn't turn around and bite him. That made him easier to string along.

Zhang Dong took a step closer to the garbage truck. "I can't help but notice this large dent in the side of the truck. A very large dent, indeed. The paint is still rough around the edges, like this occurred recently," he said. He walked right up to the spot where the elephant had slammed into the side of the truck and nearly tipped it over.

Denise looked over at Dr. D'Arnot, and she saw his eyes narrow. His already thin lips thinned more until they were almost nonexistent.

"We had a small accident. We crashed into one of the ranger cars parked in the garage. Silly me," Denise said.

There was a faint rumble in the distance. No one besides Cornelia seemed to notice. Denise resisted the urge to try to look over her shoulder. She wouldn't be able to see anything in the darkness at this point anyway, and it might simply alert her captors that she knew what was coming.

"And all around this dent, I can't help but notice these scratches. Lots of scratches. If I didn't know better, I'd say a lot of these are claw marks."

The rumble in the distance grew a little more distinct. One of Zhang Dong's men looked up for a second, but he didn't know what it was yet, so he dismissed it just as quickly.

"It's a game preserve," Denise said. "Sometimes the animals get a little frisky. They smell something rotting in the trash, and they try to get at it. Those scratches were there when we took the truck out, I guess. I sure didn't notice them at the time."

Zhang Dong turned slowly to face Denise. He stared directly at her. "Now forgive me if these questions seem repetitive, but are you absolutely sure you don't know where those creatures Dr. D'Arnot is looking for are?"

"We have a rough idea, but I couldn't tell you exactly."

Sighing, Zhang Dong turned to D'Arnot. "She's playing us. Look." He pointed to a couple of small smears of black slime stuck to the truck along the edges of the dent. "She's already encountered your creatures, my good Dr. D'Arnot."

"Probably motor oil or something," Denise said, knowing the story was getting thinner and thinner. Soon, the tenuous string would grow too thin and snap altogether.

"Denise, Denise, Denise," Zhang Dong said. "Dr. D'Arnot and his entourage only just arrived here at the game preserve. They haven't had the time or inclination to look over your folder. They don't know who you are. But I know that you know who they are. You are perfectly aware that they aren't with the military, but you asked anyway."

"What are you talking about?" D'Arnot asked.

"Does the phrase 'Malheur Island' mean anything to you, Doctor?"

D'Arnot stood stock still for a moment and then nodded.

"I can tell you it means something to her as well. She's known who you're with before you even started asking her questions."

The distant sound of feet pounding into the earth had amplified into a slow, steady drumbeat. Zhang Dong finally seemed to notice them. He looked up from Denise and out toward the night-cloaked grasslands. He signaled to a couple of his henchmen, and they started walking around the far edge of the building to investigate.

Dr. D'Arnot was too absorbed in the anger clearly brewing up inside him. He glowered at Denise. "So, it would seem my little secret is out. Unfortunate. However, your secret is out in the open now, too. And you must understand that I will have the answers I need from you. One way or the other. Now, tell me, and we can make this quick. Where are the creatures?"

Denise kept her mouth clenched firmly shut as she stared up at Dr. D'Arnot.

The Yersinia scientist tried a different tactic. With visible effort, he folded up his anger at being jerked around and trotted out the kindly benefactor voice he'd used before, as if he hadn't already spent that nickel.

"Listen. I'm here to help. It's very important that you tell me where I can find any infected creatures. They could be rampaging through the park right now. That's thousands of square miles. The sooner you tell me, the sooner my team can eliminate them. People's lives may be at stake. Now, where are they?"

Zhang Dong's men came running back around the far side of the building, sprinting at top speed. The one in front waved his arms and shouted in Mandarin.

A second later, the *Spinosaurus* burst straight through the corrugated tin walls of the supply depot from the other side, spraying equipment and building materials in every direction. The dinosaur snatched the first man up in its claws, raised him up to its giant fangs, and scissored his head off. The body had already thumped down onto the dust by the time the monster caught the next man in its oversized crocodile jaws.

"You asked," Denise said.

D'Arnot's men immediately began firing at the dinosaur. Machine pistols chattered and a couple of jets of burning fuel shot out toward the monster. The flamethrowers fell short but drove the creature back a couple of steps. The machine pistols did nothing but dimple its slimy surface.

"What is that?" D'Arnot asked a second before Denise kicked him in the groin. The Yersinia scientist crumpled up and fell to the ground. In the sudden chaos of the *Spinosaurus*'s arrival, Denise wasn't sure anyone even noticed. No one was paying attention to her anymore.

She scrambled up and over D'Arnot's boneless form and made for the armored vehicles just as the front wave of the undead horde rounded the supply depot behind the dinosaur.

Teeth flashed in the night as the creatures poured forward. Elephants. Game preserve employees. Lions. It looked like just about one of everything on God's green earth was coming at them, but horribly corrupted. The figures slashing out of the darkness looked more like Satan had built an ark and the craft beached itself near the supply depot, actually.

With Cornelia close behind her, Denise slipped away from the center of the scene and into the darkness along the periphery. She didn't have her Nitro Express or revolver anymore, not that they could do much for her in this situation. Without them, she felt naked as the battle exploded around them, though.

Normally, the Yersinia men would have done well for themselves. They had at least an inkling of what to expect, and they'd brought the proper equipment to deal with it. However, they hadn't been expecting an attack, so they were poorly positioned to bring all their firepower to bear, and the creatures had the element of surprise.

Plus, no one had been expecting to deal with forty feet of angry dinosaur. At some point, even the best laid plans of mice and men fell apart, but they tended to not so much fall apart as crumble down to their individual atoms and then catch fire when a giant dinosaur appeared in the middle of the playing field.

Of course, then again, that had been Denise's plan all along. Sometimes, it was the most haphazardly laid plans of mice and women that succeeded the best.

They couldn't stay here long, though. Either the Yersinia cleanup crew or their Triad business partners or the monsters would get them sooner or later. It was well past time to get out of here.

Denise angled around to the closest of the armored cars and pulled the driver's door open. A very surprised man in heavy, dark armor stared at her. He lunged for the pistol sitting on the seat next to him.

Before he could grab it, Denise grabbed a fistful of his collar and pulled. The man was already off balance and leaning down to grab the weapon. Denise's grip simply served as a sort of last minute course correction. The man's face smashed into the steering column, and the armored car's horn beeped.

The man tried to jerk back, blood fountaining from his nose, but Denise wrenched him out of his seat and threw him onto the ground. She hauled herself into the vehicle and grabbed the pistol for herself. It wasn't much, but it was something. Then she looked up.

Oh, *hell* yeah.

The top of the armored car had been scooped away to make way for a turret. Someone could stand behind the driver and fire the weapon at anything that got too close. In this case, the more usual machine gun had been dismounted and replaced with a flamethrower. A sunny little pilot flame waved at her.

"Don't mind if I do," she said to herself. "Cornelia, you drive." She handed the Yersinia man's pistol over.

A second later, they were moving. Nearby, the driver she'd stolen the vehicle from was shouting at a couple of Yersinia men and pointing at the fleeing war machine. The two Yersinia men turned their machine pistols toward the armored car.

Denise squeezed the trigger and an arc of burning fire caught all three of the men in its embrace. They disappeared in the burst of orange. Denise could see a tangle of blackening shapes in the flames for a second before they fell to the ground.

Behind them, the remaining Triads had caught the worst of the attack. They were standing nearest to the edge of the building and had the least time to react when hundreds of abominations suddenly appeared out of the darkness right next to them. Most of them had already been torn apart. A few were already splashed with enough slime to start to get up again.

Denise couldn't see Zhang Dong anywhere, but she was sure he was around. The flamethrower was ready if she spotted him.

Screw that guy.

With a pointy stick.

In the eye.

She watched as Dr. D'Arnot tried to scramble away on his hands and knees, trying to back away from a pair of rotting hyenas. The two creatures circled around to either side of the man, their teeth showing through what was left of their cheeks. D'Arnot scooted backwards until his back smacked up against something. It was the gooey leg of the *Spinosaurus*. The Yersinia scientist tried to lunge away, but he was stuck like a bug on flypaper. Tendrils of black slime wrapped around him and sucked the screaming man inside the dinosaur's mass.

"We need some place to go," Cornelia said. Behind them, the Yersinia team was pulling up stakes. They realized that they couldn't stay where they were. Engines roared to life. Headlights flashed. Flamethrowers spewed sizzling death.

But almost a quarter of their people had already gone down, and the rest were scrambling to get out of the way of the *Spinosaurus* and its companions. The armored cars belched to life and started moving. Anyone who hadn't already grabbed a seat was left behind and swiftly devoured.

She checked the rear of the armored car, looking for anything that might be useful. The bed was filled with a couple of crates of military-grade explosives. They basically looked like more sophisticated versions of the jury-rigged naval mine they'd confiscated from the Triad camp.

Denise turned around to ask Cornelia about the explosives when the back doors of the armored car swung open, and Zhang Dong piled in. He gripped a knife in one hand, and he swung it around as he scrabbled inside. He must have grabbed onto the back of the vehicle as it started to move and clung there until he could make his way inside.

Denise tried to back away, but her shoulder blades smacked into the flamethrower harness. Before she could duck back, Zhang Dong's knife found its way into her upper arm. The blade was cold going into her arm. Then the sensation turned into blistering, white-hot pain. Every thought and concern in Denise's brain compressed into a tiny ball and bounced right out of her skull.

She tried to push Zhang away, but it was hard in the vehicle's narrow confines. The knife simply ended up grating against her bone. Denise gasped, and then Zhang pulled the knife out of her arm, a sensation just as unpleasant as the knife going in.

Her first reaction was to step away from him, but there was nowhere to go inside the car. She stepped forward instead, moving into Zhang's space. He had just as little room to maneuver, and the tight confines made it harder for him to bring his knife back around.

He swung at her again, aiming for her neck this time. She ducked forward and slammed her forehead into his nose. There was a satisfying crack, and warm, red moisture ran down his face. Instead of sinking into her throat, Zhang's forearm smacked against the side of her neck, the knife stuck in the air where her neck a second earlier. Denise gagged, but she was alive.

Zhang Dong recoiled and bounced up against the armored vehicle's interior wall. Denise gritted her teeth. Her forehead stung, and it felt like a colony of fire ants was excavating a new nest in her arm. With her good arm, she grabbed Zhang under the chin and smashed the back of his head into the side of the car as hard as she could. She repeated the process until he went limp. Then she did it a couple more times for good measure, each thump sending a resounding pain through her bad arm. Releasing her grip, she let him slide down to the floor, unconscious.

Cornelia had the pistol in her hand, trying to aim it while half-twisted around and bouncing up and down on the rutted road. "Glad you got him. I didn't want to try shooting anything like this."

"How's my arm look?" Denise asked.

"Painful."

"I hope your nursing classes weren't expensive. It is. Will it be hard to fix, though?"

"Probably not. Some stitches and going easy on it will take care of most of the problem. You'll have a scar and a cool story for the grandkids. Maybe a little decreased mobility if you do anything too crazy with it. I can take care of the stitches when we get somewhere with a first-aid box."

"Thanks."

"You going to throw him out the back?" Cornelia bobbed her head in Zhang Dong's direction.

"Tempting, but I won't. He'd die."

"He'd do it to us. He did it to Skipworth."

"Yeah, well maybe my big problem in life is just that I haven't sunk to his level of depravity yet. I'll tie him up, and he'll be harmless. We'll only kill him if we have to."

"Fine. Here's the pistol. I can't aim it and drive, and if I could, I'd shoot him."

"Thanks." Denise took the weapon and moved to the back of the armored car to close the gaping doors.

Behind them, the remaining armored cars locked onto their taillights and started following. Behind *them*, the army of monsters gave chase. Yersinia's flamethrowers had taken a toll on the creatures' ranks, but they were still legion. Even with the flame weapons, Denise wasn't sure that the bioresearch company's hired goons would survive another onslaught from the host of monsters.

And Denise and Cornelia wouldn't survive a concerted attack from the remaining Yersinia team, let alone a surge from the creatures. Thus, they were at the front of an insane parade, like one of those educational food chain diagrams that showed the little fish about to be eaten by a bigger fish that was in turn about to be eaten by a shark. Those were a simple way to explain the circle of life to children. It was less fun when Denise knew she was the little fish in the equation.

Cornelia checked her mirrors and reached the same conclusion. "They're following us. We need to find someplace we can hole up. I could outrun the creatures, but Yersinia will be able to keep pace with me. I say we make a break for the villages and try to get to a real town. It's the only place we'll be safe." She started to bank the vehicle back in the direction of the visitor center to leave the park.

"No, wait," Denise said, experiencing an epiphany. It was a dumb epiphany, one that should have had "BAD IDEA" stamped right on the box. It was the kind of idea that made liability lawyers salivate. "Go straight instead."

Cornelia's idea was probably the better one. Get to safety and get help. Smart woman. However, that would leave the creatures inside the park for hours. Maybe days until the military first believed their story and then gathered the necessary resources to fight the monsters. In that amount of time, the number of creatures loose in the game preserve would only increase. Worse yet, they'd probably follow the armored cars and end up smack in the middle of the nearby villages.

"There isn't anyone who can help us straight ahead. It's just the mountains."

"We're going to help ourselves," Denise said as she tore up Zhang Dong's shirt to make some strips. She started tying him up with the remains of the shirt, but she saved one rag to tie around her wounded arm as a bandage. The slice Zhang took out of her made her gnash her teeth every time the vehicle hit a rut.

Cornelia looked over her shoulder to Denise. "We've got a bioweapon manufacturer's private army and monsters from the ninth circle of hell following us. You want to unpack this plan a little for me?"

Denise reached into one of the crates in the back if the car and pulled out a detonator. She waggled the device in her fingers. Behind them, the monsters soon dropped out of sight as the armored car sped away. The Yersinia team remained behind them, kicking up clouds of dust, though.

"Head for the Verschoor Dam. We're going to do something stupid."

FIFTEEN

SOMETHING STUPID

The armored car swung up the switchback roads, traveling ever upward. Tires screeched on the pavement as Cornelia took the road far too fast for any reasonable person. In the predawn darkness, the road unfolded in front of them like a huge, black snake.

Behind them, nine Yersinia vehicles raced up the side of the mountain behind them. Denise and Cornelia had been able to open up a little room between themselves and the Yersinia team on the trek up the mountain. Cornelia knew the curves and crests, and the pursuing vehicles did not. She could take the road faster, knowing what was ahead.

There was no sign of the creatures yet. The armored cars had outpaced them a long time ago. They were somewhere a few miles back still heading this way, following the promise of fresh meat as long as it took. By now, a lot of the Yersinia team was among their hungry ranks.

Denise couldn't worry about that right now, though. Instead, she already had plenty on her plate.

Zhang Dong was awake. She had to undo the gag she'd wrapped around his mouth because he threw up almost as soon as he was conscious again. Head trauma had a way of taking the fight right out of folks. Even though he was with them again, he hadn't said very much, and he'd fallen unconscious again at one point. He probably had a concussion. When he was conscious, he tended to mumble to himself in a mixture of English, Mandarin, and Italian. Denise wondered just how in the world someone like him had ended up in charge of a Triad poaching operation.

The pain in her arm had receded to something she could at least deal with. She'd taken her jacket off because the sleeve had become tacky with blood and was starting to stick to the wound. Every time Cornelia hit a bump, the stab wound still throbbed and threatened to gush fresh blood. There were a lot of bumps in the road.

Denise had something to keep her occupied, though. She'd taken one of the boxes of detonators and explosives and gone to work. Everything came with instructions, and anything that would get them blown to pieces prematurely was pointed out in big, red letters in the guide. Plus, Cornelia had glanced back and signed off that everything was set up properly, and Denise trusted her just as much as the instructions.

Now, she had a whole lot of timed explosives primed and ready to go. There were a few things she could do with them. Setting the timers and lobbing them out the back of the armored car would effectively create booby traps for the Yersinia men. But there was no guarantee she'd get the timing right. The charges might go off only after the armored cars had already passed by. Alternatively, she could push them all out at once and try to crater the road or cause a rockslide, making the path behind them unpassable.

She had something similar in mind. There was no surety that a rockslide would completely block the road. It might only slow the other vehicles down, and she would need time to set up the next phase of her plan. Having Yersinia's monkeys hop on her back again would only cause problems. She wanted to make sure nobody would interrupt her preparations for a good, long while.

"We're almost there," Cornelia said. "Ready?"

"Yeah. Just park us a little bit across and help me set up."

Cornelia rounded another corner, and they immediately found themselves rumbling across a short, latticework bridge. The bridge crossed a narrow but steep chasm. Directly below the bridge, there was a precipitous, two-hundred-foot drop down the sheer rock face before the slope rolled away down toward the foothills.

The armored car braked to a halt, and Denise hopped out the back doors. Cornelia popped out of the driver seat and helped her carry a crate of explosives over to the bridge. The strain made Denise's arm cry out, but she dragged it to the edge of the bridge supports anyway. They didn't have long before the Yersinia team showed up, hot on their tail.

Denise slapped first one charge and then another to the crisscrossing wood and metal support beams. She went down one side of the bridge while Cornelia took the other side. The military-grade explosives went in cracks and crevices, tucked anywhere within easy reach that looked like it was structurally important. Wires led out of each explosive, all of them trailing back to a plunger at the far side of the bridge.

After placing most of the explosives, Denise heard the roar of engines emanating from further down the side of the mountain. The noise grew louder and louder as the armored cars chugged up the incline and navigated the sharp turns. Denise dropped the last remaining explosives in her arms near the center of the bridge and ran back to their own hijacked vehicle.

Beating Cornelia by a couple of steps, she snatched up the plunger and ducked behind the armored vehicle for cover. "Care to do the honors?" Denise asked, offering the plunger to Cornelia.

"No, be my guest," she said as the engine noise revved up to the roar of an angry beast.

The first of the Yersinia vehicles rounded the final curve and accelerated forward before the driver noticed his prey sitting parked on the far side of the bridge. Surprised by the blind curve, he slammed on the brakes to avoid crashing directly into Denise's stolen vehicle.

The sudden braking caused a chain reaction. The second car rounded the bend only to see the first car braking. They bumped into the rear of the first car about halfway across the bridge, and the third car slewed into them.

A slight gap between the third and four car prevented the rest of the convoy from snarling up. They stopped short of the bridge, caught in a single file line along the narrow road. Yersinia personnel started to emerge from the first few vehicles, getting ready to rush up close and finish the job. At the very last second, a couple of them noticed the cables leading to various points around the bridge, and they shot back inside the armored cars and tried to reverse their way through their comrades and get off the bridge.

Denise pulled the plunger down. The night turned into a brilliant chiaroscuro painting for a moment. The center of the bridge was cast in intense light. Everywhere the light could not reach, the shadows turned as black as Satan's heart.

Parked almost directly over the bundle of explosives Denise had dropped, the forward most car simply ceased to exist. Pieces of flanged metal and shattered bone buried themselves into the side of the mountain. The second car rolled away from the blast, flipping across the bridge like a Russian tumbler, rolling right over its crew. Its flamethrower fuel supply ruptured, and the interior burst into flames as it spilled over the side of the side of the bridge, cascading downward in a streak of fire.

The last car on the bridge might have made it. It was furthest away from the epicenter of the blast. The explosion rocked it back on its rear wheels, but it bounced back down with only minimal damage to the vehicle itself, even if the man standing in the flamethrower turret had been sheared in half.

Then the bridge started to collapse. With the middle blown out and most of its supports weakened or snapped, the bridge buckled in the center. The anchors tethering it to the rock groaned and plunged inward.

Panicking, the driver of the third vehicle jammed on the accelerator and threw the car into reverse. Tires shrieked like demons as they tried to find purchase on the growing incline. The bridge sagged. The howling engine fought gravity to a standstill.

Then the stress simply grew too great, and the moorings snapped completely away from the road. The bridge folded up on itself and crashed down the side of the mountain. Timbers and girders snapped or knotted themselves into a shape Gordias himself would never be able to untie. The armored car went with the bridge, caught in the collapsing spider web of girders.

Smashing into the ground below, the inextricably tangled mass started to slide down the side of the mountain. Suddenly, a secondary explosion lit up the pre-dawn night. Even from hundreds of feet away, the blast rattled the ground under Denise's feet and smote her ears. The entire mountain seemed to shudder a little as a hot blast of wind hit Denise a second later.

Denise ducked back inside her own vehicle as gravel started to pelt down from the sky. One of the other armored cars, probably the one that caught fire, must have contained explosives, too. Small, jagged rocks plunged out of the sky and pattered against the roof of the armored car.

On the other side of the chasm, the remaining Yersinia men stared in disbelief at the spot where their colleagues had been standing just a few seconds before. Now there was nothing left but a yawning gap and a few ragged stumps of bent steel where the bridge detached itself.

The fourth car, suddenly finding itself in the lead, started to back up. The vehicles were too wide to travel in anything but single file, and they couldn't turn around on the thin strip of asphalt leading up the side of the mountain.

Driving up the road, with its curves and switches, was a test of driving skill. Driving down, in reverse, as a convoy, would take at least half an hour. Maybe more if one or more of the drivers had difficulties.

Denise wasn't under any illusions. She hoped they would give up. It would be nice if they gave up. She didn't think it would happen, though. Yersinia still had more people and more equipment. They had the upper hand in any sort of stand-up fight. All they needed was five minutes on favorable ground, and they would have eliminated the key witnesses. She knew it, and they knew it. The trick was to deny them that favorable ground.

There were two other ways up to the top of the dam. The first was an elevator that ran up the side of the dam so staff could quickly access the control room. The second was a metal staircase that ran all the way down the side of the mountain, built in case power ever cut off to the elevator. While the dam was only about one hundred feet tall, it only had to block off a particular pass between two peaks. The staircase was over a two thousand feet from top to bottom. It went from the top of the dam, down to the base, and then all the way down to the river banks below, switching back and forth as it went.

Denise guessed they'd try the elevator first. The stairs were an arduous journey that took forever and would exhaust anyone wearing thick armor. Plus, it was completely open, even if they did try to mount the stairs, they didn't know what sort of weapons she and Cornelia had. In reality, all they had between them was the lone pistol, but a good rifle would make short work or anyone attempting the stairs. She and Cornelia would hole up in the control room and wait for the second part of her plan to swing into motion.

Driving up to the end of the road, Cornelia parked their armored car outside the dam's entrance. The door to the control center was locked. Cornelia shot it open while Denise opened the back doors and dragged Zhang Dong out of the armored car. For a moment, she imagined herself dragging him over to the edge of the dam and dumping him over. Letting him splatter on the concrete a hundred feet below would be satisfying, but it wasn't in Denise to simply murder the man.

Zhang Dong's senses had come back to him. Maybe the explosions at the bridge snapped his brain back into place.

"I'm still alive? Surprising. I say, the throbbing in my head almost makes me wish I wasn't."

"That could still be arranged, if you'd like," Denise said. The front of his shirt was still encrusted with vomit. She grabbed him by the back of the collar instead and marched him out the back of the vehicle.

"No, that's quite alright."

"So, did Yersinia tell you what all is going on here? Do you know what their plans are?"

"Are you trying to, what is the term, soak me for information?"

"That's right. Don't you hate it when the turntables do that?"

"Indeed," Zhang Dong said stiffly.

Denise led her captive inside the dam's central control room. There was no one else here at this time of night. Hopefully, this would all be over soon and she could simply hand Zhang Dong over to the proper authorities, and he could go rot in a cage somewhere. Just so long as he wasn't her problem anymore. If it meant saving her own hide, she'd let Yersinia have him again, though. Staying alive was more important than justice tonight.

She plopped him in a chair in the corner. It squeaked like a dying mouse as his weight came down on it. Lower down in the dam, turbines thrummed as water spilled through them. The gentle white noise should have been soothing, but Denise didn't like that it would make it harder to hear more subtle sounds.

"Alright," Denise said. "I understand why Yersinia is here. They want the slime from Sulfur Springs so they can go back to their freak lab and freakify up some monsters. The highest bidder can have some monster cavalry for the next war. First, they have to clean up the mess their man created, though."

"That is the cut of their jib, yes."

"And you and your people were there to serve as the point men and help Yersinia pull it off."

"Well, I might characterize it a little differently."

"Oh really? And just how would you characterize it?"

"The same way I try to structure everything in my life. As a business transaction."

"Right. Just like how killing our friend was part of a business transaction."

"Ah, but it was. We entered into a mutually beneficial relationship. I protected him from his creditors. He helped me make money. I made it very clear when we entered that relationship that the consequences of breaching our contract would be quite dire."

"Using him to make money. And then you murdered him in cold blood. There's more to life than money."

"Please. I hardly need a sermon from the likes of you," Zhang Dong said. "As I said before, I read your file. You were making huge sums of money as a professional hunter, then you quit. Now you're here, making a pittance in comparison."

"It's enough. I have what I need, and I get to do something important. Not that you'd understand. You've been killing some of the rarest animals in the world just to turn a quick profit. Don't you ever think about the future?"

"Posh. People have been killing these very animals for eons. Suddenly, you want to accuse me of some moral depravity for doing the same thing at a good price. You're the one assigning morality to something that no one raised an eyebrow at a couple of generations ago."

"There were a lot more of these animals a couple of generations ago than there are now. If we don't keep people like you out, there won't be any more by the time the next couple of generations roll around."

"There you go again, so concerned about the future. Ten years from now. A hundred years from now. A thousand. It doesn't matter."

"You're obviously an educated man. How can you say the future doesn't matter?"

"How can you say it does? Have you paid attention to Russia lately? Twenty years ago, the czars were at the height of their powers. Wealth. Status. Connections. A history spanning back hundreds of years. Utterly in control of their state."

"Don't change the subject."

"I am not changing the subject. Pay attention. The czars were seated firmly in Moscow, and then the Great War broke out. By the end of the conflict, the Romanovs were all dead, summarily murdered by people who had seized power over the ruling dynasty's political miscalculations. Miscalculations that no one could see until it was too late, and the pieces had been swept from the board."

"I'm pretty sure you're changing the subject."

"And I'm quite sure I'm not. Consider the Mongols. Genghis Khan and his descendants cut a swath through Asia and created the largest contiguous land empire the world has ever known. He cut a swathe elsewhere, too. They estimate that about eight percent of all the people living in the former Mongol-controlled territories are related to him. That's approaching one percent of the entire world's population.

"They expanded out of Mongolia and into my native China, founding the Yuan Dynasty. They conquered much of central Asia. They ravaged Russia, the same country that would lose its czars to the communists half a millennium later.

"Yet, where are the great Mongol dynasties today? One of the greatest feats of military prowess in all of history, and in just a few short generations, it was all for naught. The Yuan Dynasty was overthrown by the Ming Dynasty, headed by native Chinese. Then the Ming Dynasty was defeated by invading Manchus, and gave way to the Qing Dynasty. And then the Qing Dynasty was all but conquered by the European powers, and it gave way to the current Chinese Republic, which is so riddled with warlords and petty incompetence that it's not long for this world. And of course, that's ignoring all the dynasties that came before the Mongols."

"I think I see where you're trying to go with this. I'm not buying it, though."

"Shall I provide more examples? Alexander the Great. From the western perspective at the time, he conquered the known world. The mightiest empire the world had ever known at the time. It even conquered the Greeks, themselves the heights of progress. Then he died. The ripe old age of thirty-two. All those ambitions and plans for the future he no doubt had? Poof. Gone. No more future. His empire crumbled. In a few generations, the blink of an eye, the maps were completely unrecognizable from the one he forged."

"Life's unpredictable. That doesn't excuse what you're doing. Still not buying it."

"Not buying it? What, that everything must someday fall into the ash heap of history? That all must end? That the future is a promise that never comes? Consider something closer to home. The British Empire is the largest in our so-called modern world. It stretches from hemisphere to hemisphere. The sun never sets on the British Empire, as they are so fond of saying."

"I'm familiar with basic geography, thank you. The problem I have is--"

"But look at South Africa. Right here in front of us. One of the many lands under the British dominion. You want to protect its future?"

"I'd like to do my part, which is a hell of a lot more than you're doing."

"Consider this, though. What percentage of the population here is white? Something on the order of twenty percent? Yes, I believe that's right. And blacks? Roughly the opposite. Eighty percent of the population and twenty percent of the land and banned from careers of any influence. I believe the only black people hired anywhere in this park were the ones under my employment. And let's not forget that parts of the Boer population resent British rule. They'd like to be an independent country. Does that sound like a stable system to you? Left to its own devices, would the cherished Empire continue to run, or would it fly apart into a thousand constituent parts?"

"I don't always care for my government's policies, but I'm not here to discuss political science with you. Things fall apart. The center cannot hold. I get it."

"Hmmph. W.B. Yeats. I'm impressed. A lovely poem. I think it only adds to my point, though."

"Here's the part where you're wrong, though. Yeah, sure. Things change. Sometimes for the worse. Everything has an end. Countries. Policies. Everything. Sometimes it's a good thing when they end, even. That doesn't mean it's not worth it to try to protect and preserve some of the best things. Even if they're vulnerable to disappearing into the past. Especially if they're vulnerable to disappearing into the past."

"There once was a time when I thought like you did. I was a man on the up and up. I'd studied economics at Oxford. I had a wife and two beautiful little daughters. Then one day, the train they were on hit a truck stalled on the tracks. Their carriage flipped over, and they died. I was lost for a time. The future that I'd dreamed of, that I'd been planning for, that I'd carefully pruned and cultivated, was proved an illusion in a single shattering minute."

"I'm sorry. You're still a huge asshole, but I'm sorry about that."

"That's when I realized that what really matters in life is the here and now. Worrying about what will happen in twenty years is a game for fools. About what will happen in a hundred years, all the more so. If I drive the creatures here extinct, what of it? By the time I die of old age, South Africa will be ruled by the blacks who live here after an uprising. Or the Boers. Or some other European power. Or maybe still the British, if they're lucky. The point is, it will be an issue for someone else. If I make it my duty to try to keep things as they are, I will only be disappointed, and so will you."

"You can't just live your life like there won't be consequences down the road. If everyone did that, the world would go straight down the toilet."

"The world, as you so eloquently put it, is always going straight down the toilet. That is the point. And for your erudition, I do not live as if there are no consequences to anything. That is why I so enjoy contracts and transactions. I set the rules and consequences and parameters. Your friend Dr. Skipworth understood the rules and consequences of turning against me, and yet he did it anyway. Do you also now accuse him of not thinking about the future? At least I have the good sense not to fight against things I cannot change. I merely try to shape the things I can, and I always try to shape them to my current advantage. This future you seem so intent on protecting will be different from anything you planned, regardless of your actions, and it will continue to unfold without you after you are gone, probably in ways you wouldn't approve of."

"That still doesn't mean we should all just throw up our hands and let the whole thing burn down around us."

"I regret to inform you, but it's already on fire. The only question is whether you have a route to the exit or whether you'll burn with everything else," Zhang Dong said.

Cornelia had walked up to observe the exchange. She frowned as the Triad leader fell silent. "Alright, Voltaire. That's enough philosophy for now. You can take some time to enjoy the here and now, because your butt is going to be in prison in the not-too-distant future. I want to know a couple of more practical things than how you justify massacring all the fluffy bunnies in the game preserve."

"For your information, I do not 'massacre fluffy bunnies.' I run a highly sophisticated organization encompassing dozens of--"

"Uh-huh. Don't care. What's with all the explosives?" Cornelia asked.

"Which explosives?"

"Well, Yersinia has a whole bunch of crates of military explosives. We also found a modified naval mine in your hunting camp."

"I think it should be obvious. Yersinia Bioresearch is currently engaged in something they're calling Plan C. It's not a very creative naming system, I'm afraid. In its basest essence, Plan A was to insert a man into Sulfur Springs and recover him along with the samples he took. In the event something went wrong, they would move on to Plan B, eliminating the witnesses and cleaning up any small containment breach."

"Let me guess," Denise said. "Plan C was the backup in case everything went to hell."

"Indeed. It was. If something like, well, *this* happened, my men and I were to assist Yersinia in burning the park down. A splash of gasoline in the dry grass and a small explosive charge. We were supposed to start hundreds of fires over the course of the night. Then you bumbled into our midst."

"Burning down the entire park. Wouldn't that wreck your poaching business?"

"Clearly. There wouldn't be anything left to hunt if we simply incinerated every living thing here. I didn't say I was thrilled about that possible outcome, but I was aware of it. It was in the verbal contract between myself and Yersinia. They paid well enough that I was willing to take a risk. Clearly, I misinterpreted the odds, but then again, I was never counting on job security into perpetuity."

"Do you think Yersinia will keep trying, even with the losses they've taken?" Cornelia asked. "Because I could really stand to have them off our back."

"Of course they will. They know that leaving the situation as it is would leave a mess at their door in short order. They're already under threat from the League of Nations and half a dozen major lawsuits since some of their operations came to light. Leaving their fingerprints all over this would be the final nail, so to speak. They won't stop, not while they still think they can win."

"I guess we'll just have to convince them they can't," Denise said.

"You'll have to burn down the park anyway. Those creatures are still loose."

"I think maybe we can come up with some alternatives."

SIXTEEN

DAM IT

"How's that look?" Denise asked.

"It'll slow them down, but it won't stop them," Cornelia said.

"That's the plan." Denise wiped some of the grease off her hands. The elevator running up the side of the dam was temporarily out of commission, its gears jammed. They'd thrown some equipment in there, which would take a while to pry out, but it was doable.

At least, that's what Denise and Cornelia were hoping the Yersinia team would think. With only one pistol between them, the two of them couldn't do much to defend the stairs leading up the side of the mountain. The stairs looked formidable, though. Open. No cover. No way to tell if Denise and Cornelia had a rifle.

What Denise really wanted was for Yersinia to take the elevator. She just had to fix it up so that it looked like she wanted exactly the opposite.

The equipment jammed in the gears would make it look like they tried to block off access but failed. Right now, Yersinia knew they'd had their nose bloodied. Denise needed to make sure they thought they had the advantage again, to convince them there was a path of least resistance. By fixing the elevator, victory would be within their grasp.

It was right when people believed they were on the verge of winning that they took their eyes off the ball. With the elevator cleared of debris, Yersinia could ride right up to the dam's control room and meet Denise and Cornelia with overwhelming force. The delaying tactic of jamming the elevator would be overcome, and the risks of taking the stairwell mitigated.

A simple plan. A good plan. The wrong plan.

"Alright, I think that's the best we can do. Now we just have to wait for Yersinia and our other guests." Denise had to remember that Yersinia wasn't their only problem. The men in the armored cars and black armor would get here first, and they'd be more than happy to kill Denise and Cornelia. The bigger problem, literally and metaphorically, was the undead dinosaur and its army of ghouls.

The trick would be to deal with that second problem, which would be fast approaching from the south. The horde of transmogrified monsters would be moving from the supply deport up toward the dam, roughly following the course of the river. They'd be arriving before dawn finally cracked over the horizon.

Denise looked back over her shoulder. There were plumes of dust rising up into the night sky. That would be the Yersinia men. They'd made poor progress creeping backwards down the side of the mountain. It was a shame they hadn't gotten really tangled up and arrived at the same time as the creatures, allowing all Denise's problems to eliminate themselves at once. Later than expected wasn't a bad thing, though. She could live with that.

"Time to get out of here," she said. They both took off as fast as they could up the stairs. The stitches Cornelia had put in Denise's arm stung, but she ignored the throb of pain that hit her each time she jostled up a step. Speed was more important than comfort right now.

By the time they'd reached the top of the stairs, they were both sweaty and out of breath. Cornelia's blonde hair was stuck to her forehead, and she was sucking in air. Dirt and powder marks covered her face and hands, and she'd acquired a series of scratches all over her exposed skin. Her ranger uniform was torn and equally dirty. Denise knew she probably didn't look much better. They both looked like they'd been rolled through a construction pit. It had been a very long night.

Denise looked up at the sky. Dawn was approaching. The night's darkest hours had passed. Hopefully, that was some kind of sign. More likely, it just meant she'd been up for far too long and seen far too much.

Looking down, she saw the Yersinia vehicles pull to a stop where the road ended at the base of the mountain. The men hopped out of their armored cars and started looking around, mindful that they'd already been surprised a couple of times that night.

Their vehicles sat parked not far from a series of short waterfalls leading out of the foothills and up to the dam, the source of the river. The staircase led all the way down to not far from where they were parked, but the elevator lay significantly higher up, near the base of the dam.

Denise picked up a set of binoculars she'd found in the dam's control room and watched the group get organized. The one in charge was a giant of a man, his head shaved bald. He was looking at a park map, getting his bearings and trying to decide what to do next.

He gestured to a cluster of his men and said something. Denise couldn't make out the words from up at the top of the dam, but the order was clear regardless. The men went off to lurk near the base of the staircase. They didn't bother to go up it; they simply found spots near the base that offered a modicum of cover. They were there to make sure Denise and Cornelia didn't try to escape when the main group flushed them out of the control center.

Then he made the decision Denise had been counting on the whole time. He looked up at the imposing and open staircase, something like a combination of a New York City fire escape and a grueling mountain path, and then he beckoned the rest of his men up the path toward the dam's elevator.

They moved smartly, forming tight little clusters and keeping their eyes on the bushes. If Denise and Cornelia had laid booby traps along the path, any explosion would only hit an individual group, and an ambush would be torn to shreds from multiple different angles of crossfire before it even began.

Right now, the Yersinia team didn't know exactly where the two of them were, but they were assuming that Denise and Cornelia were in the control room because it was the most defensible place. Only a couple of entrances. Thick walls. Room for cover. It's what they would do.

If Denise had more people to help defend the area, it's what she would have done, too. A good plan. A simple plan. The wrong plan. She knew perfectly well that just the two of them couldn't hole up in the control room and expect to live, not with just a pistol.

Yersinia would be thinking the same thing. Everybody was trying to keep a couple of steps ahead of everyone else on what amounted to a very small chessboard. Time to confirm their suspicions. Let them think they were that extra step ahead.

She leaned over the far edge of the dam and fired a bullet from their pistol down at the approaching men. Denise didn't bother to take careful aim. From this distance, they were out of range. Hitting anything would be a matter of chance.

She squeezed the trigger and then ducked back down behind the concrete retaining wall that rimmed the top of the dam. The response was immediate. Dozens of rounds from the machine pistols below peppered the dam. A few of them came close. Most of them didn't. They smacked into the poured concrete face of the dam, sending crumbles of dust and flatted brass down to the earth, or they shot by overhead. Denise could have paraded around at the top of the dam for a full minute, and the odds were long that anybody could hit her from where they were.

There was no need to, though. Now, Yersinia knew for sure they were at the top of the dam. They also thought they knew for sure that they were panicking and firing from well out of range. She could almost imagine the huge bald man smiling, deciding they were trapped like cats in a tree they were about to set on fire.

Now the waiting began. Denise and Cornelia didn't have any rifles, but neither did Yersinia. They'd brought weapons for close-up, dirty fighting. Machine pistols and flamethrowers. Those were good choices for dealing with monsters, but they couldn't do much in this situation. Someone would have to get close to make anything happen.

"Think it's working?" Cornelia asked. She had a special map of the park in her hands. Huge swathes of land were marked in red, with smaller sections in yellow. The rest was green. Ranger Station Thirteen sat squarely in a green section. The visitor center lay in a red area. Ranger Station Two, the supply depot, lay in a yellow area.

"They're doing about like we expected," Denise said. She peeked over the edge of the dam again. The river ran off into the night, a slit in the dark landscape leading toward the horizon. Her eyes followed the water.

Nearby was Ranger Station Thirteen, a couple of lights blazing inside. Most of its staff were already gone. Hartzell and Planck and Matheson and Ritter and Crane and De Hoog and Kirkeberg. All dead. With Denise and Cornelia out here on the dam, there were only a few people left to man the station. The last anyone there knew, Denise, Cornelia, Kirkeberg, and Skipworth had gone out to investigate why the police convoy was late. They probably thought everyone was dead. If Denise had miscalculated here, they might even be right in an hour.

Further out, she could see the remains of the visitor center. Normally, it would also have a few lights blazing, even at this hour. Right now, it was only illuminated by the last guttering flames from the fire Denise had set earlier in the night. The building's neat angles and modern design had been reduced to a barely standing pile of mixed rubbish. Entire walls had collapsed, and the building looked like it was in danger of falling in on itself.

One thing Denise couldn't see was the entrance to Sulfur Springs. The dark crevice lay in a green area on Cornelia's map. It lay just on the far side of the pass, essentially around the corner from the staircase up to the dam. Strange to think that this whole incident had started so close by, ranged all over the park, and now come almost back to where it all began.

Along the river's edge, she could see the dense tangle of vegetation that hid the poacher camp they'd raided earlier that day. Simpler times, like something out of a bygone era. What a difference twelve hours made. The black knots of foliage reminded her of something, though.

She turned to Zhang Dong. They'd brought him up to the top of the dam as well. He was still tied up and still sitting in the squeaky chair. Leaving him in the control room wasn't an option, even if he couldn't do much in his current state.

"Something still doesn't make sense to me," Denise said, turning to him.

"The meaning of life? How they put toothpaste in the tube? How plesiosaurs mated? I'm not in the mood to speculate with you," he spat out.

"Do you practice being insufferable in a mirror? Or is there some sort of self-help book on the topic?"

"It's a gift. I'm a man of many talents."

"Aside from your amazing skills, I wanted to know about something else."

"I can already tell that I won't be able to dissuade you from asking."

"At your camp by the river, we found a naval mine. Someone had heavily modified it to increase its yield, but it obviously wasn't meant to be used against ships anymore. It was more of a gigantic time bomb."

"Ah yes. A special project I commissioned."

"Yeah, about that. Why?"

"Why what?"

"Why make something like that? Yersinia was already going to bring a lot of explosives to help set the park on fire. A whole bunch of little charges spread all over the place, distributed to set the widest swaths of the park on fire. You didn't have any of those smaller explosives. You just had one really big one. It wouldn't be very efficient for starting a fire; it would probably just leave a giant crater. What was it for? In case the creatures got loose and attacked the camp?"

"Nominally, yes. A bomb that size would make a nice last ditch defense in case everything else was lost. The last couple of survivors could set it before being overwhelmed, and then the problem would be neutralized. No one would have to deal with the indignity of being infested with worms and dragged around like a mobile breeding ground, either."

"Nominally? It was nominally for a last ditch defense? Want to explain that for me?"

"Well, consider this. Yersinia Bioresearch has a well-earned reputation for not playing by the agreed-upon rules. Whether those rules are ethical or legal, they have the habit of disregarding them if it suits them."

"That's rich, coming from you."

Zhang Dong scowled. "I don't care for the law any more than they do. I never signed anything agreeing to be bound by it. However, Yersinia and I cut a deal. A deal with clear rules that we both agreed to. I would help them, and they would pay me. Simple. Clean-cut. Beneficial to both parties. I do not like it when someone gives me their word and then changes their mind."

"Like Skipworth."

"Indeed. However, given Yersinia's reputation, I decided to create a small insurance policy."

"Go on."

"It's a simple concept. If they tried to renege, I would hit them where it hurt most. They needed a sample from Sulfur Springs. It's the item at the top of their ledger, the entire reason they are here. But I read the same report they did. I read about the geology of Sulfur Springs."

Cornelia interrupted them. "Hey, there's more dust on the horizon. The creatures found us."

Denise grabbed her binoculars, her thoughts shifting from Zhang Dong's bomb to the new arrivals. Sure enough, Cornelia was right. A large cloud of dust billowed up from the horizon, wider than the one the Yersinia vehicles raised. They were moving roughly parallel to the river, coming straight toward the dam, straight to where they'd been led.

Through her binoculars, the monsters were mostly just a darker blotch moving across the dark landscape. The only thing she could clearly make out was the *Spinosaurus* at the front of the group, dripping vile liquid blackness. All the other monsters were simply a sea of indistinct, roiling movement, like a swarm of cockroaches moving across the dirt.

Kirkeberg was down in that mass somewhere. So was Skipworth. They were one with the worms now, part of the ravenous hive mind. The thought made Denise's stomach clench up.

"They're earlier than I was expecting," she said.

"Is that going to be a problem?"

"I'm not sure yet." Denise looked down at the base of the dam. The Yersinia men had also noticed the cloud of dust on the horizon. There was a great deal of pointing and gesticulating. No one down there wanted to be caught in another situation where they were boxed in by the monsters.

Someone summoned the huge bald man from the base of the elevator, and he came to look with a set of binoculars of his own. He put the binoculars down and looked thoughtful.

Denise held her breath. She needed Yersinia to stay right here at the dam. If they left now, her plan might still be able to do a little something about the creatures, but she wouldn't know where the corporate mercenaries had gone. She had to deal with them sooner, or they'd deal with her later.

The bald man slapped his underling on the shoulder and said something. Probably along the lines of keeping an eye on the approaching creatures. Then he turned around and marched purposefully back toward the elevator.

Denise breathed a little sigh of relief. They must be close to unblocking the gears. A few minutes later, a little ripple of excitement went through the men gathered around the elevator. One of them held up a bent and mashed wrench, finally pried out of the works.

"We should get off the dam now," Denise said as the Yersinia men started to step into the elevator. Their hulking leader was the first inside the compartment, but it was wide enough to fit many more of them. The elevator was designed to haul heavy equipment up and down from the control room, including massive spare parts for the turbines. Another whole squad of them probably could have fit aboard.

Their commander left a couple of men near the base of the elevator to keep watch on the approaching creatures. He also left the team at the base of the staircase in case Denise and Cornelia tried to make their escape that way. Denise caught a big grin on the man's face just before the elevator doors closed.

Time to go.

Instead of making for the control room or the staircase, Denise and Cornelia started moving up the side of the mountain pass, dragging Zhang behind them. There wasn't anywhere for them to go. It was a sheer drop on almost every side from there. The sides of the mountain had been blasted to conform to the dam's edges, and there was nowhere to escape to. But Denise wasn't trying to escape from Yersinia.

Her hands scrabbled at the hard surface. In a few places, hardy weeds and grasses clung to the side of the rock. A lot of it was bare stone, though. She just needed to make sure she was far enough away and that she had a firm grip. Her arm burned as she hauled herself up the last ledge and found the relatively flat spot she'd picked out before Yersinia arrived. It was an even plane, and there was no overhang that might come loose.

The elevator started to grind upward, moving smoothly after its gears had been fixed. It moved in a calm, stable ascent. Denise couldn't see what was happening in the enclosed metal box, but she imagined machine pistols were being given one final check. Ammo magazines were being adjusted to somewhere comfortable but easy to reach. Maybe a couple of silent prayers were going up around clutched rosaries or other personal effects. This would be the final push.

Cornelia clambered up and sat down next to Denise. She looked down at Denise's sleeve. "I think you ripped one of your stitches," she said.

Denise glanced down. A splotch of fresh blood marked her arm. The blood ran down and dripped off her elbow.

"I'll be able to take care of it soon enough. Thanks for patching it up earlier."

Zhang Dong scrabbled at the rocks below. Denise and Cornelia leaned down and dragged him up to their perch. He flopped down and sat in front of them without a word.

"No problem. Say, a little while ago, you said you'd like to bring Skipworth and me onto a project of yours. You didn't get to finish because…" Cornelia mimed kicking Zhang Dong over the ledge and off the mountain. "What was that about?"

"I'm thinking about leaving the park service and getting into the monster hunting business. Would you be interested?"

Cornelia rubbed her chin and glanced out over the grassland. The creatures were no more than a quarter-mile away now, moving surprisingly fast.

Yersinia's men down on the ground had gotten into their armored cars, and the men on the flamethrower turrets had their hands wrapped around the grips. This time, they had the better position, and they knew what was coming at them. This time, they were ready.

Denise reckoned they might even be correct about their chances against the creatures. Not the *ready for anything* part, though. They were wrong about that.

"I like you, Denise. I think you're a good person. If you'd asked me a year ago if I wanted to become a monster hunter with you, I'd have laughed in your face and said you were crazy. You might still be crazy, but it's a good kind of crazy. Sure. It would be a pleasure."

"Thanks, Cornelia."

Denise turned back to the elevator just before it reached the halfway point up the side of the dam. She squinted, not to see better, but to protect her eyes against what she knew was coming.

Cornelia had planted their remaining explosives halfway up the side of the dam, hiding hundreds of pounds of ordinance behind the elevator's tracks. The explosives were pressed up between the metal tracks and the concrete surface of the dam itself. They were utterly impossible to see from the ground.

If someone knew exactly where to look and what to look for while standing in the right spot, they might have been able to see the plunger. Obviously, none of the Yersinia men had been standing in the right spot. The plunger was strapped upside down to the elevator track.

A second after Denise squinted, the roof of the elevator hit the plunger handle and pressed it upward until it sank all the way into its base. The men inside the elevator probably heard a dull clunk and had a split second to wonder about it.

Then hundreds of pounds of high-yield explosives detonated all at once. The elevator turned into metal confetti before the massive fireball engulfed it. Concrete and chunks of warped metal blew out from the dam in a geyser of fire.

The fire was short-lived, though. A torrential gout of water shot out of the hole the explosion had blasted, quenching the flames.

Below, the Yersinia teams watching the creatures and guarding the stairs whipped around as the massive blast pounded their ears. A strong wind whooshed out, rustling the plants all around them. Debris of every shape and size rained down all around them. A house-sized chunk of reinforced concrete rolled down the hill and flattened one of the armored cars.

The gush of water in the dam grew wider and more ferocious. Cracks shot through the concrete, and more pieces started to crumble away.

Dams were deceptively brilliant things. The curved concrete face was simple looking from the outside, but the shape was designed to withstand massive pressure. The water on the other side of the concrete amounted to hundreds of thousands of tons, all of it pushing steadily against the curved wall. Some of that pressure was allowed to escape through the turbine shafts, spinning them to generate electricity, but most of it remained bottled up behind the dam. Holding an entire lake back was a massive feat that required careful engineering and planning.

The thing about all that engineering and planning was, it didn't react well to having a hole punched through it. It didn't react well at all. The even, uninterrupted shape of the dam was one of the things that allowed it to withstand all that water constantly pressing against it.

Blasting out in a brown and white torrent, the water quickly undermined the stability of the rest of the dam. Pieces gave way. More holes appeared. Spouts of water shot in every direction.

And then it was all over. The dam gave way completely, and an eighty-foot wave of water smashed through the concrete, heading straight down the side of the mountain.

Below, there was nowhere for the Yersinia team to go. Some of the armored cars started chugging away from the dam, but they couldn't outrun what was coming toward them.

The wave of water scoured the landscape, ripping boulders out of the ground and smashing them together, pulverizing trees into mush, ripping the topsoil away down to the bedrock. Raging against the sides of the mountain pass, the flood tried to take the rock with it.

A second later, the wave scooped up the armored cars and the men guarding the stairs and chewed them to shreds. Denise knew the armored cars would be bounced around inside the wave, crunched between tons and tons of debris. Even if the vehicles were water tight, the crews wouldn't be able to survive. Despite the steel armor, the cars would be flattened and torn apart in a couple of seconds. The men who weren't inside a vehicle wouldn't even last that long. They'd be like bugs inside a gravel hopper.

Denise could actually feel the mountain grinding underneath her feet as loose rock tore away. The rock groaned as debris smashed into it and etched away at its sides. Entire boulders tore off the face of the mountain and disappeared into the maelstrom below. The sound was simply a continuous roar, even louder than the explosion which originally engulfed the elevator and sparked the deluge.

A few seconds later, the crest of water slammed into the approaching monsters. Denise smiled as they disappeared, instantly engulfed by the frothing wave of destruction. The water and debris would pulp the bodies and the worms together. The tidal wave would be just as effective as the great cleansing fire Yersinia had planned.

Cornelia glanced away from the disaster to check the map she'd found earlier. The green areas indicated regions too high to be affected by the floodwaters in case of an incident that breached the dam. Yellow areas would receive extensive damage. Red areas would be completely annihilated.

The creatures were standing directly in a patch of deep maroon on the map. In a few minutes, the floodwaters would hit the remains of the visitor center and Ranger Station Two. There was no one there to evacuate, though. The creatures had turned them into dead zones. The other ranger stations were built away from the river lowlands, up on hills where they would have maximum visibility. They'd be mostly safe.

Denise sat and watched the water flow out of the destroyed dam. The flow kept coming, and it would for quite a while. There was a lot of water in the lake behind the dam. Like pulling the plug out of a full bathtub, she would have to wait some time before it all drained out. She and Cornelia watched in amenable silence while Zhang rested with his shoulders slumped.

By the time the water had gone down, the sun had peeked across the horizon. The distant sky was pink and orange, bright with promise.

Denise shifted on her rock. Her eyes wanted to droop. A dozen different aches cried out for her attention like needy children. The spot where she'd been slammed in the chest with the gasoline jerry can throbbed. She had a bruise the color of a diseased raisin where she'd been struck by part of the collapsing garage wall in the visitor center. Her stab wound kept breaking open and oozing a little bit more blood.

Dozens of little cuts and bruises covered her body. Seemingly all of them were covered in an exotic mixture of dirt and grime that would normally take years of dedicatedly avoiding showers to cultivate. Cornelia didn't look a lot better, and Zhang still had dried vomit down the front of his shirt. It had been a wild night for everyone.

Finally, the water receded down until it was no more than a couple of feet deep. The river that previously ran through the park was now more of a wide, shallow ditch. The floodwaters had excavated everything away, burnishing the landscape down to its rocky substrata. This particular section of the park would be barren scablands for years before soil started to deposit again and something else could grow. Right now, it was merely a shallow brown swamp, though.

This was coming out of her paycheck for sure.

"I think this as low as the water is going to get," Denise said. "We should head out and try to find someone who can give us a hand with him." She gestured toward Zhang Dong, who still hadn't said anything since the dam burst.

"And then we need to get your arm stitched back up."

"And then find some beds. There's going to be questions for us soon. Lots and lots of questions. We should grab some rest while we can."

Denise swung her legs over the rocky ledge and started lowering herself down the edge of the mountain. A small ledge, almost all that still remained of the dam, lay below. She scurried across it and stood at the top of the staircase. The metal stairs were too far to the sides for the floodwaters to pull them away from the mountain except near their base.

Cornelia prodded Zhang Dong down the side of the mountain and followed down soon after. The two park rangers marveled at the changed landscape, once lush and familiar but now barren and strange. Zhang simply marched along between them, resigned to his fate.

They picked their way down the staircase, moving slowly. Since she'd spent a few hours not moving much, Denise's injuries had made her stiff. She took the steps slow and gentle, feeling like an old lady.

Finally, they reached the space where the stairs had met the floodwaters. The metal was simply wrenched away from the side of the mountain, the screws and bolts used to secure it scraped away. Fortunately, the ground had shifted beneath the stairs. Huge sandbars of gravel and silt now filled the mountain pass, poking above the surface of the muddy water like the humps of a great sea serpent.

It was only a short jump down to one of the sandbars. Denise hopped down, and the sand and gravel crunched under her feet. She looked at the landscape from ground level. This part of the park looked completely different. It might never look quite right again, at least not in her lifetime.

She'd saved it, though. The park hadn't been consumed in the vast firestorm that Yersinia was planning. Nor were its creatures a writhing mass of blackened, slimy husks.

They started hopping across the sandbars toward Ranger Station Thirteen and the coming dawn.

SEVENTEEN

THE GOOD KIND OF CRAZY AND A POST-DILUVIAN WORLD

They slogged through the cold, brown water, moving carefully. Nearer to Ranger Station Thirteen there weren't any more sandbars or gravel patches they could use to stay dry. Everything had been swept away.

Seeing below the muddied water was completely impossible. Denise probed each step of the way before putting her full weight down. In a few places, the water was shockingly deep. In others, the ground was as jagged as a bed of broken glass, or it was unstable. The last thing she needed was to survive Yersinia and a swarm of ravenous monsters only to be sucked into a sinkhole half a mile away from safety.

"So," Cornelia said. "A monster hunting company. Think we'll actually get any business?"

"Maybe."

"Think we'll actually get any business from people who aren't cranks?"

"Maybe not."

"I'm in anyway. I'd rather not replay this exact scenario again, but it does feel good knowing we helped save the park. Doing something like that would be good work."

"Yeah, that's part of my thinking," Denise said. Even though she was tired down to the bone, and just about every part of her body hurt like nobody's business, she still felt good. They'd protected something worthwhile and probably saved a fair number of lives in the long run. Helping out with smaller scale problems would be nice.

"So where do you think we should set up shop?"

"I hadn't thought about it too much yet. Probably Cape Town. That's where my old safari company used to be. I've got a lot of connections there still. I didn't burn all my bridges, at least."

"Works for me. Even though I'm glad the game preserve is still mostly in one piece, I wouldn't be too eager to spend a lot of time around here after this. Once they appoint a new director for the park, I doubt he'll be very eager to have us around, either."

"Probably not. A lot of people won't want to be reminded of what happened here."

"Alright, so Cape Town it is. Got a name all picked out. Just 'DeMarco and van Rensburg, Monster Hunters?'"

"Maybe something like that. Maybe something a little more circumspect, just so we get fewer crazy people and hucksters telling us Dracula is in their basement. DeMarco and van Rensburg Specialty Hunting Services?"

"Specialty Hunting Services. I like it."

They squelched their way further along the newly carved river channel. Denise was almost to the shore when she felt it. She stopped for a second to see if it would continue or not. Cornelia and Zhang Dong continued a few steps ahead. They hadn't noticed yet.

"Hold on a minute," Denise said. "I think the ground might not be done settling over here yet." They stopped and turned around, and then they noticed it too.

The ground quivered slightly beneath them, trembling like a living thing. It stopped for a second and then started up again, a little stronger.

"Let's book it out of here," Cornelia said, making for the closest stretch of scabby jagged shore. Denise was only a few steps behind her, moving as fast as she dared. She hoped she wouldn't step right in a hidden underwater divot and snap her ankle or trigger a destabilizing slide into a pit. Moving along the ragged stone shore would be even harder than through the water, but maybe it would be safer. The rumbling beneath them intensified.

Denise suddenly looked up. She'd been so focused on her footing and the rumbling that she hadn't been paying attention to something else. She could hear Cornelia's feet splashing through the muck, and she obviously knew what her own feet were doing, but there was a third set of footsteps splashing away from them, moving quickly in the opposite direction.

She spun around. "Dammit."

Zhang Dong was moving as fast as he could through the calf-high water. His arms were still bound, but Denise had cut his legs free earlier so they could march him toward the ranger station. Now he was moving in long, awkward strides toward the far away opposite shore.

Normally, Denise could probably run him down and catch him. The water would slow them both down, but he hadn't gotten too far yet, and he would have a difficult time squirming up the rocky edges of the former river channel with his hands tied.

However, the ground shifting under their feet changed everything. Zhang Dong was willing to take the chance that something would collapse under him. The alternative was the rest of his life in prison anyway, so a slight chance of being sucked under probably seemed pretty good in comparison to making a break for freedom.

Denise wasn't willing to take that same chance just to drag him back across the unstable river bed.

"Cornelia, hand me that pistol."

"What? Why do you need...aw crap. Here. Be my guest."

Denise had caused a lot of deaths in the past few hours. She didn't especially like that fact, but it had been justified. It was the Yersinia team or her. She hadn't killed Zhang Dong, though. He'd been unarmed and tied up. There wasn't any need to kill him, and she didn't fancy the idea of shedding blood needlessly.

He was a killer. He'd murdered Skipworth and the real Dr. Thornber and plenty of others, but Denise wasn't an executioner. She would have been happy to let the justice system run its course. There would be problems if Zhang Dong escaped now, though. No doubt he'd be back with more poachers later, for one thing. For another, he'd remember his treatment at Denise's hands, and she knew he wasn't the sort to let bygones be bygones. Someday, he would come after her with a vengeance.

The pistol landed in her open palm. Her fingers clamped around the grip and found the trigger guard without looking. She swung the weapon around and lined up the sights. She focused on the spot between Zhang Dong's shoulder blades. Narrowing her eyes to focus against the dawn's glare on the water, she started to tighten her finger around the trigger.

Suddenly, a plume of water shot up directly in front of Zhang Dong. He skidded to a stop and nearly fell down. He started to backpedal straight toward Denise as a swell of water rose up behind him.

Something breached out of the water, sand and gravel sliding off as it rose to the surface. For a second, it almost looked like a U-boat rising to the surface as it prepared to launch a torpedo at some unsuspecting merchant ship. Then Denise saw the bones and the black slime clinging to it.

The *Spinosaurus*, its bones broken in a dozen different places, clawed its way out of the muck directly in front of Zhang Dong. Part of its lower jaw was missing. One arm had been wrenched away. The spines along its back were shattered. Entire sections of its ribcage were broken or torn away.

Somehow, it was still moving, though. Multiple skeletons clung to its sides too, like shipwreck survivors grasping whatever debris would keep them afloat. A lot of the black slime had been wiped from the bones, leaving them bare. The *Spinosaurus* now looked more like some museum's osteology department had been glued together by pranksters than the mass of oily black ooze it was before. Human and animal skeletons were molded onto the dinosaur bones.

In the brief glimpse she got of the creature, she realized that the animals closest to the dinosaur must have all joined together when they were all tumbling around inside the floodwaters. Being bashed by stones and scraped along the ground had destroyed most of the creatures. However, some of the worms were able to survive by banding together into a sort of multi-species monstrosity. The great majority of the worms had still been crushed and swept away into oblivion, but there were still enough left over to operate in one final form.

A huge claw erupted out of the water, rose high into the air, and smashed down directly on top of Zhang Dong. Even above the noise of the huge splash, Denise could hear every bone in the man's body shatter all at once. The claw flattened Zhang Dong into the water. The *Spinosaurus* used its remaining arm to leverage itself up out of the mud and silt.

That was the trembling and quaking that had sent them scrambling for the shore. The ground itself wasn't unstable. There was something underneath the ground trying to work its way to the surface. It had finally succeeded.

"Well, shit," Denise said as the *Spinosaurus* and its friends freed themselves from the water and stood up. Already knowing it wouldn't do any good, Denise fired the pistol at the monstrosity. She squeezed the trigger again and again until the chamber clicked empty.

The *Spinosaurus* swung its head in her direction and took a slow, creaky step. Denise threw the empty pistol at the monster.

It was over. Neither one of them had anything else to fight with. They didn't have any more bullets. They didn't have any more guns. They'd used all their explosives. They couldn't fight the freakish accretion of bone and slime with their bare fists.

The dinosaur took another step and then another, moving slowly without as many worms to aid its locomotion. Denise and Cornelia splashed toward the shore. There was no way they could outrun the thing, but they tried anyway.

Denise heard huge splashes behind her with each step the *Spinosaurus* took. Small waves washed against her legs as it upset the course of the river when it moved.

She risked a glance back, afraid she'd see a huge grimace of broken and shattered razor teeth right behind her. What she saw was confusing for a second, then a relief, and then she realized it was probably even worse than seeing a mouthful of teeth.

The *Spinosaurus* wasn't following them. It was moving up the river toward the dam, apparently showing no interest in chasing the two of them. But then Denise realized where it was no doubt headed. The creature was almost certainly foregoing chasing them to go back to Sulfur Springs.

If it made it to that cavern, it would be able to sink back into that lake where the worms originated from. From there, it would only be a short matter of time until it had a brand new skin of slime. It would emerge again, ready to wreak more havoc across the park, just as strong as ever.

Denise looked at the sun creeping above the horizon. Search-and-rescue crews would no doubt be in the area soon, but Denise was never able to contact the Army. The phone lines at the visitor center were down, probably cut by Yersinia so they could initiate their operation without interference from the outside. If ambulances and police arrived in the area as the *Spinosaurus* emerged from Sulfur Springs again, it would be a massacre. Even if everyone managed to get clear before that, the monster would start building another horde around it, making it that much harder to kill it.

Cornelia dragged herself over the line where the flood had pulled all the plant life and soil away and collapsed into the grass. Denise was only a few steps behind her. Ranger Station Thirteen lay not far ahead.

"We've got problems," Cornelia said.

"Tell me about it. If that thing makes it to Sulfur Springs, we'll just have to deal with it all over again."

"You're the one who wants to open a monster hunting business. There's a set of dinosaur bones walking around, getting ready to rejuvenate into a slime monster. Is there anything we can do about it?"

"Maybe. Let's get to the ranger station and see what sort of supplies we can muster." They trudged as fast as their wet clothes and tired bodies would allow. A few minutes later, they found Ranger Station Thirteen, quiet and abandoned.

Denise poked her head through the open front door. There was a blood stain on the floor near the front entrance. Oh no.

Now Denise understood why the Yersinia team had been slower than expected in getting back to the dam after she blew up the bridge. They must have gotten back down the side of the mountain in decent time but then made a detour. Ranger Station Thirteen was the closest one to the dam, the one most likely to notice strange activity near the dam. Either the rangers here tried to interfere or Yersinia decided to take preventive measures against being interrupted.

The walls were full of bullet holes. They were clustered around the front entrance but extended further inside. With Denise and Cornelia gone, there had only been four rangers at the station, and at least two of them never knew what hit them. Brady and Van Zandt lay by the front door, both stone dead. Young and Schmidt were a bit further inside, also dead.

Denise shook her head. She'd seen these people less than a day ago, and here they were butchered. She had gotten along with some of them better than others, but they all meant well in their own ways. Brady was newly engaged. Young was planning to quit and start a restaurant. Now they were all dead. Any of the discomfort she felt about killing the Yersinia biocontainment team evaporated in a cloud of sorrow and impotent rage.

Feeling her throat starting to close up, Denise moved toward the station's armory. "First thing's first," she said, fighting a hitch in her voice. "We're going to need guns. Big guns."

"Right," Cornelia said, her voice quiet.

They walked down the main hallway. The door to Kirkeberg's office stood open. The giraffe head mounted on his wall had been knocked off and lay on the floor behind his desk. The armory laid just ahead, the door closed. Denise fished out her keys and opened the door.

She grabbed an elephant gun off the rack and started filling her jacket pockets with shells. The heavy brass slugs rattled as she dumped them out of the box, and she could feel their weight.

The tug of the shells in her pockets suddenly made her realize that she still had no real plan. The *Spinosaurus* presented the same threat it always had. Would they really be able to destroy it with only guns? The flood had severely damaged it. Maybe the guns would be enough, but Denise wasn't sure.

She grabbed a revolver off the shelf, checked it, and slid it into her empty holster. The sidearm felt pitifully inadequate for what they needed to do. Regardless, she snatched up a couple of speed loaders. Better to have and not need than to need and not have.

Stepping back out of the hallway, she saw Van Zandt's legs sticking out into the hallway on the other side of the station. She decided to take a different route out to the garage so she wouldn't have to step over Van Zandt again. "I'm going to get a car running so we can get out of here and after that dinosaur," Denise said.

"Okay. I'll be there in a second," Cornelia said, still loading herself down with ammunition.

Denise went the long way around the station. She walked past the open door to the examination room. The smell of hastily scrubbed burnt

179

flesh and gasoline wafted out to greet her like an old friend. For a brief second, it even overpowered the coppery odor that prevailed in the rest of the station.

She walked past, her nose already abused enough by that smell. Then she stopped and took two steps back to look inside again.

The naval mine they'd confiscated from the poacher camp was still in there, along with the equipment they'd recovered from the fake Thornber's expedition out to Sulfur Springs.

Zhang Dong had never finished explaining why he'd acquired the thing. All he'd said was that he didn't trust Yersinia to hold up their end of the deal, and something about the geology of Sulfur Springs.

Denise frowned. The geology of Sulfur Springs...

She walked over to the piles of stuff they'd collected from the failed expedition into the caves a few days ago. The report they'd found secreted away in the fake Thornber's luggage still sat on the table. Denise picked it up and thumbed back to the secret addendums.

Skipping past the sections on the weird lichen and other elements in the cave system, she scanned the document for the paragraphs about the cave's structure.

Then she saw it. She suddenly understood what Zhang Dong had meant.

He'd been concerned about Yersinia double crossing him and reneging on their deal. Nominally, he and his Triads didn't have any leverage over Yersinia if that happened. They were just the local branch of a broader criminal gang. They couldn't exactly go through the court system and complain that they'd been stiffed when they agreed to help Yersinia gather the raw components for a possible biological weapon.

They did have other options, though. The hydrothermal vents inside Sulfur Springs fed the system and allowed the worms to thrive in isolation for millions of years, but they were also a structural weakness. Each vent and crevice was like a crack in an eggshell. If they were seriously disturbed, if perhaps a giant hole was blown in one of the vents, it wouldn't be so very different from what happened at Verschoor Dam. A major explosion could uncover the massive power locked beneath the surface, and once it was uncovered the whole thing would probably go up in smoke. Yersinia wouldn't be able to get their samples anymore. Zhang Dong's trump card.

Cornelia walked past the entrance to the examination room and then backtracked. "What are you doing in there? We need to get out there and stop that thing."

Denise turned to her, the report still in her hand. "Help me load this bomb into one of the trucks. I've got a plan."

EIGHTEEN

WELCOME TO HELL; ENJOY THE BUFFET

The *Spinosaurus* beat them to Sulfur Springs. Denise saw its bony tail disappear inside the cavern entrance just as she pulled up to the base of the trail. She'd been forced to take a long, circuitous route around to avoid areas that had been flooded.

She didn't dare try to drive such a heavy vehicle over areas that might still be unstable, but it had cost them a lot of time. Now, they would need to move all the quicker. If that monstrosity and the minions clinging to its body were able to reach the lake of worms inside Sulfur Springs, they'd simply reemerge and raise absolute hell again.

Maybe someone would have to burn down most of the park to contain them, if that happened. That person wouldn't be Denise or Cornelia. They'd be the first to die if they allowed that thing back out.

They hopped out of the truck and dashed around to the back. Despite the rush, they slowly, carefully lowered the naval mine down on its dolly. Denise felt the sutures in her arm tear a little more as she strained to set the explosive device down on the ground without dropping it. Fresh blood trickled down her arm.

Far in the distance, she could see flashing lights moving closer amid a cloud of dust. Those would be the police and emergency services. Obviously, despite the cut phone lines, somebody found a way to get word out about the flooding. The other ranger stations were probably just finding out the visitor center and original police convoy had been destroyed. She and Cornelia were the only ones left who could tell the full story about what happened last night.

The emergency vehicles were still too far away to help, though. They would reach Ranger Station Thirteen shortly, but it would take them a good, long while to navigate out to Sulfur Springs. By then, it would already be too late. The whole damn cycle would have already started anew. Denise and Cornelia would simply have to do this without backup.

Grunting, they set the bomb down on the ground and started wheeling it up the incline. Denise walked in front, guiding the dolly with one hand and holding her new Nitro Express in front of her with the other. If anything leapt out at them, she wanted to be ready.

The naval mine wobbled on the dolly as they moved over the uneven ground. Cornelia laid a steadying hand on it from behind. If it rolled off and down the hill, it would take precious minutes to drag it back up. Not to mention the obvious concern that it might blow them to smithereens.

"So how does this thing work?" Denise asked.

"Okay, see this lever here?" Cornelia pointed to a sort of crude control console grafted onto the side of the bomb. "It's pretty simple. All I have to do is pull that, and then we'll roll the whole thing into the lake. The lever starts a timer. When that timer counts down, it'll complete the circuit, and the whole thing goes up."

"How long do we have after we activate it until it blows?"

"Two minutes. Plenty of time for it to roll to the bottom of the lake and settle. We just have to pull the lever, roll it off, and then get out of there."

"Alright. We can do this."

As they approached the entrance to the cavern, the air grew fouler. Denise could increasingly smell the noxious fumes belching out of the cavern. The fact that the worms could thrive on anything that made her stomach want to do gymnastics told just how different they were from her on a biological level. For all intents and purposes, evolution had turned them into aliens.

Denise and Cornelia slapped the gasmasks they'd grabbed from the fake Thornber's supplies over their faces and secured the fasteners. The air lost its noxious undertone but took on a rubbery, chemical tang that wasn't a whole lot better. Denise knew they if they tried to go down into the caves without the masks, they'd end up down on their knees retching and poisoned. They'd die before they ever made it to the slime lake.

Stepping up to the edge of Sulfur Springs, Denise pointed her elephant gun down into the darkness to make sure there wasn't anything waiting for them just inside. No teeth flashed at her. Empty eye sockets didn't swivel around to stare at her. The entrance was deserted. She shouldered the Nitro Express and got a good grip on the sides of the dolly.

"With the knees. On three. One...two...three!"

Actually dragging the bomb down into the hole took several more precious minutes. Minutes they didn't have. Denise's arms trembled slightly from the strain as she set the bomb and dolly back on the ground.

She could hear the skeletal dinosaur somewhere up ahead, its bones scraping against the rocks as it moved. The tunnel was only barely large enough for the beast to move down. Its claws clacked and scratched against the hot stone.

Denise took position in front of the bomb again and whipped her rifle back around. The cave was warm and damp. Sweat immediately beaded on her palms, making her grip on the rifle slick. She wiped her hands on the front of her jacket, and the ammo in her pockets jangled.

"Let's go," she said, her voice sounding strange in her own ears. The gasmask muffled her words but also added a strange buzz to them. It sounded like a swarm of flies trying to imitate human speech.

Cornelia nodded, and they started wheeling the bomb forward as fast as they could. In places, the cavern floor was uneven, marked with divots or uneven patches where rock had eroded away.

Their flashlights led them forward, picking their way downward. Denise could still hear the dinosaur somewhere up ahead. Judging from the volume of the noises, they were gaining ground on it. Hopefully, the tight confines meant it wouldn't be able to back up to attack them with its fangs or claws very easily.

Soon, Denise started noticing a strange red lichen along the floors and walls. The stuff closer to the entrance was stunted or dead, little more than individual tufts of moss. A lot of it looked pretty sickly.

After a few hundred more feet though, the lichen was bushy and robust. Long, drooping tendrils hung from the walls like tentacles. It sprouted up from the cavern floor in dense patches of red. Pushing the dolly and bomb through certain sections was like wading through the dense reeds surrounding a cistern.

The task was made marginally easier by the patches that had been trampled down by the *Spinosaurus*. Denise didn't need years of working in the field to recognize that something huge had crashed through here recently. The lichen-like plants were crushed in regular footprints almost large enough to bathe a child in.

Something suddenly occurred to Denise. The patches of lichen grew denser and freer the deeper they went into the cave. The entrance area was completely bare of the strange plant life, and it only grew in mangy spots further in. Anywhere there was so much as a whiff of fresh air, the plants had difficulty growing.

That made a certain amount of sense. The ecosystem down here wasn't built around sunlight or oxygen, but she hadn't really considered the corollary to that. Just as she needed a gas mask to survive for any amount of time down here, the things down here couldn't survive the influx of oxygen over the long term.

The engineers who blasted this place open trying to build Verschoor Dam, the same dam she'd blown to pieces just a few hours before, had probably doomed everything down here. The gases that had built up down here over the eons were now escaping out into the atmosphere and new surface gases were seeping inside. The outside world was toxic to anything specialized enough to live down here.

Most likely, the worms weren't just using the dead bodies they collected for food, although that was how they temporarily sustained themselves. They were using the bodies as scouts, amassing more and more corpses to search a broader and broader area.

They weren't just looking for prey; they were looking for a new home. Their spawning ground since time immemorial had been breached, and it was slowly becoming more and more inhospitable as oxygen leaked inside. They were like demonic little refugees searching for a new Hell after a leak in Heaven's basement started leaking holy water into their space.

In that moment, Denise almost felt a little pity for them. Almost. Blasting open Sulfur Springs had probably doomed them to extinction, and they were searching for a new habitat with similar conditions. Unfortunately for them, their environment was unique. Once their sanctuary was breached, it was all over for them with due time. They could survive for a time on the outside by infecting the dead and riding their bones around, but even then, the outside world would kill them off eventually. They were nomads fleeing a corrupted homeland, doomed to die out in the wastes. Everyone involved would have been a lot better off if Sulfur Springs simply remained sealed for another million years.

Given what had already happened, Denise couldn't pity them too much, though. They were a threat to every living thing around them. Their quest for new lands to colonize would lay waste to the entire region if it was left unchecked. Zhang Dong's bomb was just the check that they needed.

Just ahead, Denise's flashlight revealed a length of bony tail. The bones whipped out of sight a second later around a corner. The cave system looked like it opened up into a massive chamber just ahead. That must be where the lake was. They were nearly too late.

"Leave the bomb. Let's go," Denise said. They needed to get there fast. Denise didn't know exactly how long it would take to reconstitute the dinosaur bones into the giant slime monster that had spent the night terrorizing the park, but she suspected it wouldn't take long. From what she'd seen the worms worked fast. They could organize and have a dead body up and moving about in a couple of minutes. That didn't give them much time.

Denise charged forward, smacking through the chest-high lichen bushels. She carried her elephant gun at the ready.

Rounding the corner, she turned and saw the *Spinosaurus* standing right in front of them. Its dark, ossified bones clacked together as it moved toward the black lake directly in front of it. Fresher, lighter-colored bones hung off the dinosaur at weird angles. Some of the bones were human skeleton fragments. Others were parts of animals. The worms had simply glommed together whatever they needed to retain a certain amount of critical mass and survive the flood. They'd probably lost ninety percent of their numbers on the dinosaur skeleton, but they still had barely enough power to control it by banding together with other worm-infested corpses.

Such behavior seemed remarkably intelligent and perceptive for animals that couldn't have much brain matter. Then again, ants weren't that smart, and they dug elaborately engineered tunnel systems and rafts. Bees weren't necessarily any smarter than ants, but their hives were masterworks of geometry and group coordination. Maybe intelligence didn't have much to do with it.

Skidding to a stop, Denise raised her Nitro Express and fired. The gun punched her in the shoulder, and she had to brace herself not to fall over. Inside the cavernous space, the sound of the gunshot was horrifically loud. The massive boom echoed back and forth through the enclosed space.

The bullet shot out and punched into the dinosaur's exposed femur. Fossilized and brittle, the bone burst like a fragmentation grenade. Chunks of bone blew outward in every direction.

Denise broke the Nitro Express open to reload. Even as she did so, she saw a pseudopod of black slime shoot down and try to wrap around the shattered length of bone, to splint it together long enough to limp back into the lake.

But there weren't enough worms left on the bones to hold them together. The femur held together for an extra second and then collapsed under the weight of the rest of the dinosaur. The entire mass tottered to the ground with a crash nearly as loud as the elephant gun. Cornelia opened up and put a round through its spine, blowing the vertebrae apart like fireworks.

The sounds of the guns came again and again as Denise aimed for joints and bones the dinosaur could use to support itself to get back up. Individual hunks of bone flew into the black lake, but she wasn't worried about those. A few bone shards couldn't walk over and bite her face off. If the *Spinosaurus* got back up, it would do worse than that to her.

Her hands worked automatically, plucking fresh ammo out and stuffing it into the gun after firing each shot. Her shoulder was numb except for a blast of pain every time she pulled the trigger. Her ears rang like they were trying to pick up some strange radio signal.

Bits and pieces of the dinosaur blew apart. The worms thrashed at the bones, trying to make them walk or at least crawl, but every time they moved, Denise and Cornelia unleashed another salvo. Some of the smaller skeletons fell off into the lichen, and Denise blasted them, too. Others continued to cling tight like baby possums to their mother.

They didn't stop firing until the bones were little more than a pile of fractured rubble. Slime dripped from the still bones, roiling across the cavern floor to the edge of the lake where it drained down into the depths. The undead dinosaur was now merely dead, joining all its ancient cousins in the sweet embrace of oblivion.

"We did it," Cornelia said, sounding as if she herself didn't quite believe it.

"Hell yeah, we did," Denise agreed. "Now let's go get that bomb and finish this."

The two of them walked back to the mouth of the tunnel, beating back strands of overgrown lichen as they moved. Every single part of Denise's body complained at her as she moved. Cuts, bruises, and scrapes snarled at her with each step. Now that she'd stopped firing the elephant gun, it felt like her arm was about to fall off at the shoulder. Her arm was bleeding again, and she felt a little woozy from lack of sleep.

Even so, she grabbed the front of the dolly again and started lugging it forward, helping to guide it through the strange terrain. She strapped her elephant gun across her back. She was almost out of ammunition for the weapon, but she shouldn't need it anymore.

They wheeled the bomb around the pile of debris that had been the *Spinosaurus*, steering well clear of the slime that continued to dribble off its bones.

"This looks like a good spot," Cornelia said. "The slope is gentle but smooth. I can pull the lever and then we can just roll the dolly right down into the water. Gravity will do the rest. You ready for this?"

Denise looked out over the bubbling black lake. In a lot of ways, it was oddly beautiful. The stone columns rising up out of the slime supported the high-domed ceiling. Stalactites hung from the ceiling and dripped water down. Her flashlight couldn't even shine to the far end of the cavern.

They would be the last people to ever see this place. In a few minutes, after millions of years of isolation, it would be gone. They would be the only two souls who ever saw the cathedral of stone down here and lived long enough to tell people about it.

A pity. If Mother Nature wasn't a crazy old crone, this place would be a beautiful shrine to the wonders of the natural world.

They had to destroy it, though. Maybe the oxygen seeping in from the surface world would kill all the worms eventually, but first, they would almost certainly try to escape again. And even if they couldn't, Yersinia Bioresearch would want to send another team here sooner or later, one way or another, for another shot at gathering samples.

It had to be done.

Denise turned back to Cornelia. "I'm ready. Let's take care of this once and for all."

Cornelia nodded and reached out to grasp the bomb's activation lever. Then she started screaming.

Denise nearly jumped out of her skin. The sound of Cornelia's shriek, muffled though it was behind her gasmask, was an awful thing to hear. She looked every which way as Cornelia lost her balance and fell down.

Cornelia smashed into the side of the dolly, knocking it over. The roughly spherical mine rolled off and bounced onto the stone floor. It bounced once, and then started rolling down the incline. It hit a rock and bounced again, landing squarely in the black quagmire in front of them.

Denise watched hopelessly as the metal sank into the tarn, the lever still firmly wedged in the safety position.

There was no time to worry about that now, though.

Grabbing her elephant gun again, Denise turned back to Cornelia. Something had her by the leg. It was a human skeleton, a small amount of black goo still sucking at its bones. The skeleton must have been flung off the *Spinosaurus* when they first started firing at it, and it had gone unnoticed until it crawled up behind Cornelia.

One bony hand was wrapped around Cornelia's ankle, and its teeth were stuck in the back of her calf. There wasn't much flesh left on the body itself, and its legs were missing, evidence of how badly it was damaged during the flood. Now the worms needed Cornelia's flesh if they were to repopulate the skeleton.

Just before Denise fired the Nitro Express at the shambling ghoul, Denise noticed one last thing about the skeleton. It had two very distinct holes in the back of its skull, each one not much larger than a single fingernail. Those were bullet holes, clustered together in the back of the head.

Dr. Lyndon Skipworth.

Denise blew the skeleton away. The oversized elephant gun round caught the skeleton in the top of the head and traveled down the length of its spine. Pieces of bone shot away as Skipworth's mortal remains violently disarticulated themselves in the blink of an eye.

Swearing, Denise bent down to help Cornelia. There was black slime smeared all around the edges of the dripping red wound. As Denise watched, some of the goo slithered inside the torn flesh and attached itself to the raw meat there. Bone shrapnel also jutted out of Cornelia's leg like a bizarre pin cushion. Some of the shattered bone was tipped in black, like a poisoned arrow.

Cornelia was breathing hard and fast, each gasp shallow and pained. Denise couldn't see her mouth behind the gas mask, but she knew her teeth were gritted in pain from the sound of her voice.

"Denise," Cornelia said.

"Don't move. I'm going to get you to safety. To help. Here, I'm going to drag you onto the dolly and roll you out of here. Everything is going to be fine," Denise lied.

Oh shit. What was she going to do? What the hell was she going to do? Ragged fingers of panic tore her thoughts apart like cotton candy.

"Denise, there's no time for that," Cornelia said. "We're going to have to do something a little different." Cornelia panted out each word.

"Give me—Oh crap. I can feel them working their way up my leg from the inside. They'll be in the bloodstream soon. Give me your belt."

Denise tore her belt off and handed it over. Cornelia took it and cinched it tight above the knee.

"Okay, we're going to do something a little unpleasant here." Cornelia twisted around.

Denise could actually see the slime festering inside the torn half-moon of flesh, already starting to feed on the skin and muscle.

Cornelia twisted back, her own Nitro Express in her hands. Her finger trembled. "I need you to do it. The barrel is too long for me to hold the gun properly." She hissed as the worms worked at her exposed nerve endings, their pincers macheteing into her flesh one bite at a time.

"To do...it?" It suddenly dawned on Denise what Cornelia was talking about. The momentary sense of panic gave way to grim, stomach wrenching certainty. There was only one way to deal with this.

God help them both.

"A field amputation," Cornelia said. "Hurry. I can feel them working their way up inside me." Her voice came in a pained snarl.

Denise took the massive rifle, held the barrel against her friend's knee, and fired.

NINETEEN

LEVIATHAN

Denise drove the truck straight through the water, hazards be damned. If she drove the long way around to Ranger Station Thirteen, Cornelia would be dead of shock and blood loss by the time they arrived. She might die from those things regardless of which route Denise took. She pressed even harder on the gas. The truck roared and streamers of brown water shot up from the tires.

She hit the rocky shore on the far side of the river bed and the truck clawed its way up the side of the hill toward the ranger station. Grass and shrubs smacked against the front grill as Denise powered forward.

Beside her, Cornelia was breathing in quick, hiccupping bursts. Her skin was pale and sweaty. Denise had ripped the gasmask off, and she could see that Cornelia's eyes looked huge and staring. Her head kept listing to one side or the other as if her neck couldn't support the weight anymore.

The truck blasted up the side of the hill and slammed to a halt directly in front of the ranger station. Police and emergency services personnel gawped at the mud-spattered vehicle screeching to a stop directly in front of them. Several police officers stopped wheeling a gurney carrying Brady's body out of the ranger station and stared.

Denise hopped out of the still running truck and rushed around to the passenger side of the rumbling vehicle.

One of the cops finally snapped into action. "Wait, who are you? Were you part of this station? Who murdered these people?" He sounded unnerved at discovering a park outpost full of dead rangers. The police and emergency services probably came because of the burst dam, without realizing that Yersinia was ever even here. Denise couldn't blame him, but she had other priorities right now.

"You," she pointed at one of the medics.

The man looked around, as if trying to figure out who else she could be pointing at. She was aware that she'd just driven up to the scene of a major, unexplained crime and probably looked like she was out of her mind. She beckoned the man and he took a reluctant step closer.

Then he saw Cornelia inside and the blood dripping out of the door and onto the ground. He jerked and gestured to the other medics. They rushed forward and prepared a gurney. Working with practiced efficiency, they hauled Cornelia out of the truck cab and onto the gurney. Denise caught a quick glimpse of tattered flesh and jagged bone, and then Cornelia was gone. The medics whisked her into an ambulance and took off.

Denise marched straight toward the medic who looked like he was in charge of the group. He held up a hand in her direction. "Ma'am, please. There are dead bodies. We need space to--"

"Will Cornelia be okay?"

"Who?"

"The woman I just arrived with. Will she be okay?"

"It looks like you got her here in time to save her life. 'Okay' might be a relative term after that. Obviously, we won't be able to reattach the leg, and the damage looks fairly severe. We might have to amputate more to make sure everything is properly--"

Denise had heard what she needed to hear. She'd done what she needed to do. Now it was time to do the other task that needed to be done.

She walked toward the front entrance of Ranger Station Thirteen. A crowd of cops at the door tried to stop her, but she waved her game preserve identification badge at them. "Emergency measures," she said.

Instead of walking back to the armory to refill her pockets with ammunition, Denise made a beeline for the examination room. She dragged the crate with the diving suit out to the truck and threw it in the back. Then she went back and grabbed the harpoon gun. Tossing that into the truck too, she took off again, leaving a crowd of confused-looking police officers in her wake. She'd go back and tell the story about what transpired last night later. First, she had unfinished business in Sulfur Springs to attend to.

Her thoughts zipped through her head with frantic speed, alternating between relief that Cornelia would live and recriminations that she hadn't seen the skeleton creeping up behind her in the first place. Skipworth. Kirkeberg. Cornelia. Matheson and Ritter. Director Prescott and the staff at the visitor center. She had managed to stuff the genie back inside the lamp, but the costs had been enormous.

This time, she'd finish it. She'd do it right and put an end to this damn nightmare. The dead, the very dead the worms had defiled, would be avenged. Just as importantly, Yersinia Bioresearch would find that all their efforts were for naught.

Her mind still flushed with oppressive thoughts like bats flapping about inside an attic, Denise parked the truck in front of the cave entrance again and fetched the diving suit crate. Checking the equipment, she adjusted the suit over her clothes and unspooled the air hoses. Then she donned the heavy brass helmet.

Inside the helmet, the world suddenly took on an eerie echoing quality. Glass portholes in the front and sides gave her a limited view of the world, but she had two huge blind spots to either side of her face. She had to continually rotate her head back and forth, panning from side to side, to see everything in front of her.

Finally, she grabbed the harpoon gun. The extra harpoons went in an oversized quiver on her belt. The weapon was heavy and unwieldy. All the dead bodies had been destroyed, but Denise didn't want to go into that lake without some weapon in her hands. If she actually needed the harpoon gun, she was in deep, deep trouble.

Last, she grabbed a waterproof flashlight. She started walking forward, and soon, the darkness of Sulfur Springs engulfed her again. Flicking the flashlight on, she trudged down the same rocky hallway as before.

The suit was heavy on her abused body. Clunky and awkward, it wasn't meant for significant use on land. Each step she took resulted in a heavy thud against the ground, and she had to walk in an awkward waddling shuffle. The added weight of the harpoon gun only weighed her down even more.

All Denise could hear was her own breathing, harsh and loud inside the confining suit. Soon, she could also hear the crunch of lichen under her feet. The plant life grew tall and wild, and then Denise entered the system's main chamber again.

Everything was just as Denise left it. The *Spinosaurus* skeleton still lay in a broken heap. Brass shell casings still littered the floor. Blood still spattered the stone near the edge of the tarn. The ragged remains of Cornelia's lower leg still sat near the edge of the lake.

Denise briefly wondered if she should pick it up for Cornelia before she realized what an absurd thought it was. They couldn't reattach it, not with that sort of damage. Even if they could, it was slowly turning black with worms, so it was unusable. What would she even do with it? Have it mounted on the wall?

Taking a few more heavy steps forward, Denise stopped at the edge of the lake. She checked her air supply one last time, even though she knew it was working fine. She checked her harpoon gun, even though she'd already inspected it while walking down the tunnel. She checked her suit for any leaks, even though she knew she'd be able to smell any breaches in the suit. She checked her air supply again.

She was delaying and she knew it. Would the worms be able to eat through the dive suit's material? Unlikely. The suit was thick and rubbery. There was no way for them to get inside. Even if they were smart enough to launch a concerted effort, it would take them a good long while to chew through the material, and she didn't need a good long while. She knew where the bomb rolled in, and finding it shouldn't be hard.

Her heart did jumping jacks in her chest anyway. Taking a deep breath, Denise took a step forward and placed one foot into the lake. Her foot met with a little resistance, like she was stepping through applesauce. The slime bubbled a little around the edge of her suit, but the worms didn't seem realize there was food hidden behind the thick material. If they did, they showed no signs they knew how to get to her.

Denise took another step forward and then another, the sea of worms rising up to her knees. The suit pressed a little more tightly against her skin with the pressure of all their bodies against it.

The water was warm. But for the mass of flesh-eating worms and poisonous atmosphere, it might almost have been pleasant.

Another step and the lake came up to her chest. The bottom of the lake gave way fast, basically turning into a sheer, black pit. She couldn't see through the mass of worms, so she had no idea what the drop off was. She had to feel ahead with her feet.

Not knowing what lay directly ahead of her, lurking beneath that darkness, made her want to turn right around and march back up the shore. She wanted to keep going until she was out of the tunnel and into the bright sunlight again. She wanted to strip the heavy diving suit off and go wrap her arms around herself somewhere quiet.

She took another step forward instead, the worms rising up to her chest. Gripping the harpoon gun tight in one hand, she kept her flashlight locked in her other fist. The diving suit clung tight around her, like she was slowly being eaten by a massive snake, slipping into the tight confines of its belly one inch at a time.

Gnashing her teeth, Denise took the final step, and the whole word was blotted out. Perfect darkness enveloped her helmet. She couldn't even see her flashlight beam through the mass of worm bodies.

The only sound was a gentle grating noise. Denise stopped and listened for a second, wondering what it was. Then she realized that it was the noise of thousands of hard little armored plates bashing against the sides of her brass helmet.

Everything was black. She couldn't even tell where the glass portholes were in her helmet, even though she knew they were right in front of her. Everything was simply blackness and that infernal sound, like being trapped in a metal coffin as sand was slowly poured over the top. Good God, this is what it must feel like to be buried alive.

Denise suddenly realized she'd been holding her breath. She let out a whoop of air and dragged in a big, sucking gust. She needed to normalize her breathing. The air would go funny as she descended if she only breathed in fits and starts.

She closed her eyes and didn't move for a moment, focusing on simply controlling her breathing. The darkness behind her eyelids made no difference. It was the same darkness that was inside her helmet.

Breathe in.

Breathe out.

Breathe in.

Breathe out.

Denise opened her eyes again. The blackness made no difference now. She focused her mind on what she needed to do. All she had to do was walk down the incline, find the bomb, pull the lever, and climb back up and out of the lake. Easy. A walk in the park. Just out for a stroll. The only difference was that she was underwater.

And surrounded by millions and millions of--

She cut that thought off before it could go anywhere. There was no need to think about that right now. The fact that she was still alive at all showed she was safe. All she needed to do was move quickly and with purpose.

And that purpose was simple. She'd move forward for her friends and colleagues. For Cornelia. And Skipworth. And Kirkeberg. And all the others. She just needed to push forward a bit further.

Moving forward, she took another step, and the blackness suddenly cleared. The worms formed a layer of slime at the top of the lake, but they didn't extend more than a few feet down.

Denise swept her light back and forth. Everything was still mostly black. There was no light down in the caves, and even if there was, the layer of worms cavorting across the surface would block it out from down here.

There were three sources of illumination, though. The first was Denise's flashlight, it sent a narrow cone of white-yellow light out across the rocky floor in front of her. The water cut the beam short everywhere she shone it, illuminating little more than her next few steps. Powerful as it was, it was still almost useless against the greater, crushing darkness.

The next source was a glowing red spider web further down in the depths. Denise realized that there were fingers of magma crisscrossing the floor of the chamber. None of them were very wide. They were simply gossamer red threads down in the very deepest crevices.

In places, spires of basalt rock rose up like steeples. They merged and pushed against each other like flying buttresses. Dark soot and bubbles pumped out of several of them, superhot geological effluvia from below. Around each active hotspot, a black funnel of worms floated down from above and went after the nutrients in the coal-colored ejaculate. The scene looked like tornadoes on an alien planet.

A slight current hit Denise. It wasn't strong, but the water had been almost entirely still before. She shone her light around, looking for whatever could have caused the change in the water, but there was nothing. The current died down a second later, as if something had whisked past and she'd only caught its wake.

She licked her dry lips and kept moving forward. The sooner she was out of here, the better.

The final source of illumination was the plant life that had sprung up under water. Near the smoking spires, bioluminescent tubes and fronds wavered in the eddies produced by the black smokers. Each spire supported a little island of beautiful, glowing plants. Pale, off-blue light winked at her from the strange biomes.

With each step she took, the water grew a little warmer. She was moving closer to the black spires, to the source of the heat. Down here, there was nowhere for it to dissipate to. Sweat poured down her forehead as the temperature climbed to levels she'd find in a desert.

Then she spotted it. Zhang Dong's bomb lay just ahead. It had come to rest at the base of one of the spires, rolling through a small forest of glowing plants. It had left a clear trail of darkness where it crushed the delicate fronds.

Breathing a little sigh of relief, Denise bee-lined toward the bomb. It only lay about fifty feet ahead.

It would be a shame to destroy such a strangely beautiful place, but it had to be done. Perhaps if groups like Yersinia weren't interested in harvesting the worms for their own ends, the game preserve could protect and study the area. There was almost surely much to be learned about the more obscure chapters of life down here. Scientists could spend years studying the lichen alone to learn how it worked.

Denise slowed a little. This would be the last chance anyone ever had to savor the view down here. Might as well make the most of it.

Then she noticed something.

Off in the distance, one of the glowing islands of plant life went dark. Denise narrowed her eyes. What in the world? The glow reappeared again a second later.

That's when she realized what had happened: something had passed in front of the glowing garden. Something big.

She tried to estimate the distance between herself and the glowing biome that had momentarily disappeared. The darkness made it incredibly difficult. It was like staring out into the night sky and trying to eyeball the distance between herself and the various stars. Scale and distance were fickle things when all the other points of reference were cast in blackness.

The relatively tiny size of the glowing patch told her it was fairly distant, though. Then, another, larger glowing patch disappeared from sight for a moment. That was closer. The thing was moving her way.

Oh hell.

Denise scrambled down toward the bomb, her every step slow and leaden. She had to push against the weight of the water as she moved. It was like walking into a strong wind, slow and exhausting. The temperature only continued to climb as she drew closer. It was like standing in the middle of an asphalt parking lot on a hot day now, deeply uncomfortable, even dangerous if stretched over a long time.

She reached the outer edge of the knee-high forest of glowing plants and entered the false safety of their cheerful glow. A second later, a huge wall of chitinous plate swept past her, barely illuminated by the soft blue glow of the plants. The creature, whatever it was, had just passed by her, almost close enough to touch. It knew she was here.

Denise realized she was making a high-pitched keening noise deep in the back of her throat and forced herself to raise the light upward. The thing was already gone, moving somewhere through the outer blackness. It was probably circling back now that it had seen her.

She'd only gotten the tiniest glimpse at it. All she could see for sure were rows and rows of black, armored plates, thick as tank armor and darker than sin, covering a long, sinuous body. Her quick glance told her the thing was absolutely gigantic. Just the length she'd seen was as long as an orca, and she hadn't even seen the head.

A couple more steps took her up to the bomb, laying face up next to the smoking black spire. The lever was right in front of her.

Denise's instincts wanted her to freeze, to hide somewhere, but there was nowhere to go. The only patch to safety lay back up the wide open slope up to the lake's surface.

Not only that, but the temperature immediately next to the black smoker was near to boiling. The water shooting out the top of the spire had come from deeper below in the earth, blasted out by the heat of the fiery magma below. Staying put wasn't an option. She'd be partially cooked in five minutes and dead in ten. The thick material of her suit could insulate her against some of the heat, but not for long.

Just standing still was an excruciating experience, like her outer layer of skin was being peeled off in great, stinging sheets. She could already feel the sensation penetrating down from her skin into her soft tissue. Sweat gushed from her every pore like someone wringing out a wet rag.

What had she been thinking coming down here? This place was death. The atmosphere was choking. The upper surface of the water was populated by a gelatinous layer of living slime that wanted to colonize her body. Who cared how beautiful it was when the deep below was populated by whale-sized monsters and burning heat? She should have left the situation alone.

Fear started to claw at her. Her breathing was fast and jagged. Should she pull the lever and make a break for the surface? Would she even have a chance of making it if she did that?

She put one hand on the bomb lever. One way or another, she couldn't stay down here any longer. That wasn't an option. If she let her emotions paralyze her, she'd boil away inside the suit.

A flicker of movement appeared in front of her. The creature had circled all the way back. An array of saucer-sized, black, goggling eyes stared at Denise from a thick-plated exoskeleton. Long antenna ran back from its face almost like a catfish.

Denise stared at the vaguely insectile leviathan for a moment that lasted an eternity. Maybe it wasn't hostile. Maybe it was just curious. The creature was even larger than the *Spinosaurus* Denise dispatched earlier, but size wasn't everything. Elephants were big, and they were herbivores. She liked elephants. Whales were big, and they mostly ate krill. She liked whales. Maybe this thing was like a whale, just wondering what she was doing her. Perfectly friendly. Not even a threat.

The creature's multi-segmented mouth opened up like a blooming rose, revealing hundreds of spiked teeth. It swished its body back and forth and shot forward.

Nope. Not friendly.

All Denise's worst suspicions were confirmed the second she saw those teeth. Earlier, she'd thought about how strange it was that the worms were organized enough to control an entire human body, however inelegantly they did it. She'd mentally compared them to ants and bees.

Of course, one of the reasons ants and bees were so organized was because they had a queen. Denise suspected she'd just met the worms' queen, and she was a real bitch.

She snapped the harpoon gun up and fired it. The long, metal prod shot out amid a stream of bubbles and lodged directly in the queen worm's open mouth.

Instead of snapping those awful fangs down over Denise, the worm queen writhed and shot over her head instead, nearly sweeping Denise up off her feet with the current from her passing.

This was it. This was her chance. Denise yanked the lever on the bomb and started moving as fast as she could up the side of the incline, which wasn't very fast. The bomb was now primed. She had two minutes to escape. Her skin tingled unpleasantly as she moved away from the most immediate source of heat. It felt like her skin might slough off her bones if she moved too quickly.

She had to move quickly though, fighting gravity and the weight of the suit the whole way. If she didn't move fast enough, she was sure the worm queen would come back and stuff Denise down her gullet. Even if the giant monster didn't eat her, the concussive blast from the massive naval mine would travel through the water and either blow her apart or pop her internal organs like party balloons. Even if she somehow survived the blast from Zhang Dong's naval mine, this whole space was about to fill up with goddamn lava. Any which way, it was time to get out of Dodge and fast.

She brought her weapon up and stuffed a new harpoon into the launcher. Cursing under her breath, Denise tried to shine her flashlight in every direction at once. She whipped her neck back and forth to make up for the helmet's blind spot. Yet no matter how she twisted and turned, she could never see much more than a narrow strip of light a few feet in front of her.

The black veil of worms near the lake's surface was getting closer as Denise did her best to scramble back up the incline. If she could just get to the surface, she'd have a good chance.

Through the left porthole on her helmet, Denise saw another glowing patch flicker out of existence for a second. The worm queen was circling around. That patch of plants was way too close; Denise knew she'd never be able to make it to the surface in time.

She swung the harpoon gun and flashlight around, searching for the massive creature stalking her through the blackness. There was actually sweat splashing around inside her suit, sloshing around her feet with each step. Her eyes seemed to creak in her skull as she looked from side to side. The tendons in her neck strained a little as she swiveled her head back and forth to check her blind spots. Her body was in bad shape after the previous night and nearly baking alive inside the diving suit. She felt like half the fluid left in her body was simply the remnants of spent adrenaline.

Teeth lunged out at her from the left. The huge, gaping maw could easily swallow her up in one massive bite and have room leftover.

Denise had just enough time to swivel the harpoon gun around and fire. The jagged metal spike shot out and embedded itself directly in one of the worm queen's eyes. The soft black orb burst like a balloon, spraying ichor and vitreous fluids.

The worm queen swerved away from Denise again, that huge, freakish mouth snapping closed as it thrashed in sudden pain. A wave of water bombarded Denise, nearly plucking her off the side of the incline.

She had to drop the flashlight just to grab onto the side of the rock. The light spun away, twirling around and around as it fell into the darkness below.

Balls. Denise reloaded the harpoon gun as she moved closer to the surface. She was almost there now, nearly to the blackness that constituted the layer of worms. Looking around, she searched for any signs of the worm queen, but she couldn't see anything.

Glancing back toward the bomb, she tried to figure out how much time had passed since she activated the lever and started the countdown timer. It felt like a couple of decades. She quickly realized that she had no idea. At least a minute must have passed, and they had to be closing in on two. Scaling the incline was hard work, and using one arm to carry a harpoon gun instead of climbing was only slowing her down.

She reached the layer of worms near the surface, and her head was surrounded by pure blackness once again. The strange noise of the tiny worms scrabbling at her brass helmet filled her head, but she couldn't see anything.

This must be what it was like when the worms managed to colonize a live body. The victim could feel their limbs moving and their body working, but they couldn't see anything if their eyes had already been eaten away. There would be only the sense of movement and the sound of the worms tapping away at the inside of their skull.

Denise's head broke through the surface. She still couldn't see anything, but she could feel the sudden change in pressure. The suit didn't suck at her body anymore. She reached up and swiped a hand across the glass lens on the front of her helmet. A smeared, dark version of the cavern appeared in front of her.

Summoning a little more strength, Denise forced her legs to move faster, to pump harder. She waded out of the lake, the worms sucking at her like a sheet of sticky tar. Finally, even her feet were clear of the edge of the lake.

More than anything else, Denise wanted to take off her helmet. A stitch throbbed in her side, and her body kept telling her it wanted to puke from all the exertion. Taking the helmet off here would be just as deadly as jumping into the queen worm's jaws, though. It would just take longer to die.

Now she had to get out of here before that bomb went off. Denise turned around for one last look at the lake of sludge.

She noticed a ripple across the surface moving toward her. The ripple turned into a wave, and the wave turned into a black wall of slime. Denise turned around and started running as fast as the diving suit allowed as the queen worm smashed its way up to the surface and beached itself on the shore, harpoons still buried in its mouth and the remains of one eye.

The giant worm goddess shrieked, a noise that made Denise's ears want to throw up, and her eyes want to scream, and her bowels want to go blind. It started pulling itself out of the muck, trundling up onto the shore with grotesque undulating motions.

Denise ran past the remains of the *Spinosaurus*. A few seconds later, the worm crushed the old bones beneath its bulk. They splintered and cracked beneath its enormous, armored weight.

Denise's run wasn't much more than a determined shuffle. The diving suit was heavy, and slime clung to its every fold and crevice, only weighing her down more and making the suit's movements awkward and sticky. She bashed her way through the thick patches of lichen, moving as much by touch as sight in the cavern's darkness.

Suddenly, she felt the ground quake beneath her feet. She stumbled and almost went down on her knees, but she recovered and continued heaving herself down the tunnel.

A giant plume water shot up from the lake, flying straight up. Before the plume of water had even settled back down, the edges of the lake receded for a second before a second wave, even larger than the one the worm queen generated when she beached herself. The black tsunami swept forward and battered the cavern walls. The water splashed its way up the tunnel, washing out shortly behind Denise's heels.

Even as she moved though, the water was already sinking lower in the lake. The bomb had blasted a huge hole in the lakebed. All around Denise, the ground continued to shake and rumble. One of the pillars in the main chamber shook itself loose and crumbled into the water, generating another violent wave.

A strange glow suddenly suffused the chamber and tunnel. Denise risked a glance backward. The queen worm was still squirming after her, squelching her body along the stony surface. Denise could barely see around her.

Even so, she caught a tiny glimpse of what was happening back in the main chamber. There was a bright light glowing from somewhere down below the surface, and it was getting bigger and brighter. It shone through the surface layer of worms like a spotlight covered with a length of burlap cloth.

The water roiled and bubbled. Waves crashed back and forth as if a tempest had broken out inside the chamber. A second later, a finger of red hot magma burped to the surface. It fell back down into the water a second later, but it told Denise everything she needed to know.

By now, the entire subterranean lake was starting to boil as the bottom collapsed and millions of tons of liquid hot rock poured up toward the surface.

The queen worm screamed again, this time with an even more awful shriek. Her cry had a slightly different tone, as if she could sense the sudden distress of her multitude of loyal servants. She thrashed and wriggled after Denise, her mouth gaping like the express elevator to Hell.

More lava bubbled to the surface, bring great gouts of steam with it. Boiling water from deeper down in the lake was trying to escape upward. The body of water was essentially turning upside down as the bottom heated too rapidly to dissipate and exploded upward. The surface of the lake wasn't even black anymore as it roiled and jumped like a sack full of tortured animals.

Glowing red magma started to pour down the tunnel entrance behind Denise and the queen worm. The temperature inside the caves suddenly doubled and then tripled. Denise suddenly felt like she was down by the black spire again, on the verge of being baked alive.

The lava hit the lichen, and the plants instantly burst into flames. Denise could suddenly see quite well as the tunnel went from dark and sunless to alive with crackling flames. There wasn't enough oxygen down here for the flames to last very long, but the extreme heat guaranteed at least one fat gout of fire each time the magma engulfed a new patch of lichen.

She was pretty sure that exerting herself in such high temperatures was rapidly giving her heat stroke. Her head throbbed with the beginnings of a brain-splitting headache. Every inch of her skin was drenched in sweat, and her heart felt like it might explode in her chest. Nausea threatened to clamp her throat up, and she felt like she might faint dead with each extra step she took. There was no stopping, though. To stop or even slow was to die.

She beat her way through the worst of the lichen. What was left of the red plants merely clung to the ground in little tufts or patches. She could actually see a glimmer of real sunlight ahead. All she had to do was keep going.

Behind her, the queen worm suddenly sped up. She scooted forward at a surprising speed for something so big and ungainly. She seemed to have lost interest in Denise, too.

Denise realized that the lava must be creeping closer, close enough to singe the worm queen's rear end. She was now the very last of her species, and even she was about to be extinct if she couldn't squirm faster than the lava.

Of course, Denise would be extinct, too if she couldn't move faster than the giant, armored worm. Even if the queen worm didn't snatch her up into her mouth parts, she would simply be crushed beneath the worm's enormous weight. Anything that was left over would be burnt up a couple of minutes later.

But the worm queen was gaining on Denise. Using everything she had, Denise dragged herself toward the sunlight. She tried to focus on the blinding streamer of light as it drew closer, tuning everything else out. It grew in size from a pinprick to a button to a walnut, getting closer with each painful step.

The worm queen refused to be tuned out. She was only feet behind Denise, her mass making the ground rumble as she moved. She squirmed down the tunnel like a massive steam roller. Behind her, the oozing lava consumed everything behind the panicked monster.

Denise was almost to the cave entrance, but realized she wasn't going to make it. There just wasn't enough time. She couldn't coax any more speed out of her legs. She could barely even keep herself upright, let alone move faster. The queen worm was right on her heels, and the lava was right behind the worm. She was sizzling in her suit, the sweat evaporating from her skin as soon as it appeared.

She still had the harpoon gun, though. Maybe there was still one thing she could do to save herself.

She didn't turn around to try to shoot at the worm. From only a few feet away, she wasn't sure she'd be able to hit anything vital. With her arms feeling like strangled spaghetti, she wasn't even sure she could aim steady enough to hit any target that presented itself. The queen worm had already shown she could take a smaller wound and keep on moving.

No, instead, Denise raised the harpoon gun and fired the harpoon directly into the stone in front of her. The harpoon shot out and embedded itself into the rock at an acute angle. Running right past the expended harpoon, Denise dropped the gun. She could barely hold it anymore anyway, and she didn't have time to reload it.

Behind her, the queen worm screamed in unholy fury. She was too broad to move around the harpoon. It was angled upward like a spearman trying to unseat a soldier on a horse. If she tried to slither over it, she'd impale her softer underbelly on the blunt end of the harpoon.

With the lava creeping up behind her, she didn't have much choice. She tried to roll over the harpoon anyway. The spike immediately speared into her flesh. As she squirmed forward, it worked like a filleting knife, tearing her guts out down the middle as she moved forward. Heaps of innards tumbled out in steaming piles.

Even through her helmet, Denise could hear the sounds of ripping, tearing meat behind her. The worm had gotten herself stuck on the spike, her own weight only driving it deeper into her body. An awful banshee shriek filled the cavern as the monster wailed out in agony.

Denise reached the edge of the cave and started climbing upward. Her fingers felt like sticks of jerky as she struggled to get them to wrap around handholds. Every single part of her body was screaming at her, and her heart beat was a distant throb that pulsed in her ears like pagan drums dedicated to some alien god. Her vision flickered in time with her heartbeat, fading out around the edges and hiccupping back into painful focus with each new convulsion from her overworked heart.

The lava reached the worm's tail. Her keening wail turned into a scream that threatened to burst Denise's eardrums. Steam rose everywhere the lava touched the worm queen's armored hide. Her black plates started to turn from black to red. One by one, they burst like popcorn dropped into a fire.

Even where the lava hadn't touched yet, steam shot out from between the worm's armored plates. Its flesh was being sublimated into superhot blood steam, and the burning gas needed somewhere to escape. Teakettle noises filled the tunnel as more and more steam shout out from between the worm's remaining plates. Her remaining eyeballs popped like overcooked potatoes, spraying burning liquid in every direction.

The scream kept coming from the worm's gaping mouth, but it wasn't a voluntary noise anymore. Now it was the sound of hot air and steam roaring out through the nearest exit it could as the worm's remaining insides bubbled, melted, and turned to furious steam vapor.

Denise clambered all the way out of Sulfur Springs just as the worm queen's body completely overheated and lost all its structural stability. The expanding vapors brewing inside her body became too much, and she ruptured. Organs and flesh splattered the inside of the tunnel walls as the lava pooled around the worm queen, embracing her quivering form.

Finally free of the dark confines of the tunnel, Denise tore her helmet off and took a heaving breath. She gagged and nearly collapsed at the smell still emanating from the cave. Taking shuddering steps down the side of the hill, the air quickly cleared.

Denise dropped the diving helmet in the dirt and limped over to her truck. She unfastened the clasps on the rest of her suit and shimmied out of it. It fell to the ground, and she shook it off her feet and left it crumpled on the ground.

The lava was just starting to brim out of the hole where Sulfur Springs had been, the front edge of the magma turning black as it hit the colder outside air. More lava burped out and covered the cooling chunk. Soon, the whole hillside would be a drying basalt flow.

Dragging her tired bones into the truck's driver seat, Denise sat behind the wheel but didn't bother to turn on the ignition or close the door just yet. She let the African sun shine down on her as she looked back over the landscape.

The river valley had been all but swept away, leaving behind mud, brown water, and jagged rock behind. In the background, the Verschoor Dam was only a few pieces of ragged concrete that had managed to cling to their moorings in the mountain. Nearby, a crumpled hunk of metal poked out of the rocks; Denise thought it might have been an armored car's axle at one point, but it had been tied into a pretzel. It would be covered in lava by the end of the day. In the distance, she could see the crumbled remains of the park's visitor center.

The poachers, including Zhang Dong himself, had been wiped out. The team sent by Yersinia Bioresearch to collect samples and eliminate evidence were all dead. The worms, including their giant queen, had all been cooked and rendered extinct.

All in a day's work for a professional monster hunter. She started the truck and drove away.

THE END

Jonah Buck wanted to study eldritch knowledge and commune with pale, semi-human creatures that flit across the sunless landscape to terrorize the living, so he became an attorney in Oregon. His interests include history, exotic poultry, paleontology, monster movies, and professional stage magic. Special thanks to Lila.

www.ingramcontent.com/pod-product-compliance
Lightning Source LLC
Chambersburg PA
CBHW031956170626
46807CB00006B/2511